# RECKLESS
# GIRLS

## RACHEL HAWKINS

HarperCollins*Publishers*

HarperCollins*Publishers* Ltd
1 London Bridge Street,
London SE1 9GF

www.harpercollins.co.uk

HarperCollins*Publishers*
1st Floor, Watermarque Building, Ringsend Road
Dublin 4, Ireland

This edition published in Great Britain by HarperCollins*Publishers* 2022
1

First published in the USA in 2022 by St. Martin's Press,
an imprint of St. Martin's Publishing Group

Text designed by Kelly S. Too

A catalogue record for this book is available from the British Library

ISBN: 978-0-00-849558-9

Printed and Bound in the UK using 100% Renewable Electricity
at CPI Group (UK) Ltd

MIX
Paper from
responsible sources
FSC™ C007454

This book is produced from independently certified FSC™ paper
to ensure responsible forest management.

For more information visit: www.harpercollins.co.uk/green

For Daddy and the *Rachel K*

# PROLOGUE

Salt water and blood taste the same.

She'd never thought of that until now, until she was drowning in both, blood gushing from the wound in her temple, the sea rushing into her mouth.

Both are warm, tangy.

Both threaten to consume her.

It's dark, but she can hear the waves lapping against the side of the boat, hear the frantic arguing somewhere above her. Moments ago, that argument mattered to her, but now she only cares about the pain in her head, the stinging of the salt, the ache deep in her chest.

In a way, it's easier to let go. To let it happen.

Isn't that what she's been doing this whole time? Isn't that what led her here, to this lonely spot in the Pacific Ocean, woozy and drowning and alone?

She breathes deeply.

It hurts, water rushing in where there should be air.

But after the pain, there's a kind of peace. It's over now. All of it.

She slips under.

She doesn't come back up.

Up until World War II, Meroe Island was best known for the shipwreck that gave it its name. The sailors of the HMS *Meroe* were marooned on the island for more than five months, and the handful of survivors were eventually tried in England for the murder of their shipmates. Dark rumors of cannibalism surrounded the trial, the details of which were considered too gruesome to even be mentioned in newspapers. Only one of the eight survivors, a Lieutenant Thornton, was convicted. His hanging drew a crowd of thousands, including such luminaries of the day as Lord Byron and J. M. W. Turner. Meroe Island became a sort of grim footnote in the annals of nautical history until the 1940s when its strategic location made it useful to Allied forces in the Pacific. Since then, it has been more or less abandoned, although in recent years, it's become a popular destination for a more adventurous brand of traveler.

—*Hidden Histories, Traveler's Press, 2010*

# NOW

---

OVER 60 OF THESE BLANK
PAGES IN THIS BOOK

# ONE

Sometimes I wonder if people on vacation think they're actually on another planet.

Or maybe just another dimension?

It's the only explanation I have for the shit that I've seen in the six months that I've worked at the Haleakala Resort in Maui. And I'm not just talking about the weird stuff you'd expect—sunburned couples asking if I'm interested in "joining them later that evening," the groups of women who wear coordinated tank tops emblazoned with the phrase GO-GETTERS! while they spend several thousand dollars on tequila shots and eventually get into a weepy argument at the lobby bar, or the douchey Wall Street bros who leave lines of coke on the bathroom counter, then accuse the maid who serviced the room of snorting them.

Those were all messes I ended up cleaning up—one way or another—but I'm talking about the truly unhinged moments, like the guy who offered me $200 if I'd eat a whole pineapple in front of him (I didn't), or the senior citizen who spent the entirety of her weeklong vacation in her suite ordering adult movies off the

TV and endless french fries from room service (honestly, good for her). There was also the time I went to clean a room where some frat guys had stayed, and found concentric circles of urine all over the carpet (someone's dad whipped out an Amex to pay for the replacement after I provided management with photographic evidence of the damage).

Which brings me to today, as I stand in the middle of the Makai Suite, looking at the array of sex toys laid out on the bed, considering where this particular moment falls on the spectrum of disgusting, disturbing, and deranged.

"This is so fucked up," Maia mutters next to me, her arms still full of damp towels. "It's like Stonehenge, but with dildos."

I snort, already pulling on a pair of gloves. "To be fair, I only see two—okay, no, three—dildos. That one"—I point to the hot-pink disc on the right—"is a vibrator, and that purple thing is . . . yeah, I don't know what that is, but anyway, good for these people, they're clearly having a lovely time here on the island."

Maia shakes her head, moving back toward the laundry cart. She's shorter than me, and the skirt of her uniform hangs down past her knees. It should make her look dowdy or frumpy, but Maia is incapable of that. She looks like a hot actress on some CW show who is merely deigning to play a maid.

"I'm not against anyone having a good time, Lux. I just sometimes think they forget that, like, people *will* see this shit."

"Or they wanted us to see this shit," I counter, pulling a plastic bag stamped with the hotel's logo off my own cart. "Maybe that's part of their whole deal."

"Gross," she replies with a shudder, and I pick up the pink vibrator, dropping it into the bag.

"Prude."

"Weirdo," she says before disappearing into the bathroom. I grin at her, and turn back to my task.

Maia is new here at Haleakala, just started last month, and

while I like her a lot, I have a feeling she'll be gone within a couple of weeks. I've been here long enough to realize that the housekeeping staff tends to fall into three categories: the lifers, ladies who have been here ten years and will be here for another thirty; the "this is a temporary thing, but I've been here a year," crew; and finally, girls like Maia who think working at a five-star resort will be fun, not too much work, and will earn them a decent amount of cash.

I was supposed to be in the third group, but after six months, I'm worried I'm sliding into the second one.

I'd come to Hawaii for a guy—which, I realize, sounds stupid—but I feel like any woman who'd had Nico Johannsen ask her to meet him in Maui would've bought a plane ticket on the spot.

And besides, it hadn't just been the guy himself—it had been what the guy was offering. A chance to travel, to sail around the world, to finally have some experiences.

An adventure.

"Livin' the dream," I mutter, surveying the bed, unsure how to proceed. Should I lay all of the toys out on a towel on the bathroom counter, the way we do makeup brushes?

Suddenly, all I want to do is leave. Tear off this uniform, abandon my cleaning cart, walk out of the resort, and go back home.

But where even is that now?

Technically, I live in a tiny ranch house on the south side of the island, a place Nico and I share with two dudes he works with at the marina, plus their girlfriends. Except we don't even have a room there—we sleep on a mattress they put out in the living room at night. The whole place constantly smells like salt and sunscreen, and the sheets always feel a little damp and gritty. The six of us share two bathrooms, with wet swimsuits dripping from the shower rod, and towels with little dots of mildew because nothing in that place ever seems to stay dry.

Home was supposed to be Nico's boat, the *Susannah*.

Even thinking about it hurts, imagining it in its dry dock, with a big fucking hole in the hull. Nico had sailed her down from San Diego after we'd met, and I'd flown to meet him here. One-way ticket, my entire life packed into one roller bag and a backpack.

But when I'd gotten to Wailuku, I'd learned that not only had the *Susannah*'s engine busted on the trip over, but when Nico had it moved to the marina where it could be fixed, an accident getting it off the trailer had pierced the hull, a repair Nico didn't have the funds for.

Correction, Nico wouldn't *ask* for the funds to repair it. His family has more money than God—they run this massive law firm, personal injury, litigation, shit like that—but Nico wants to make his own way in the world on his own terms.

It's a really admirable quality, when it isn't also wrecking our plan and keeping me stuck here, cleaning up strangers' sex toys.

*Maybe the boat is cursed*, I'd said to him just the other night, whispering against the warm, salty skin of his neck as we huddled on our mattress, rain pattering on the tin roof.

*Maybe it's you,* he'd murmured back. *Letting a woman on board a ship was thought to be bad luck back in the day.*

*Maybe you're an asshole,* had been my reply, he'd only laughed and kissed me, and then our tiny, sandy mattress hadn't seemed so bad. Nico was good at that, distracting me, his unflagging optimism bringing me out of those spirals of worry and doubt and *what the fuck now?* Nico didn't worry about the future—and if an uncharitable voice in the back of my mind occasionally hissed that Nico didn't *have* to worry about that kind of shit because I was always doing it for him—I ignored it.

Or, I tried to.

Anyway, before the *Susannah* and Hawaii, I'd been in California, but that had never felt like home to me, not really. I'd moved there with my mom from Nebraska when I was twelve, and when she'd died eleven years later, I'd just stayed in San Diego because I couldn't think of where else to go.

Now, at twenty-five, all of it is starting to feel like a series of wrong turns and missed chances. Heading left when I should've gone right. Zigging when I should've zagged.

I strip the bed and shove the sheets in the bottom of my cart. I hear the door to the suite open as Maia goes into the hall to get more towels or shampoo that smells like bananas and hibiscus.

"So, do you think I should make these assholes a festive towel sculpture shaped like a cock?" I call out to her. "I know a swan is the normal thing, but given their tastes—"

Behind me, someone clears their throat, and I straighten to see two people standing in the foyer, a man wearing a Hawaiian shirt in violent shades of red and green, a woman in a matching dress. They're holding mai tais, their faces bright with embarrassment or sunburn or both, and I offer a weak smile.

"Aloha?"

An hour later, I'm standing in the parking lot of the Haleakala, in my cutoff shorts and T-shirt, my uniform and name tag back in the hands of my boss—well, former boss now—Mr. Chen, and while I should be freaking the fuck out, I tip my face up to the sun and smile.

No more sheets. No more towels. No more stray fingers "accidentally" brushing my ass. I've wanted to quit for over a month now, but there's something freeing about having the choice taken out of my hands. It's not my fault the Sandersons walked in when they did. Not my fault they'd left all that stuff on their bed in the first place.

Not my fault that I don't have a job anymore.

Now, I just have to tell Nico.

# TWO

"Gotta say, losing my job because of a dildo is a first."

Since I'm officially unemployed, I can meet Nico at his favorite lunch counter on the island. He sits across from me, smelling like salt water and engine grease, but still so handsome I can feel it in the pit of my stomach, my knees. He's got a red bandana holding his sandy hair back from his face, and his skin is tanned and smooth, a tattoo curling around his bicep.

If I'm honest, the tattoo is more than a little douchey. Typical white dude tribal shit that doesn't actually mean anything to him, but three days after we met, he added a curling *L* to one edge of the tattoo for me. That was sweet, at least.

*He* was sweet.

He still is, of course, but it was different when I first met him. When our relationship was heady and new, the calm he radiated was a welcome balm after years of dealing with Mom's cancer: the hospitals, the chemo side effects, the screaming fights with my dad over the phone.

Nico is the kind of guy who can say something like, "Don't

pick up what you don't need to carry," and you actually believe it—that he's figured out some better, more enlightened way of living—and you don't even want to punch him.

Well, you don't *always* want to punch him.

Now he just slurps his soda and nods at me. "Job was bullshit anyway."

"*Such* bullshit."

"And you can have another one, like, tomorrow," he goes on, pointing at me with his cup.

I stab at a noodle and shrug. "Why don't we look at how much we've saved up? Maybe we can finally get the *Susannah* fixed?"

He doesn't answer that, just rolls his head from side to side in this gesture that I've seen a thousand times from him. It basically signals a mix of "eh" and "we can talk later," and frustration suddenly shoots through me.

There's no getting away from the fact that Nico is happy here. He says that he wants to keep traveling like we'd planned, but the more time passes, the more I can see him settling in, putting down roots. He likes his job at the marina, and working with boats. He makes friends everywhere because he's that kind of guy, so all his coworkers love him (hence us having a free place to stay). If anyone can "bloom where they're planted," it's Nico.

I'm not sure I've ever bloomed anywhere. Sometimes I wonder if I even can. Maybe that's why the idea of never being planted in the first place is so appealing to me.

Or maybe I'm just sick of cleaning up other people's shit, sometimes literally.

I poke at my food and glance toward the counter, where the line has finally thinned. It's nearly two, which means they'll close soon, and Nico will go back to the marina while I'll go . . . back to the house, I guess? Sit on the couch, wait for Nico to come home?

That's almost more depressing than cleaning hotel rooms, and

I suddenly have the tiniest pang of regret for what happened today. Maybe I should've really apologized to the Sandersons, groveled even. Begged Mr. Chen for another chance.

But I can't let myself go down that road, because if I start regretting one thing, there will be a thousand other decisions to second-guess. Quitting school, the way things went down with my dad, those lost years of partying with friends who weren't actually my friends. The aimless way I'd drifted through life—until I'd met Nico.

"I met a couple of girls today," he says, pulling me from my thoughts.

I look at him, raising my eyebrows. "And you're telling me this because . . . ?"

"Well, they were looking for a boyfriend while on vacation, and I decided that seemed a lot more fun than fixing boat engines, so it looks like I'll have a new job soon, too."

I give him the finger and slurp some more noodles. "Seriously, Nico."

Grinning, he winks at me before pushing his empty plate away. "Seriously, Lux, I met these two girls. Americans. East Coasters."

He says that with enough disdain that I lift my eyebrows. "We can't all be gods of Southern California, Nicholas."

I expect him to laugh, but I spot a little irritation in the wrinkle that appears on the bridge of his nose. I don't know if it's the gentle teasing about his background or the use of his real name, but in either case, I wave my hand, not wanting an argument. "Sorry, go on."

He lets it drop. "Well, they were looking to charter a boat for a few days, but the dude they were supposed to talk to wasn't there, so we got to chatting instead. I think they might hire me."

I'm not exactly the jealous type—with a boyfriend who looks like Nico, you kind of learn not to be if you don't want to lose your mind—but I still feel a weird flutter of apprehension. "Hire you to sail a boat for them? Take them around the island?"

He shrugs, leaning back in his seat. Outside, it's started to rain, a soft drizzle that I know will be over in a few minutes and leave the air thick and sweet smelling. "I guess? They asked if I wanted to get drinks tonight and talk it over, and I told them I'd bring my girlfriend."

"Look at you, you loyal motherfucker," I tease, and he grins at me again, reaching across the table to take my hand in his, kissing my knuckles.

"More like terrified you'd cut my dick off in my sleep if I met two girls at a bar without you."

"Loyal *and* smart."

The rain picks up, slapping hard against the roof, and Nico glances outside before turning back to me. He has beautiful eyes, deep brown, and they crinkle at the corners as he smiles.

"I figure if they don't hire me for the job, they might at least buy us a couple of beers, and it's not like I have anything else going on tonight."

"Same," I say, then laugh. "I mean, fuck, now I don't have anything else going on at any point, ever."

I hate that it doesn't sound like a joke.

# THREE

The girls picked a tourist bar, because of course they did.

Pineapple Pete's is too crowded, and I can smell that particularly noxious mix of sunscreen, beer, and duty-free perfume that always hovers over these kinds of places. With my luck, I'll run into the Haleakala guests who got me fired today.

Nico had gone back to work after lunch, cleaning up and changing at the marina and leaving me to get ready back at the house. But since our roommates were also going out tonight, I had to fight for shower time and a space at the mirror, which means I'm running late and my hair is still wet in one spot in the back. I don't know why I even made an effort to look nice—Nico will just be wearing the extra shorts and T-shirt he keeps in the bag he takes to work. It's not like I care about impressing some rich college girls on vacation, but I still found myself pulling out my favorite dress, the yellow one with the halter neck and tiny embroidered birds along the hem, the one that swirled around my knees and always made Nico's eyes linger a little longer on the curve of my hip, the hollow of my collarbone.

I've always loved when he looks at me like that. I've loved it from the first night I met him, in a bar not that different from Pineapple Pete's in terms of low lighting and shitty beer, but a whole world away, otherwise. I'd been waitressing at a place near the beach in San Diego, and Nico had walked in one night. He'd just bought the *Susannah*, and was fixing it up, before sailing to Baja, then down the coast of Mexico, off into the Pacific, to who knew where. Hawaii, Tahiti, maybe even as far as Australia.

*We'll still get there,* I tell myself as I weave through the crowd, searching for Nico. *This is just a little hiccup, and then we're on our way like he promised.*

I see him standing near the back at one of the high tables that doesn't have any chairs. He spots me and lifts a hand, already holding a beer, and the two girls standing across from him turn to look at me.

They're not scowling, which I guess is a good start. In fact, their smiles seem genuine, not sugary sweet and fake as fuck. They also don't look like most of the wealthy college girls we tend to see here. No floral prints, no shiny lip gloss. The one on the right has dark hair gathered up in a messy bun, and the one on the left, her hair several shades lighter, is wearing jeans and a tank top, her face bare of makeup.

Nico comes around the table and pulls me in for a kiss, his breath warm and smelling like the beer he was drinking. "There's my girl," he says, his hand briefly sliding down to squeeze my hip.

"Please tell me you've already ordered me a drink," I reply, rising up on tiptoes to nip at his lower lip, and he grins, nuzzling his nose against mine.

"I can go grab you one now," he says, and I glance at the girls, both of whom have turned away from us to talk to each other.

"I'll come with," I say, but Nico shakes his head, tugging me over to the table.

"No worries, babe," he says, a phrase I hear so often I nearly mouth it along with him.

The girls at the table are watching me, and Nico nods at them in turn. "Brittany," he says to the one with the bun, "and Amma," the girl in jeans, "this is Lux. Lux, Brittany and Amma." Another grin, this one slightly goofy. "I'm gonna grab a couple more beers."

He disappears back into the crush of people, leaving me standing there at the edge of the table, looking at Brittany and Amma.

Brittany speaks first. "Lux," she says. "Like *The Virgin Suicides*."

I'm surprised—and more than a little pleased. No one has ever made that connection when they hear my name. Usually they just ask if it's a nickname, or short for something. "Yeah," I say. "My mom really loved that book."

"Kind of a bummer of a character to be named after?" Brittany says, but she's smiling as she tilts her bottle to her mouth.

"I know," I reply. "When I finally read the book when I was thirteen, I was like, 'Mom, what the fuck?'"

Brittany and Amma both burst out laughing, and I suddenly realize how long it's been since I've talked to people who weren't my coworkers or Nico's. Even back in San Diego, I'd started losing touch with my friends as soon as my mom got sick.

Funny how fast that happened, how easy it was for people I saw every day to fade away, disappear, become nothing more than a bunch of Instagram accounts I still followed. And I didn't blame them. My life had become sad and depressing, and no one knew what to say to the girl who was suddenly taking care of a sick parent instead of sitting next to them in sociology.

After Mom died, I'd thought about reenrolling, but everyone I'd once been close to was already at least two semesters ahead of me. It had felt too much like starting over again, and it had been easier to get a job, to just focus on putting one foot in front of the other—and making rent.

"So, Nico says you've been in Hawaii for almost a year?" Amma asks. Up close, I see that she's not quite as pretty as Brittany, but she has full lips and high cheekbones. In the dim light of the bar, her eyes are dark and hypnotizing.

"Six months," I say, then wonder if Nico had exaggerated to make himself seem more familiar with the waters around the island. I quickly add, "Nico had been to Hawaii many times before we moved here, though, and he's done a lot of sailing in the area."

On family vacations, that is, staying at the nicest resorts on the islands, places where I wouldn't even be able to get a job scrubbing toilets. I don't mention this. I'm assuming that they only see Nico as a beach bum, a friendly guy with a great smile and an even better body who works on boats and definitely has no idea which fork to use at a fancy dinner.

"What about you?" Brittany asks. As she reaches up to tuck a stray lock of hair behind her ear, I notice a tattoo on her wrist. "Where were you before this?"

*In the After.*

I wonder what that means, if anything. Maybe it's just a lyric from a Taylor Swift song I can't bring to mind.

"I grew up in Nebraska," I tell her. "But me and my mom moved to San Diego when I was a kid. That's where I met Nico last year. He told me about his whole plan of sailing around the South Pacific. About how there were hundreds of islands that didn't even have names, places that were barely on maps." That had been the part I'd liked the most, if I was honest. The idea of going somewhere almost completely unknown.

"And you followed him?" Amma asks, cocking her head to one side.

I don't like the way she says it, but it's true. I hitched onto Nico's dream because coming up with my own felt impossible, back then. Dreams were for people with money and time, people who didn't feel hollowed out from watching the only person who loved them die in agony. Dreams were for people who had choices, opportunities. I didn't believe I had any of those things.

But it's not like I'm going to confess as much to Brittany and Amma. Instead, I shrug and smile. "I mean, you've seen him, can you blame me?"

Brittany laughs and nods, but Amma is still studying me. I feel like there's more she wants to ask, but then Nico is back, four beers dangling from his fingertips.

"So," he says, setting them down on the table. "Did you two tell Lux what we were just talking about?"

"We were getting to know her first," Brittany says, giving me a little conspiratorial wink, like we're already friends.

Nico squeezes in close to me, grinning as he sips his beer. "Babe," he says, "you're gonna love this." He nods at Brittany. "Show her."

Reaching into her back pocket, Brittany pulls out her phone. "Amma and I met freshman year of college," she begins, and Amma nods.

"Western civ. So fucking boring." Brittany smiles. "But ever since, we've been talking about taking this big trip once we graduated. This is our last stop, and we wanted something special. Something different than what every sorority girl on vacation in Hawaii puts on their Instagram. Something . . . off the beaten path."

She hands me her phone, and I realize I'm looking at a map. But it's all light blue, the entire screen is nothing but ocean. It actually takes me a second to spot the tiny sand-colored dot in the middle of all that emptiness.

"It's an island," Amma says to me.

"An atoll," Brittany corrects.

"An atoll is an island," Nico says, leaning over my shoulder to look at the map. "Made of coral. They're all over the place in this part of the world. During World War II—"

I hold up a hand. "Nico, I love you, but men talking about World War II gives me hives."

Brittany laughs loudly, throwing her head back, her teeth very white in the glow from the Bud Light sign above our table. "Okay, I knew I liked you because of the cool name, but now I *really* like you."

Amma smiles, but I see her posture stiffen slightly, and her gaze slides away for a moment.

"Anyway, I know this place," Nico tells me. "Meroe Island. Named after a ship called the HMS *Meroe* that was wrecked there in the 1800s. The coral caused a lot of ships to go aground in the area. But the *Meroe* was the first big one, so I guess it got naming rights."

"Did anyone survive?" Amma asks, propping one elbow on the table.

Nico shrugs. "The wreck? Yeah, pretty much everyone. But the island got them in the end. Crew of thirty-some dudes, whittled down to eight guys by the time they were rescued. There's not much life out there to sustain you for long. You can fish, but the jungle is pretty rough from what I hear. And there's no fresh water."

"And you want to go there why?" I ask, handing Brittany her phone.

She shoves it back into her pocket. "I read about it a couple of years ago on this travel blog. Nico's right, it's hardcore and everything, but it was also . . ." Her gaze goes a little dreamy, slightly unfocused. "I don't know. It looked so beautiful. And remote. A real escape, you know?"

She laughs then, self-conscious. "Plus, it seems cool. To spend a little time off the grid." She smiles and rolls her eyes. "I know, you're probably thinking I've seen *The Beach* one too many times."

"No," I say, sipping my beer and grinning. "I was thinking you read *The Beach* too many times. You strike me as a book-before-the-movie kind of girl."

She clinks her bottle against mine. "Fuck yeah."

"The guy we wanted to take us wasn't at the marina," Amma adds. She's peeled the whole label off her bottle now and is tearing it into small pieces. "But Nico was, so Brittany decided it was fate."

"It *is* fate," Brittany insists. "Extremely excellent fate that has brought us not just Nico, but also Lux."

I stare at her, confused, and then look at Nico, grinning at me like an excited kid on Christmas Eve.

"What do you mean?"

Her eyes are bright as she leans in even closer. "Come with us."

# FOUR

"You're not really going to say no, are you?" Nico asks in the darkness.

We're on our mattress in Greg and Josh's living room, my head on Nico's shoulder as I trace patterns on his bare chest. We had several more beers with Brittany and Amma, then the four of us had found another, better bar, and I'd had more vodka shots than I should have. But Brittany and Amma had been paying, and it had been easier to drink and dance than give a serious answer about heading off on this little *Robinson Crusoe* trip of theirs.

"I don't get it," he continues, putting a hand behind his head. "All you've wanted is to get out on the water, and now you're like, *'I need to think about it'*?"

I push myself up on one elbow, looking down at him. "I want to get on the water with *you*," I tell him. "I don't want some two-week-long cruise with a couple of college girls looking for a good time. Besides, don't you think it's weird that they met me for, like, three seconds, then were suddenly inviting me on their vacation?

You, sure. They need someone who can drive a boat. But me?" I shake my head.

He frowns, and I reach down, smoothing away the wrinkles above his nose with my thumb.

I know why he doesn't get it. I mean, he's right: I've been dying to get off the island, and it's not like I have a job holding me back now. But there's something about the entire proposition that is making me hesitate, something that I don't want to put into words.

Instead I ask, "Are you going to say yes even if I say no?"

Nico sighs, and I trail my hand down to his tattoo, letting my nail scrape against that elegant cursive *L* woven in there just for me.

"Babe," Nico starts, and that's when I realize that yup, he is absolutely going to say yes even if I say no.

I sit up, dragging the sheet with me even though it's hot, my hand fumbling on the floor for the joint I'd rolled earlier. I'd planned to smoke it then, but my head had already been spinning, and then Nico's hands had been on my waist, and I'd dropped it.

The lighter flares, briefly illuminating the nearly empty living room, and the smoke I exhale looks blue in the dim light.

I sit there, arms resting on my upraised knees, for a long moment before the silence becomes too much for Nico.

"I thought you liked them," he finally says, plucking the joint from my hand and taking a hit before handing it back.

"I did," I reply, still not looking at him. "I do."

"So, come."

"And do what?" I ask. "Serve drinks?"

Scoffing, he lies back. "They weren't like that."

"But they could be," I say, imagining how much that would suck. How much I'd liked feeling like the old me tonight, joking and drinking—the Cool Girlfriend, not the girl serving beers or towels.

I want to hold onto the version of me that's just another

carefree twentysomething. The me I pretended to be when I first met Nico, and lost sight of the moment I landed on Maui and our plan got sidetracked.

Sometimes it bothers me that I'm the one always thinking about our future, about what it will take for us to have a more comfortable lifestyle, while Nico seems perfectly happy fixing boats and taking out the occasional charter. It's like we got to Hawaii and became different versions of the people we were in San Diego.

I shake my head, wanting to dispel that thought. It's been forever since I've smoked, and it's clearly fucking with my head.

"We should focus on repairing the *Susannah* and heading out," I remind him. "Having our own adventure instead of tagging along on someone else's."

He takes the joint back, sucking hard, and I recognize the stubborn set of his jaw.

"The pay is too good to pass up, Lux," he says, shaking his head. "What they're willing to pay me for a couple of weeks of work could get us out of here the day I come back."

I blink at him. "Seriously?"

Nico nods. "Seriously. Fifty grand, Lux. To sail them out to some atoll, let them get their *Blue Lagoon* on, and come back."

Fuck.

I slide back under the sheets, my foot brushing his shin.

He's right—he can't pass that up. *We* can't pass that up. We need a new engine, and the holes in the hull repaired. Plus, we haven't restocked any rations since Nico's sail from California. That money will go a long way.

*It's money he could've had months ago with one phone call to his dad,* a voice in my head whispers.

Nico's never been specific about just how rich his family is, but I looked them up not long after we met—dug around the law firm's website, some Facebook profiles of cousins, even his sister's Instagram.

They're Fuck-You Money rich. Houses in California, in Vail, in Florida rich. Fancy apartment in New York rich. And they probably have millions more in the stock market.

Nico once told me that he walked away from his family because of all the expectations: that he'd go to law school, and that he'd eventually be a partner in his dad's firm. He hated the idea that he was just, as he put it, "a cog in the machine." I guess I can appreciate that—there's even a part of me that thinks it's noble, to resist falling into a life that your parents have just created for you—but there are also times when it's frustrating as fuck.

The past few months have been full of those times.

And then something else occurs to me. What if Nico comes back with all that cash and decides, hey, if he could get a few more jobs like that, what's the point of ever leaving Hawaii? Where would that leave me?

"Make them pay for the *Susannah* first," I finally say, and he looks over at me, surprised.

"What?"

"Add it to the cost. Tell them you'll give them a much better, more authentic experience on your own boat, but it needs some repairs. I mean, how long will it take?"

Nico tilts his head back, looking up at the ceiling. "Jesus, a couple of days at most? The issue has always been money, not time. Dom has a new engine he'll sell me, I can do the fiberglass work myself . . ."

He trails off, then drops the joint in a little jelly glass of water by the side of the mattress. "If we take the *Susannah*, will you come?"

When I don't answer immediately, he pulls me closer, my breasts pressed against his chest, his breath warm on my face. "I want you there, babe. They want you there. What's holding you back?"

"Do you think it's gonna end in some weird sex thing?" I ask, and he grins.

"I definitely hope so."

When I punch his shoulder, he just laughs, rolling me beneath him.

"You just want me to see you in action," I joke. "All pirate-y and hot. Making them call you 'Captain Nic' or something."

"Oooh, say it again," he teases, his knee nudging my thigh open as I kiss him, smiling against his mouth.

The *Susannah* fixed, with enough money left over to stock her well. One job, and then finally—*finally*—the adventure I'd signed on for could start.

About fucking time.

# BEFORE

"Golden Boy is back."

Cam, another waitress at the Cove, smiles suggestively at Lux as they pass in the narrow hallway by the kitchen, both their trays heavy with empty glasses, ketchup-smeared plates, balled-up napkins.

And even though Lux is exhausted, her feet throbbing and her hair smelling depressingly like french fries, she feels a little sparkle shoot through her.

She's felt it every time she's seen him these past two weeks, and sometimes she thinks she looks forward to that sensation—the jolt of awareness that reminds her she can still *feel* something, besides sad and tired—more than she does actually seeing the guy.

But now, as she sneaks a peek around the wall at the bar, she remembers that no, actually seeing him is pretty fucking great, too.

It's not just that he's hot. Hot guys are a dime a dozen, and his specific brand of hot—that sun-kissed California boy, all tan biceps and white teeth and streaked blond hair—isn't particularly notable, either. Lux went to college with guys like that, sees them here in the Cove nearly every night.

But Golden Boy is different.

Lux doesn't know why exactly. Maybe it's the fact that he's usually alone when he comes to the bar, that he's not part of some loud, jostling group of guys ordering pitchers of beer and tipping in loose change.

He almost always has a notebook with him, too, and as Lux

watches him now, he pulls it out from the canvas bag slung over the back of his seat, tucking his hair behind his ear as he opens it up, a stubby pencil in one hand, a dark beer at his left.

"He asked about you tonight," Cam says from behind her, and Lux turns, frowning.

"Bullshit."

Cam laughs, shaking her head. "No, for real. Okay, he didn't say, 'Hey, where's Lux McAllister, my future wife,' but he did ask if 'the redheaded waitress' was working tonight."

It's silly, probably, to feel such a flush of pleasure at such an innocuous comment, but Lux blushes the whole way back to the kitchen, her pulse leaping around crazily as she sets her tray on the counter near the sinks.

Cam is right behind her, and nudges Lux's foot with the toe of her sneaker. "Go talk to hiiiiim," she sings, and Lux is already waving her off.

"And say what?"

"Say you heard he was looking for you."

"Yeah, guys love it when you talk like you're in a Western from 1956."

Cam laughs again. "Fine," she says. "Tell you what. He's in my section. I'll pick up table eight in yours, and you can have him. Deal?"

Lux almost tells her no, and later, much later, she'll think about this moment in the kitchen at the Cove, the smell of fried fish around her, steam rolling over the industrial sinks, the clatter of silverware, the cooks bantering back and forth in Spanish. It doesn't feel important then, doesn't feel heavy or loaded. It's just the chance to talk to a boy.

How can a thing as small as that change your entire life?

"Deal," she says to Cam, smiling and reaching out her hand to shake on it.

GOLDEN BOY LOOKS UP WHEN she approaches his table, and his smile slices through everything.

It seems stupid, to feel so happy just because a cute guy is smiling at her, but Lux has learned to take these unexpected moments of joy where she can find them.

"Did my waitress tell you I asked about you?" he asks, ducking his head, grinning a little sheepishly. His eyes are a warm brown, his hair longish and curling around his earlobes, and it shouldn't be so charming, this human golden retriever thing he's got going on, but it is.

It really, really is.

"Maybe," she says with a little shrug, and he winces, rubbing a hand over the back of his neck.

"Great. So there goes any chance of you thinking I'm actually cool, right?"

"Oh yeah, right out the window."

His smile deepens, and Lux sees that he has dimples because of *course* he does.

"Well, shit," he says with a sigh. "See, I was gonna do this whole thing of chatting with you, asking interesting but not invasive questions—"

"Naturally," Lux replies, her cheeks hurting with how hard she's trying not to burst into a giddy grin.

"And then," he goes on, "at the very end of the meal, I was going to very smoothly ask for your number. But since that's blown to fuck now, I'm just gonna skip to the end and tell you I think you're gorgeous, and I'd really love to take you out sometime."

Lux's heart is beating hard, and her stomach is basically a butterfly garden at this point. Still, she's having too much fun to give in quite so easily. "You don't even know my name," she reminds him, and he points at her name tag.

"I do now. Lux. Which actually makes how uncool I'm being even harder, because *goddamn,* that is a very cool name. I knew you were out of my league."

He leans back in his chair, and Lux notices the way his T-shirt stretches across his broad chest.

"I'm Nico," he says, and she puts a hand on one hip.

"That's also a cool name."

"It's a nickname for Nicholas."

Lux screws up her face, pretending to think. "You know, that does lose you some cool points, but on the whole, still a good name. I'll allow it."

He laughs then, laughs like a kid, throwing his head back. "I take it back," he says. "Don't give me your number. Marry me."

"Let me see how well you tip first."

When was the last time she flirted with a guy? When was the last time she felt like the Lux she'd been before, the one who always had a quip on her lips, the quickest and sharpest of all her friends?

Years.

Years and years. But here she is, doing it so easily with this guy.

She'll eventually work out that this is Nico's superpower, making people instantly feel like the best, most comfortable versions of themselves. But right now, standing by his table on a Thursday night, she doesn't know that, doesn't understand that the light turned so brightly on her shines on everyone he meets.

Gesturing at the notebook still lying open on the table, Lux asks, "What are you writing?"

The light is soft in this little back corner, but she still sees him blush a little, and it might be then that she falls in love with him.

He turns the notebook to her so that she can see the page. There's a list of food that doesn't sound very appetizing—she sees

Spam listed in all caps—as well as a series of numbers, a crudely drawn map.

"I sail," he explains. "Got a twenty-five footer I've been working on. Planning to take her to Hawaii as soon as I can, so." He sweeps a hand over the page. "Logistics, basically."

Lux doesn't know much about boats other than that she likes looking at them. She may have grown up in California, but she has Midwestern roots. Her parents were both born in Nebraska, and her dad still lives there, with his new wife, and his new kids.

It had been Lux's mom's idea to come to San Diego after the divorce, wanting a fresh start, a place that was all theirs. And that had been great until she'd gotten sick Lux's sophomore year of college. Pancreatic cancer, sudden and devastating, nowhere and then everywhere. Her mom had fought hard, though. They'd given her six months, and she'd lasted three years, but every one of those years had been a struggle, so much that when she'd finally died, Lux had felt a guilty surge of relief.

*It's over now,* she'd thought. *At least it's finally over.*

It had been, but it had left Lux with a strange three-year gap in her life. The last time things had been normal, she'd been twenty, going to UCSD, leading a fairly typical life—classes, parties, the occasional hookup.

Then the phone call. Her mom's voice shaky on the other end. Her whole life upended overnight.

The three years between that phone call and the night Lux packed up her things and left the rental house she couldn't afford anymore had been a blur, and she emerged from them to find she hadn't managed to hold onto even the smallest part of her life before. Friends had gotten tired of never-returned texts and phone calls, they'd never had any family in California, and her dad . . . well, she'd blown any chance of them actually having a relationship right the fuck up.

Lux has been sleepwalking ever since—working to pay the rent on a run-down apartment she shares with three other girls, and thinking only as far ahead as the next week, sometimes just the next day.

But as she stares at Nico's drawings, something in her seems to wake up.

"How long would that take?" she asks, and he shrugs.

"To Hawaii? Three weeks, could be a little longer, little shorter. Depends on a lot of things."

"You're going alone?"

Lux tries to imagine how it would feel to be in the middle of all that water, all on her own, the only thing between her and death a fiberglass hull and her own skills. It seems terrifying, but also . . . exhilarating?

"I guess that depends on a lot of things, too," Nico replies, smiling up at her, and Lux's heart does a neat flip in her chest.

The rest of the evening goes by in a haze. She has other tables, but she's constantly aware of Nico, her eyes repeatedly drawn to his dim corner of the restaurant. When her shift ends and he's still there, waiting for her, it's like the sun coming out.

It's like her entire life is suddenly starting over again.

# NOW

# FIVE

Wait, so you don't actually like boats?"

Brittany and I are in the canned-goods aisle at Foodland, stocking up on supplies. The repairs on the *Susannah* are nearly finished, and we leave as soon as possible—hence the shopping trip. Amma had decided to stay at the marina, wrinkling her nose at the suggestion of going to the store.

I wonder if something as mundane as grocery shopping doesn't fit into Amma's idea of what an adventure should be. I get it, but since I also like not starving, I'm happy to fill the cart with non-perishables—like soup, canned vegetables, nuts and crackers, plus plenty of Hawaii's beloved Spam. And water. Nico has a purification system on the boat, but we're still taking gallons, big plastic jugs full that will rest in the boat's small hold. It's a three-day sail to Meroe, then they want to spend two weeks on the atoll—Nico had convinced them that after being at sea for seventy-two hours, they'd want a little more time on land before turning around and doing it all over again.

And that's if everything goes to plan—which, as Nico has reminded me several times, nothing ever does.

So, I grab more soup.

"It's not that I dislike boats," I tell Brittany now. "It's just that
they're Nico's thing."

She nods, leaning over the handle of the cart. Her hair is loose
today, sweeping her shoulders as she peers down at our haul.
"Okay, so what is your thing?" she asks, glancing up at me.

The PA system is playing a Muzak version of "The Greatest Love
of All," and my hairline prickles with sweat as I make a show of
studying the cans some more, like I'm suddenly really invested in
picking out the right brand of chickpeas.

The million-dollar question, right there. What *is* my thing?

The truth is, when your world is falling apart, you stop having "a thing." You get so focused on just making it through each
day that "interests" or "ambitions" kind of go out the window.
You definitely don't have time for passions. Getting to nurture a
love like Nico has for boats and the sea is an indulgence I haven't
had time for in years. Before Mom got sick, I'd had all kinds of
interests: I ran track when I was in high school, I played guitar
when I was a little kid, and I've always loved reading—from the
classics they make you read in school to those true-crime paperbacks with the really lurid covers. I'd decided to major in English,
but I picked up a guitar again in college and was thinking about
switching to music education when Mom called to tell me about
that doctor's appointment.

Sometimes, I still think about that other Lux, the one who
didn't get her world upended. The one who might be sitting in
some music room right now, surrounded by little kids, teaching
them scales. It's a pretty picture, but something about it never sits
right with me—I can't even imagine being that person, not really.

"Travel," I finally settle on because saying something like "freedom" is too cheesy to bear and "survival" is too honest, too sad.

"What's your favorite place that you've been so far?" As she pushes the cart down the aisle, one wheel squeaks loudly.

"Well, I haven't been that many places yet," I say with a shrug, my cheeks hot. Now Brittany is going to realize just how pathetic my life is, and I'll go from being Nico's cool girlfriend to some loser chick tagging along while her boyfriend does the cool shit. "To be honest, I've mostly just read a lot of travel guides."

I'd actually collected them for a while, a hobby I'd developed in middle school and carried on into adulthood. My bookshelf—back when I still had one of those—had been full of them, their neat white spines lined up, bold place names in bright colors. *Australia. Istanbul. Romania. Thailand.*

That last one had been a gift from my mom her last Christmas. It was the only one I still had.

Brittany smiles. "Yeah, that was me before."

I glance back at her, eyebrows raised. "Before what?"

She blinks, then shakes her head a little. "Before I met Amma."

"You guys met in college, right?"

"Mm-hmm," she says, looking over at one of the shelves. "UMass. Intro to western civ. Hey, what kind of pasta should we get?"

She holds up two boxes, one of regular spaghetti, one of penne, before tossing both into the cart with a shrug. "Guess we might as well have it all." She continues picking up boxes of farfalle, elbow macaroni, even egg noodles, and piling them all in with our cans of soup and beans.

"You guys must be really close to decide to travel together," I say, thinking back to my own friends from college. There wasn't a single one of them I would've picked to travel the world with.

Brittany nods, but she still isn't looking at me, and I'm getting the uneasy feeling that she doesn't really want to talk about how she and Amma began their adventure together. Which is weird, because I haven't picked up on any tension between them, and Jesus fuck, if they get in a fight while we're out on the boat . . .

By now, our cart is mostly full, and Brittany steers us to the checkout while I text Nico.

*Got everything.*

*Awesome,* is his immediate reply. *Pretty much done here, too. Think we can leave this afternoon.*

⟋⟋⟍

It's NOT EVEN NOON BY the time Brittany and I get back to the marina, our arms full of reusable grocery sacks. The *Susannah* floats in her berth, smaller than other boats nearby, but shiny and white. Her newly painted red trim is cheerful, and my heart does a little flip in my chest, the same way it had when I'd first seen Nico.

He's standing at the bow, his hair pulled from his face with its customary bandana and his smile bright as he waves at me. "How did it go?" he calls, and I gesture back toward the car.

"All the Spam we can eat," I promise, and his grin widens as he presses a hand to his bare chest.

"Woman after my own heart."

"Spam?"

Amma emerges from the cabin, and even though it's stupid, there's something about seeing her there, in her bikini top and shorts, her expensive sunglasses taking up a third of her face, hair caught up in a messy bun, that makes something dark and animal briefly rise up in me. She looks good standing there, she looks *right* next to Nico, both of them exuding a comfort with their setting and their bodies that I've never felt. That I certainly don't feel now in my cargo pants and Tevas, with a white button-down thrown over my tank top as extra protection from the sun.

"Can't be a snob about Spam when you're at sea," Nico says, oblivious to my dark thoughts as he makes his way over to the dock, one hand on the line as he casually vaults himself off the ship. His boat shoes make a thump on the planks, and when he comes over to me, he smells like sweat and salt, plus that faint metallic tang that always clings to him when he's been working in the marina.

"You ready for this?"

"Ready as I'll ever be."

"Awesome," he says again, and then he nods back to the boat. "Will you do me a favor and take those bags over to Hal's office?"

Hal is the marina manager, an older guy with skin like leather and the bluest eyes I've ever seen. The boat sways slightly under my feet as I cross the deck and heft the bags Nico had gestured to.

One, a red duffel bag, is filled with what look to be stray parts—bits of broken metal and a couple of rusty tools.

The other, another reusable grocery sack, is a lot lighter, and when I glance inside, I frown.

"Um, these are mine?" I say, hefting the sack, and Nico turns back to me, shading his eyes.

"Babe, you don't need that many books on one sail, come on. They were taking up too much space in the cabin."

There are maybe a dozen paperbacks here, some newer ones, but also my mom's old Agatha Christies, and that Thailand travel guide, nearly every page dog-eared.

I hadn't just put them on the boat to read—they'd been part of my efforts to make the space a little homier, a little more *mine*.

Nico has also stuffed one of the throw pillows I bought into the bag, as well as a couple of framed photos. One is of the two of us when I first got to Hawaii, standing on the beach, our arms around each other, my freckled skin pale against his tan.

The other is of me and my mom when I graduated high school. We're both squinting because the sun is so bright, and I remember that we had to ask my friend Mallory's mom to take that picture for us, since we didn't have any other family there.

It's one of the few keepsakes I brought with me from San Diego, and it's been sitting in my suitcase the entire time we've been crashing on that living room floor. I was excited to finally have a place to put it on the boat.

And now it's been shoved into a grocery bag.

"Hal will hold onto them while we're gone," he goes on, then gives me that patented Nico shrug. "It's not a big deal."

It's not. It'll be here when we get back. And I get that space is at a premium with four of us on the boat. Still . . .

Amma comes over, looking down into the bag. "Oh, it's not that much stuff," she says, then raises her head to call to Nico. "Besides, I actually forgot to bring a book. We can easily make room in our cabin."

She takes the bag out of my hand with a bright smile, setting it back on the deck, and I smile back at her. "Thanks."

Nico just shrugs, affable as ever. "Fine by me, then."

I know that Nico didn't mean anything by it, and I don't want to spoil the day, so I drop it, taking the other bag to Hal's office. Within an hour, we're pulling out of the harbor, leaving the tall forest of masts behind us, motoring past yachts a hell of a lot bigger and fancier than the *Susannah*. Brittany and Amma stand at the bow, their arms loosely around each other's waist, wind blowing their hair. If my phone weren't belowdecks, I'd be tempted to take a picture of them, put a pretty filter on it, and give it a sappy caption. That's exactly what they look like right now—an aspirational social media post.

As the boat slides out into the open water, my stomach dips. For the first time, it's really sinking in that we're *doing* this: we're heading out for a literal deserted island with these two strangers, and I don't know if what I'm feeling is excitement, fear, relief, or some giddy combination of all three. I just know that as the *Susannah* glides across the glassy water, something in my chest finally seems to loosen.

"It beeeegiiiiins," Brittany sings out, lifting her arms and spreading them wide as she tips her head back.

"Fuck yeah!" Nico hoots back, and Amma looks over her shoulder at both of us, smiling.

*It begins,* I echo in my head.

And I don't just mean this one trip.

# SIX

I knew the *Susannah* was small, but I'd never really felt just *how* small until that first night, when all four of us were down below.

The main cabin is both kitchen and sitting room, with a sink, fridge, and a small stove on one side, and a cushioned bench that wraps around a table on the other. That table is also our bed tonight. It folds down to be level with the bench, then we can slide the back cushions over it, turning it into a serviceable if not very luxurious sleeping space.

There's also a small cabin at the stern containing a V-berth. It's exactly what it sounds like, a mattress in the shape of a V, curving into the lines of the boat. Brittany and Amma will sleep there, and honestly, I'm glad we're getting the table-bed. The cabin is tiny with a low ceiling, and even though there's a hatch and Nico has installed a little fan on the wall, it still gets pretty stuffy.

Other than that, there's just a tiny bathroom—the *head*, as Nico keeps reminding me—at the other end of the boat, some storage cabinets, and that's it.

In addition to "decorating" with my books and photos, I'd

made a curtain for the window in the little cabin, and bought a cheerful pineapple rug for the kitchen. Still, there's no escaping the fact that it's cramped.

Brittany and Amma don't seem to mind, though. As we eat our dinner—the first of dozens of meals of rice and beans ahead of us—they say over and over again how cute everything is, with Brittany taking photos of the space from every angle.

"How long have you had this boat?" she asks now, taking a sip of bottled water.

Nico is sitting across from her, next to me, and puts his elbows on the table as he looks around. "Bought her a couple of years ago. Been fixing her up ever since."

"Why the *Susannah*?" Amma asks. She only ate about half of her dinner before pushing it away.

Nico shrugs. "The boat had a stupid name when I bought it. *Zephyr Breeze.* And, like, a zephyr is a breeze, so what the fuck? Anyway, I was dating this girl named Susannah, so . . ."

I already know this story, but every time I hear it, my chest tightens uncomfortably. It's something about the way he just waves her off despite naming a whole fucking boat after her. And it makes me wonder if someday, some other girl will look at that *L* on Nico's arm, and he'll give that same shrug and say, "It was for this girl I was dating, Lux, it wasn't a big thing," and that'll be it.

"I thought it was bad luck to rename a boat," Amma says. She leans back in the booth, pulling one foot up onto the cushion and wrapping her arms around her knee. "Might be tempting fate."

She's smiling a little, teasing, but I'd never heard that before, and I glance over at Nico.

"Some people say that," he replies with a nod. "But I don't know. Never been much for that superstitious shit."

He smiles suddenly, bumping me with his shoulder. "Anyway, the person you should be asking is Lux. The *Susannah* is her boat, after all."

I roll my eyes even as Brittany sits forward. "Wait, seriously?"

"No," I say. "Well, technically. On paper."

A couple of months ago, I came home to find Nico had a bunch of paperwork for me to sign, transferring the boat into my name. Apparently Nico's dad had called, and they'd had some big talk about taxes or something. Honestly, I didn't really understand much of it, and Nico kept insisting it wasn't a big deal, that it would make things "easier" on us financially if the boat were in my name. So that's how I technically became the legal owner of the *Susannah*.

Not that it meant much—it was still very much Nico's boat.

Leaning forward, Brittany props her chin in her hand. "Okay, so now we know about the boat, but what I *really* want to know about is you two." She gestures between us. "Tell me everything. How you met, was it love at first sight, all the really personal, dreamy shit."

I laugh at that, and Nico grins, throwing an arm around my shoulders and pulling me in closer. "Oh, totally love at first sight. For me at least."

I roll my eyes even as I smile. "He's lying. We met while I was working at this restaurant with *the* ugliest uniforms you have ever seen. No man has ever fallen instantly in love with a woman in khaki shorts."

"I did," Nico insists. "I went back every night for two weeks just to see you in those khaki shorts."

"Of course, my coworkers and I felt sorry for him because as you can see, he's super homely," I add, making Brittany and Amma laugh, as Nico jokingly jostles me.

"Anyway," Nico goes on, "I finally sacked up and asked about her, and she came to my table, and that was that."

"We've pretty much been together ever since," I say, smiling at the memory of that first night, remembering the thrill I'd felt when Nico slipped his hand in mine, that sense that, finally, I was anchored to something. To someone.

Brittany is still smiling at us, her eyes bright. "I love everything about this," she says. "Meant to be."

I lean my head on Nico's shoulder, feeling the familiar, solid warmth of him.

*Meant to be.*

I wasn't sure if I completely believed in that kind of thing. Fate, destiny. I think Nico walked into my life at the right time, and I think he liked that I needed rescuing, that he could offer me something I wanted so much. Not just another person to share my life with, but adventure, new experiences.

Nico continues, "The first time I saw those sad eyes of hers, I was a goner."

I lift my head. "Sad?"

He's never said that to me before. He usually jokes that it was my bright red hair that caught his attention, the pale milkiness of my skin.

"Mm-hmm," he says now, taking a glug from his bottle of water. "Every time I came in, even when you were smiling, you just looked really sad. I wanted to know why, I guess."

Brittany is still smiling warmly, but I don't like the picture he's painting, the sad girl moping around a seafood joint, waiting for the right guy to ask about her tragedy.

"I mean, yeah, that was a rough time, but I wasn't exactly going around crying," I say, scooting away a little. "I was holding it together despite . . . all of that shit."

"What shit?"

Amma is watching us now, her elbows on the table. "My mom got sick five years ago," I say. "Cancer. I'd dropped out of college to take care of her, and then once she was gone, going back to school was a lot of work, and—"

"Was she your only family?"

Brittany's brows are drawn close together, and there's something in her expression that tells me she actually cares about my answer.

"Kind of?" I shrug, uncomfortable, my neck going hot. "My parents got divorced when I was eleven, after my dad decided to become a living cliché and knock up his secretary."

"Jesus." Amma exhales, and I nod.

"Right. So the two of us moved to California for a fresh start while he started his brand-new family in Nebraska. And when Mom got sick, me and my dad weren't talking, so yeah. I guess she was it for me."

I don't tell them about the phone call I made to my father, close to the end. Money was running out, Mom couldn't even eat anymore—her bones had started jutting out beneath her papery skin—and her insurance was refusing to cover in-home hospice care.

I don't tell them how calm his voice was on the other end of the phone.

*Your mother made a choice, Lux. She didn't want me in her life. Neither did you. So now you both need to live with that.*

Just the memory of it—of the shame and the rage and the total disbelief that he could be that cruel, that I have that man's DNA in my blood—makes my stomach clench.

"Anyway," I say, making myself smile, "it sucked, but it all led me here, you know? To Nico and the *Susannah*. If I'd stayed in college, I would've had a B.A. in English lit and probably still ended up as a waitress, only with a lot of student debt."

"Sailing to a deserted island does sound better than that," Amma says with a nod, and I turn away, grateful that she's found a way to graciously end the conversation, but still feeling more than a little raw.

Through the small cabin window, I can see that the night sky has grown dark, and Nico stands up, stretching. "I'll take first watch."

Brittany looks up. "Watch?"

Nico gives her a smile that I've seen before, the one that's a little condescending, not showing any teeth, his dimples deepening. I've never liked that smile, and it's especially unsettling from this perspective. Suddenly, I catch a glimpse of what he must've been like before, back when he wasn't Nico the Cool Boat Guy, but rather Nicholas Johannsen III, growing up in La Jolla with his lawyer dad, his Botoxed mom, his fancy prep school uniform, and his expensive car.

It's a jarring reminder that despite living together in tight quarters for the last six months, there's still a lot that I don't know about my boyfriend.

"We can't just all go to sleep," he tells Brittany. "Someone has to keep an eye out."

"But . . ." She gestures at the radio panel, the radar that sits on a little shelf jutting out from the wall between the sleeping cabin and the main galley. "It's the twenty-first century. Isn't everything basically done digitally now?"

"Some of it," Nico says, crossing his arms over his chest, his skin very brown against the ragged sleeves of his T-shirt. Only now do I see that the faded letters on the back read, JOHANNSEN & MILLER FAMILY PICNIC 2011.

"But nothing is better than these," he goes on, forking his fingers and pointing at his own eyes. "And trust me, the last thing you want is to miss an alarm and have a container ship bearing down on you at two in the morning."

I've heard this particular warning before, and I know where Nico's going with it.

"Lot of those big-ass ships get back into port and find the rigging of smaller sailboats tangled up in their bow," he says, and there's a little bit of a gleam in his eye as he smacks one palm against the other, pushing. "They just creamed some boat in the dark, and never even knew it."

If he'd expected the girls to look alarmed, he must be disappointed because Brittany looks unfazed. "Well, we definitely don't want to be creamed," Brittany says, and Amma snorts into her water.

Nico looks a little at a loss. I get up from the table, collecting our dishes. "I'll relieve you at three," I say, and he slips an arm around my waist as I pass, bringing me in for a quick kiss on the cheek.

"Perfect, babe. Thanks."

He swats at my ass before jogging back up the steps to the deck, and I turn to Brittany and Amma, my cheeks a little flushed. Is Nico always this . . . bro-y? I mean, I definitely knew he had tendencies. But there's something about seeing him through Brittany's and Amma's eyes that makes me feel like I have to say, "This trip is clearly bringing out his inner Sigma Nu."

Brittany smiles and waves me off. "He's a good guy," she says, and Amma nods, folding her arms on the table.

"Not bad to look at, either."

The words don't make me jealous, only proud, which is maybe a little pathetic.

"Do you need any help with those?" Brittany asks, nodding at the plates, but I shake my head.

"No, I got this. Go on up to the deck. The stars are unreal, I bet."

They don't need to be told twice, and I hear Nico call out to them as they emerge above.

Without three other people in here, the galley actually feels a little open, and I take a deep breath, relishing these few moments alone.

I wonder if I maybe should've let the girls find their own boat, a bigger one where we weren't all on top of each other.

But no, it's worth being a little crammed. The *Susannah* is finally fixed. And as soon as we're back from this trip, Nico and I will be free to start our own adventure, and it won't feel claustrophobic. It will feel . . . cozy.

Homey.

Besides, in two days, we'll reach the island—*atoll*—and there will be plenty of space. Too much, probably.

After rinsing the dishes in the little pump sink, I go back to the table to collect the water bottles, sticking my fingers in the necks to gather them all up. As I do, I glance at Brittany's phone, still lying on the table. The lock screen shows a picture of Brittany and Amma with their arms around each other's shoulders, the Colosseum in the background. Their smiles are broad, but they both look a little paler than they do now, thinner, too— Brittany almost alarmingly so, her cheekbones standing out so much that they create their own shadows. Amma's knuckles on Brittany's shoulder are almost white, her fingertips digging into Brittany's skin.

Frowning, I lean in a little closer, but before I can study the photograph further, I hear feet on the steps again, and quickly turn back to the sink. I'm rinsing out the bottles when Brittany appears in the galley, reaching for her phone.

"Just wanted to get some pictures of the sky," she says, then looks again at the sink. "You sure you don't need help? I feel bad."

"Don't," I assure her. "I'll be up in a second."

"Okay, but you'd be up in *half* a second if I help," she says, and I find myself smiling back at her. They're just both really nice— not what I expected girls like this to be.

Brittany joins me at the sink, close enough that our hips bump as she reaches for one of the plates. The pump sink doesn't have the best water pressure, but we manage to clean the remaining plates and forks pretty quickly, and then I'm on the deck with all of them, staring up overhead.

There are so many stars that they almost seem fake, and I rest one hand against the mast as my eyes try to take it all in. The sea is open and empty all around us, the sky stretching out overhead, and it's all so clear, so vast, that I can see the curve of the earth, and suddenly I understand why Nico enjoys this so much.

I don't feel small or scared or alone. I feel part of something bigger.

And when I look over at Brittany, her face tipped up to the sky, I see a grin stretching wide across her face.

# BEFORE

Brittany is crying again.

Amma lies on the bottom bunk, listening to the sobs above. They're muffled because Brittany has buried her face into her pillow or the wall or a blanket—she tries to hide it, but this isn't the graceful crying that girls do in movies, silent tears tracking down pale faces. This is full-body shit, shoulders shaking, tears spraying, nose leaking, throat aching.

Amma knows because she's done her share of this kind of crying.

The bunk room is uncomfortably warm even with the windows open, the night outside hot and still, and Amma hears a dog give two short barks, the only sound other than the sobs.

She and Brittany had picked this hostel because it was cheap, and at the time, a twenty-minute train ride outside of Paris hadn't sounded that far, plus it was a good use of their Eurail passes. But Amma hadn't thought about how lonely it might feel out here in the suburbs, how the pace and noise and lights of the city might keep this kind of breakdown at bay. The quiet here is too thick, too heavy, and the old lady who runs the place has a curfew, which means they were all in their bunks by midnight, the doors locked.

*We should've spent a few extra euros and stayed in the city,* Amma thinks, punching her pillow down. But their money is already starting to run out and they never had that much to begin with.

Brittany gives another choking cry, and from across the

room, one of the other American girls staying in the hostel sits up. Amma thinks her name is Taylor or Hayden, something like that. She's from South Carolina, Amma remembers from the brief conversation they had over the shared dinner of sandwiches and soup in the rustic kitchen, and her accent is thick as she snaps, "Girl, whoever he is, he's not worth it. Shut up and go to sleep."

Amma is up almost before she realizes it, tossing her pillow back on the bunk, anger surging through her blood so quickly it almost makes her dizzy.

"Back the fuck off," she says, her voice sharp and too loud in the silent room, and the girl above Taylor or Hayden from South Carolina sits up, too.

*"Les nerfs!"*

Amma's French is shitty, stuck somewhere in eleventh grade, so she doesn't know what that means, but she's assumes it's telling her to calm down or shut up. Or maybe it's some uniquely French phrase that conveys both.

But Brittany is already sliding from the bunk, her purple plaid pajama pants riding up one slender leg as she mutters, *"Je suis désolée, je suis désolée."*

*I'm sorry, I'm sorry.*

That, Amma does know—she's always thought *désolée* is a weirdly intense word for *sorry.* But as Brittany slinks from the room, still sniffling, her pillow clutched to her chest, it's the only word that fits.

*Desolate.*

It's the feeling that she and Brittany have both been trying to outrun. With each new destination, Amma keeps thinking that maybe *now* they'll have escaped it. On the first flight from Atlanta to London, she'd imagined all that sadness, all that grief, slipping away from them to pool on the runway, a sludge of loss they could leave farther and farther behind with each stamp in their passports.

But it slips back in at night, and no sight, no experience, seems able to exorcise it.

The floor is gritty beneath Amma's feet as she follows Brittany into the hallway. As she leaves the bunk room, she hears a murmur of voices and she knows they'll leave tomorrow. This first night has already marked them as the Weird Ones—the "girl who cries" and "her psycho friend"—and that is fatal in these kinds of places where words like *vibe* and *chill* are paramount.

*Fuck them,* she thinks, crossing the empty living room as she hears Brittany unlock the back door. *If they only knew, if they only understood . . .*

The hostel has a small back garden with wrought-iron furniture and a few potted plants, and Amma finds Brittany standing in the middle of it, her face tilted up to the sky as she sucks in deep breaths, her pillow lying in the grass at her feet.

Her hair is pulled back from her face, and Amma notices the sharpness of her chin, the hollows underneath her cheekbones. She's getting thinner again, though she's still not as thin as she was when Amma first met her. Sitting in folding chairs in a church basement, Amma had thought Brittany looked sick. Beautiful, sure, with all that dark hair and those big hazel eyes—but brittle and insubstantial, like the slightest thing would break her.

Brittany is tougher than that, even with the midnight cry-fests. Amma knows that now.

She turns, sensing Amma's approach, and she wipes at her face. "I'm sorry," she says immediately, and Amma shrugs.

"You said that already. But in French, so I guess it doesn't count."

Brittany gives a watery chuckle before groaning and plunging her hands into her hair. "God," she sighs. "Am I going to cry all over Europe?"

"You're entitled to it," Amma says, stepping closer and putting an arm around Brittany's shoulders, hugging her against the side of her body. The night is warm, but Brittany's skin is cold, and she shivers a little as she presses in closer to Amma.

"I thought it would get better," she says, her voice quiet, and Amma feels her own throat grow tight.

She's not like Brittany—crying doesn't come easy to her, nor does it seem to help. Tears never leave her feeling relieved or soothed, just exhausted and vaguely ashamed, like she gave in to something she shouldn't have. A guilty purge rather than a cleansing catharsis.

"It will," she tells Brittany now. "I mean, we're only on the second week of this thing. You have to give it time."

Brittany steps away from her, scrubbing a hand over her face. "You sound like Dr. Amin."

Amma knows she does, and she kind of hates that, but the leader of their grief group is the voice in her head at moments like these.

*Give it time.*

*Nothing you feel is wrong.*

*There will always be a* before *and an* after*, and you have to learn to live in the after.*

That was the one Brittany liked the most. "In the After" is tattooed in curling script on the inside of her wrist now, slightly hidden by the beaded bracelets she's currently wearing. She'd gotten the tattoo just before they'd left on this trip, a pledge to enjoy life again.

That's what traveling around Europe was supposed to be about: seeing new things, exploring new places, and cementing the bond between them with new memories. Otherwise, they were only friends because the same horrible thing had happened to each of them. They wanted to be friends because they'd chosen each other. They wanted to have a story they could tell that wouldn't make people wince, their eyes widen, their lips wobble with sympathy or, worse, pity.

*We'll tell people we met in college,* Brittany had said. *Instant best friends.*

*In the same history class,* Amma had added. *Maybe a sorority. Did the backpacking thing our senior year.*

They could almost see it, this fun house mirror version of themselves, where they were normal.

Now, Amma hugs Brittany again, wrapping her other arm around her. "Tomorrow is going to be better," she says.

Brittany practically shoves Amma away as she says, "Jesus, did you just follow me out here to be a human fortune cookie?"

Another thing Amma is getting used to, these sudden shifts, as though every mood Brittany ever has is always right there at the surface, waiting to burst forth. Amma understands it, but that doesn't mean she isn't tired of it.

*No, I followed you out here because you were crying like a lunatic again, and you're the one with a fucking fortune cookie saying* literally *inked on your skin, so maybe take a seat, Britt.*

The harsh words are right there on her tongue, so heavy she can almost taste them, and Amma imagines how good it would feel to say what she actually thinks—but it would only last for a few moments, and then the regret would set in. Besides, they still have two more weeks on this trip and one more country to get through together before they head back home to New Hampshire. A fight now would just ruin everything.

"I'm just trying to help," Amma says instead, the words pale and weak, and Brittany sighs as she wraps her arms tightly around her body, hugging her elbows. Her skin is faintly blue in the moonlight, and once again, Amma wishes they'd stayed in Paris where they could ease this tension with a late-night drink or a mad dash through the city streets, finding boys named Etienne and Alexandre to flirt with in dim cafés.

Instead, they're in the sad backyard of a sad suburban hostel, and when Brittany says, "I don't think you can help. I don't think anyone can," Amma thinks to herself, *This was a mistake.*

She tells herself she means choosing the hostel.

But she knows better.

For such a small atoll, Meroe Island is overstuffed with legend. Named for the HMS *Meroe*, a frigate that was shipwrecked there in 1821, the atoll is, from the water, a veritable Eden, a child's storybook ideal of an island. There is little hint of the dangers that await you once you have set foot on its sandy beaches. Impenetrable jungle and a dearth of fresh water are the first challenges, but there are others. The fish that swim in the lagoon are beautifully and brightly colored, yet poisonous, and therefore inedible. A small but deadly species of shark swims through the crystalline waters. Insects buzz and bite, carrying with them all manner of tropical fevers.

And yet for all that, perhaps the most dangerous element of Meroe is what the island seems to do to those who tarry there too long. A sort of madness sets in when one is away from society for too long, when one looks out to the horizon and sees only sea and sky.

—*Rambles and Recollections: My Travels in the South Pacific*
by Lord Christopher Ellings, 1931

# NOW

# SEVEN

My morning watch on the ship ends as the sun comes up.

The sky almost looks like it's on fire, and the soft pinks I'm accustomed to are instead a blazing red, bleeding into orange.

The colors are reflected in the glass-like surface of the ocean all around us, and even though it's beautiful, my stomach sinks.

*Red sky at night, sailor's delight. Red sky at morning, sailors take warning.*

It was one of the first things Nico taught me when he was teaching me about sailing. Looking at this bloodred sky right now, it's hard to imagine a storm heading our way, but I can almost smell it on the air, a hint of a cold, metallic tinge.

Nico pops his head out of the cabin and frowns. "Fuck," he mutters, and then he's gone again.

Alarm skitters up my spine, and I follow him below.

He's sitting at the table in the galley, scowling at a weather radar map open on his laptop. When I come closer, he taps at a big blob of green on the screen. "There it is," he says, and the simple phrase makes my knees watery. "Not too big, and if we alter course now, I think we can mostly skate around the edges of it, but . . ." He releases a breath, ruffling his hair. "I'm not gonna lie, it's gonna get a little gnarly."

"What exactly is your definition of 'a little gnarly'?" I ask, folding my arms across my chest, but before he can answer, the door to the cabin opens. Brittany appears, with a loose and faded T-shirt slipping off one of her tanned shoulders, her dark hair a tangled mess as she looks at us with sleepy eyes. "Something wrong?" she asks, and I shake my head even as Nico says, "We're just in for a bit of rough weather."

That wakes her up. Her eyes go wide, and she turns to say something to Amma, who I can see sliding out of the bed behind her.

"What do we need to do?" Amma asks.

Nico pauses. "Look, I'm going to do my best to keep us out of the worst, but you should go ahead and get dressed, and grab life jackets. And even if you don't usually get seasick, take some meds now."

He goes to the counter and pulls out the red plastic medical kit, grabs a blister pack, and tosses it to Amma.

"And be sure to stay below," he tells them both. "Just hunker down."

Then Nico lifts his eyes to me, his expression as serious as I've ever seen it. "You're with me, babe."

The words warm me even as real fear takes hold.

We're a team.

We're in this together.

━━━◦◦━━━

IT COMES ON SLOW, THEN all at once.

The first sign is the way the air gets colder, enough that I'm eager to slide on the slicker Nico gave me. I have a life jacket on under that, and the entire getup is bulky, and only made worse by the fact that I also have a nylon belt around my waist, clipping me into the ship.

*That's* what suddenly makes it feel real for me: the idea of wind and waves that are strong enough to send me over the side, with this one strap the only thing between safety and all that ocean.

I've had sailing lessons, both from Nico back in San Diego and in Maui. Sometimes Nico teaches me, sometimes it's one of the guys at the marina, and I've gotten a lot more comfortable on the water, enough so that I've taken a boat out on my own several times now. But all of those lessons had happened on calm water under bright blue skies.

This is different.

Within a few hours, the sky goes so dark it almost feels like night. The wind that slaps me in the face is cold, the rain that slithers inside my jacket even more so, and I feel like the whole world has turned upside down, almost literally.

Nico is at the wheel, his feet planted firmly, and I blink, my vision blurry with rain and seawater. I tell myself it's better being out here on the deck, that if I were below like Brittany and Amma, it would drive me insane to not actually see what was happening.

But as I watch a wave swell up in front of us, higher and higher, I close my eyes instinctively. I don't want to see this, don't want to witness climbing that wall of water even as I feel the *Susannah* begin to rise. The wind is howling so loudly that I can't hear what Nico is shouting to me, and I try to stay on my feet even as the boat tilts at a crazy angle.

This is not how I want to die, swept overboard into that roiling water.

The deck is slippery as I clutch the handholds bolted to the sides. The sails are down, obviously, but our engine is still running, propelling us through the water, and I slowly make my way to Nico, shouting to be heard over the fury of the storm.

"What can I do?"

Water is streaming over his slicker, and his hands are red, knuckles white from where he's gripping the wheel. "We've got to try to keep her steady!" he shouts back. "If she turns sideways . . ."

He doesn't have to finish the sentence.

If the *Susannah* turns to starboard or port, one of these waves can roll her, and then it's over.

I put my hands alongside his on the wheel, feeling the incredible pull of ship and sea, and through the sheets of water pouring over us, I see the cabin door open.

At first, I think it's just the force of the ship that's pulled it, but then I see Brittany's dark hair, a bright orange life jacket, and she's moving slowly out onto the deck, ducking her head against the wind and water.

"Fuck!" I hear Nico shout, and he jerks his head at me. "Get her back inside. She's not clipped in."

I let go of the wheel as Nico grunts and grips even harder, and slowly inch my way toward her.

"Get back down below!" I yell, but she either can't understand me or doesn't care, because she's on the deck now, looking around in amazement or shock, I can't really tell.

"Brittany!" I yell again, and finally she turns and looks at me.

"I'm sorry! I just couldn't stay down there!" she shouts back, shaking her head. "Not knowing—"

"Okay, well now you know!" I shout back. "It's scary as fuck!"

She laughs, even though she looks pale and green, and I move closer, urging her back toward the cabin door.

It happens so fast.

One minute, I'm on my feet, my hands out in front of me, the next, the ship is lurching, my feet are slipping, and I'm falling.

The deck tilts, and I see white-capped, frothy water rising up at my side, and I'm sliding toward it.

*NO!*

It's the only thought in my frantic mind as I scramble for purchase, a constant litany of *no no no NO NO NO*.

My feet flail on the wet deck, desperate for something, anything to grab on to, and I clutch at the lifeline around me even as the nylon pulls through my fingers, tearing skin.

I hear a distant pop, and for a second, I think I've broken a small bone in my hand. It's only when the tension around my waist gives way that I realize my line has snapped.

There's nothing tethering me to the ship.

My hands sting, wet with seawater and blood, but I plant both palms down on the deck, trying to stop this slide into nothingness. Red streaks follow me down, and I watch almost from a distance as the water turns them pink, washes them away.

I dig my hands in harder even though there's nothing to grip, and then my foot hits the side of the boat, hard, and then my ankle is over the side, my shin, my foot dangling over nothingness, I'm sliding . . .

There's another sharp lurch, and I slip forward again.

The *Susannah* rights itself just as I'm about to be tipped over into the sea, and I roll back, away from the edge, panting hard.

"Lux!" I hear Brittany shouting, and out of the corner of my eye, I see her trying to move closer.

My hands are screaming, and I think I might have broken one of my toes, but I lurch to my feet anyway, shoving her back. She stumbles into the cabin, and I shut the door, leaning against it and letting my legs give out as I slump to the deck.

In seconds, I'd gone from scared but alive, to nearly dead.

I search through the wind and rain for Nico, but he's hidden from my view now that I'm sitting, and I wonder if he saw me nearly go over.

It's not like he could've done anything. But still, it had only been Brittany's cry I heard, not his.

THE WIND BEGINS TO DIE down first, the rain slowing until it's little more than a drizzle, and then it's just . . . gone.

The whole storm seems to have vanished as quickly as it appeared, the sky overhead suddenly turns blue again instead of gray, and the sun beams brightly down on us. It's over.

I'm still sitting there on the deck, sweating inside my slicker, trying to wrap my mind around how quickly things changed. At the wheel, Nico laughs, already unbuttoning his jacket. "Jesus Christ." He scrubs a hand over his hair, sending droplets of water flying. "That was fucked up."

It was, but Nico says it so cheerfully that I don't think he really understands how scary it was for me, how dangerous, and I feel anger well up inside me, pressing against my breastbone, making my hands shake as I cross the small distance between us.

"We could've died," I say. "I almost *did* die. Did you even see how useless this fucking thing was? I almost went over the side!"

I hold up the frayed end of my safety rope, and he frowns, taking it between his fingers. "Shit, babe," he says, and I feel tears suddenly well up, my throat tight.

"But you're okay, right?" he asks, looking at me with those brown eyes, and . . . the truth is, I am. Scared, sure, and my hands still really hurt, but he's right. It could've gone really badly, but it didn't.

Behind me, I hear Brittany and Amma making their way up on deck. I don't want to fight in front of them, don't want them to see me as the Shrieking and Very Uncool Girlfriend, and so I let it drop, because what else can I do? The storm has passed.

I shake my head and lean into Nico, wrapping an arm around his neck. "I'm okay," I say firmly, and his smile returns.

Brittany throws her arms around me, squeezing me tight. "Holy shit, you were so badass!" she says, and when she pulls back, I see genuine admiration in her face.

Turning over her shoulder, she calls to Amma, "Did you see this bitch? Nearly went over the side, was all, 'Not today, motherfucker!' She pushed herself back on board and—"

"The boat righted itself," I say, shaking my head. Now that the terror is fading some, it almost feels kind of silly. Only one leg really went over, and those toes I'd been sure were broken are now just sort of dully throbbing. I can wiggle them in my shoes.

Brittany turns back to me. "No, you full-on pushed yourself back on board. I'm telling you, it was awesome." She takes my shoulders in both hands, grinning in my face. "You're a survivor, Lux."

"No one wants to die like that, trust me," I say. "You would've done the same thing."

Brittany shakes her head. "I don't think so. Honestly. Some people would've been too scared to do anything but let go. It's easier, you know?"

I nod because I do know, and I'm suddenly really tired, all the adrenaline draining out of me.

"Baptism by fire," Nico adds with a grin, throwing an arm around me, and I try not to think of that moment when I was sliding and my hand was reaching for nothing, my blood streaking across the *Susannah*'s pristine white decks.

Of how I had put my life in Nico's hands, and he nearly let me go.

# BEFORE

There's a girl on Nico's boat.

In the month since Lux walked out of the Cove holding Nico's hand, she's seen people on board the *Susannah*. Nico has a never-ending rotation of friends stopping by, but they've always been guys, men who look a lot like Nico. Tanned, beautiful, teeth so straight and white that they can only be the result of thousands of dollars of orthodontia. They all smell like Nico, too, that mix of salt and motor oil that Lux has gotten so used to.

There's never been a girl before.

But there's one now. As Lux makes her way down the dock, arms full of grocery bags, she sees her, a girl with long dark hair standing on the deck of the *Susannah*. It's late afternoon, early evening, really, and she is limned in golden light. She's wearing a floral sundress that flutters against her legs, and there's an expensive-looking leather tote hanging from one shoulder. Her arms are folded tight across her slender torso, and as Lux watches, one hand darts up, swiping at her cheek beneath huge sunglasses.

She's crying.

Nico is standing across from her, one hand braced on the mast, his face set in an expression Lux hasn't seen yet.

He looks . . . bored? But there's also something about the stiff way he's holding himself, the rigidity of his posture, that sets little alarm bells ringing in her head.

Lux is hit with a memory, of sitting in the front seat of her mom's Honda Civic, the day they left for California. She was twelve, slumped in the passenger seat, watching through the window as her parents stood in the front yard of their house.

*Except it's* his *house now,* she remembers thinking. Her mom had been saying something, shaking her head, but her dad had just stood there, his posture casual, hands shoved in pockets. Everything about him had felt like a locked door, and Lux knew her mom no longer had the key.

That's how Nico looks right now. Whatever this girl is saying to him, he's nodding and listening, but she's not getting in.

Lux has nearly made it to their slip, her sneakers quiet on the faded wood of the dock, and Nico sees her, lifting his chin slightly in her direction even as the corners of his mouth briefly turn down.

The girl turns around, and even behind the sunglasses, Lux can feel her eyes taking in everything about her: her red hair, the groceries in her arms, Nico's blue plaid button-down thrown over her bathing suit top.

The girl's lips purse, and then she faces Nico again.

"So, I guess we're done, then," she says, and he tilts his head back, looking up at the sky. "We've been done, Suz."

"Right."

The girl rests a hand on the mast before going to step off the boat, her wedge sandals squeaking on the deck.

As she passes her on the dock, Lux is hit with her scent, something fresh and clean, which seems to hover around her in a mist.

"So, you're the newest project," she says, and Lux is momentarily speechless. "He's a big fan of projects," the girl continues, and now there's something ugly in the curl of her mouth, something disdainful. "Good luck."

With that, she's gone in a swirl of her skirt, that cloud of expensive perfume, leaving Lux holding a bag of wilting lettuce and rapidly melting pistachio ice cream.

Looking to Nico, she raises her eyebrows. "Wanna fill me in?"

He sighs, coming across the deck to take the groceries out of her hands. "It's nothing."

"Didn't seem like nothing."

"We dated for a little bit, she was pissed at how it ended, guess she thought she needed to tell me so in person. Again."

Lux follows Nico onto the *Susannah,* the deck swaying gently. "After a month?"

When Nico just looks at her over his shoulder, Lux tries to ignore the sudden coldness in the pit of her belly.

"I mean," she starts, shoving her hands in the back pockets of her shorts, "we've been together for a month now. So, obviously, you two broke up before that."

"Right, like I said," Nico continues, reaching out with one hand to slide open the door to the cabin, "it's nothing."

Lux follows him down the steps into the cabin, the light dim, squinting as Nico begins putting the groceries away.

He leaves for Maui in a week, maybe two, and they haven't talked about what that means for them. It's new, after all, this thing. Yeah, it got really serious really fast—Lux is more or less living on board the boat these days, which is definitely an improvement over her shitty shoebox of an apartment—but maybe Nico has always just seen this as a temporary arrangement.

Lux knows she loves him, even though she hasn't said it out loud yet. There's never been anyone like Nico before, not for her. Sure, she's dated other guys, but it was never serious, never this *all in* feeling she has with him, like they're real partners.

A team.

She thinks he might love her, too, but she keeps waiting for those magic words—*come to Maui with me.* So far, nothing.

She thinks of the person she used to be, the brave girl who thought she was tough, who didn't think the world could touch her—the person she was before her mom died. That girl would have just come right out and asked: *Hey, can I come with you?*

Sometimes she can feel the question pressing against the back of her teeth, and a part of her brain says to just go for it, for fuck's sake, so what if he says no?

But this other Lux—this newer, still fragile Lux—is too scared of popping the bubble she's been able to live in the past month, and so here she is, just . . . waiting.

*Suz.*

Nico had called her Suz.

Leaning against the wall, Lux crosses her arms over her chest. "Was that Susannah?" she asks. "As in, the namesake of this boat, Susannah?"

Nico still has his back to her as he puts bananas in the little mesh bag hanging over the sink, and she sees his shoulders rise and fall.

"Yeah, that was her," he says, "but it was—"

"Nothing, yeah, I know," Lux replies curtly.

Turning around, Nico braces both hands on the sink. "We dated in college," he says, looking her in the eye. "For a couple of years. We were young and stupid, but we were together when I got the boat, and I named it after her because I'm a romantic dude. As you well know."

He gives her a little grin at that, the one that makes his dimples deepen, and even though she hates herself for it, Lux feels a little of her anger drain away.

Nico is good at that.

Stepping forward now, he takes her hands in his, lifting one to kiss her knuckles. "Want me to rename it?" he asks. "The *Lux*? The SS *McAllister*?"

Rolling her eyes, Lux lets him pull her in, his arms going easily around her waist. "Maybe," she says, and he grins again as he leans in to kiss the tip of her nose.

"Or, better yet, how about you come with me to Maui in a week?"

Lux's heart leaps.

There it is, the question she's been waiting for. She knows she's going to say yes, but there's still something dark hovering around the edges of her joy. Why did he have to ask her now, when she still feels like there's something he's not telling her about Susannah?

She thinks again about the girl's tears, about her snarling lip.

*So, you're his newest project.*

What does that even mean? And why would a girl he'd broken up with months ago be here crying on his boat, still so hurt, so angry?

Nico kisses her then, softly, quickly. "You're thinking so hard," he says, reaching up to push her hair back from her face.

"I just . . ." she starts, but she doesn't want to finish that sentence, doesn't want to bring up Susannah again.

She doesn't want answers she knows she won't like.

*Don't be stupid. Life is short. There's nothing here for you. Go to Maui.*

So she does.

# NOW

# EIGHT

We see the island a full day before we'll be able to reach it.

It's visible in the distance, looking like nothing more than a pile of clouds at first, all smudged and vaguely gray-ish, but within a few hours, I can see spots of green, and my heart thumps against my ribs as I stand at the bow, fingers curled around the guideline.

Suddenly, this trip makes a little more sense. Why Brittany and Amma wanted to come here, why Nico loves life on the water so much. It feels like magic, charting a course to a place, then watching it slowly materialize in front of you.

Brittany appears beside me, her long hair pulled back from her face, and she reaches down to squeeze my hand. "What are you going to do first?" she asks. "After we've anchored?"

I laugh, shaking my head. "No idea. A musical number, maybe? Accompanied by some crabs and tropical birds?"

That makes her laugh, too, and she gives my hand another squeeze. "Perfect. Nico?"

She calls back to him, and from his spot at the wheel, he leans over slightly, cupping one hand around an ear. "What?"

"She wants to know what you're going to do first!" I call back. "When we get to the island!"

His expression shifts, that blinding grin flashing across his face. "Haven't decided yet. Nudity feels pretty high up there."

The storm threw me, would've thrown anyone, but now things are back on track. We're safe, our destination is in front of us, and two weeks of doing absolutely nothing—not cleaning hotel rooms, not scrubbing a sink, not waiting my turn to use the shower in a mildewed bathroom—stretch out like a fucking red carpet.

I can't wait.

HOURS LATER, WE'RE THERE, AND as the *Susannah* makes her way to the island's natural harbor, I stare at the shore in front of us. It's not like beauty is anything new to me—I've been living in Hawaii for the past six months, after all. But there's something different about Meroe, something wilder. It looks like a kid's drawing of a deserted island, all tall palm trees and sandy shore, the water and sky contrasting but equally brilliant shades of blue.

We have to motor in because of the currents, and as our boat chugs over a swell to enter the harbor, the push is strong enough that, for a second, it feels like the boat is moving backward. Like the island is pushing us away.

At the wheel, Nico's expression is steely, his hands gripping tightly, and I wonder if he felt it, too. Probably not. Like he said, Nico isn't superstitious. But I catch Amma frowning as we finally glide into the harbor.

And then I see it.

Like I told Brittany back in Maui, boats are not my thing. I've seen all kinds and have never been all that impressed by any of them.

But this boat is very different.

She's a catamaran, well over forty feet, glossy white against all that blue-green, her sail an even deeper, clearer blue than the sky. Fitting, because that's her name, stenciled on the side.

*Azure Sky.*

Looking at her, I feel the same way I did the first time I saw Nico. Like the world has suddenly gotten a little bit bigger.

"Fuck me." I hear Amma breathe at my side, and she scowls at the ship.

She and Brittany had been trying to do something other than the usual tourist thing by coming here. The fact that other people have already found the island—beaten them to it—is clearly bugging Amma.

Nico has killed the engine, letting the *Susannah* rest idly on the smooth, clear water as he looks over at the *Azure Sky*.

"What a beauty," he says with an appreciative smile.

But Amma is already turning to Brittany, her expression stormy. "I thought no one ever came here."

Brittany just shrugs, pushing her sunglasses up onto her head. "I thought so, too, but, I mean, it's the twenty-first century. If we can find things, so can other people. It's not really that weird that someone else is here."

Amma doesn't seem satisfied by that response, her frown only deepening, but then someone steps out onto the deck of the catamaran.

Even from a distance, I can tell he's rich. Working at the resorts in Maui gave me a kind of sixth sense when it came to the type. His hair was probably once brown, but he's been outside enough to give it that sun-streaked look women pay a lot of money for. Aviator sunglasses, mirrored, reflect the blue, blue water, and he flashes a million-dollar smile as he lifts an arm to wave to us.

"Ahoy!" he calls out, and I can practically feel Nico roll his eyes behind me. Still, he waves back at the guy, just as a woman makes her way up onto the deck to join him.

She's also blond, hair whipping in her face as she leans over the railing to gaze out at us. She's wearing cutoffs that ride up her tan thighs, and an oversized button-down that probably belongs to the guy. Sun-kissed and beautiful, they look like an ad for hard seltzer, and I feel grubby in my own loose-fitting shorts and an old V-neck.

Beside me, Amma's hands have clenched into fists as she stares at the couple. Her lips are a thin line, white around the edges, and when I nudge her with my elbow, she startles like she'd forgotten I was there.

"You okay?" I ask.

"Relax," Brittany says to her friend. "The more the merrier!"

"That's not it," Amma says quietly. By now, the man is climbing into the small dinghy attached to the side of the catamaran, clearly planning to come over and say hello in person.

"Bet they have some quality booze on that boat," Nico mutters in my ear as he slings an arm around my waist. He smells like sweat and sunblock, and the skin on his nose is peeling just the littlest bit. I don't even want to know how I look. A crust of salt has settled on my skin, and I know my hair is a wreck.

The tender idles next to us, the guy still grinning. "Welcome to paradise!" he calls, and I realize he's Australian.

Of course he is.

"Hey, thanks, man," Nico says, and the guy gestures at the side of the *Susannah*.

"Permission to board?"

"Aye-aye," Nico replies, and within a couple of minutes, the guy is standing there on the deck of our boat, somehow making it feel dingier with his own general shininess.

"Jake Kelly," he says, offering a hand to Nico, who shakes it before introducing all of us.

"So, what brings you all the way out here?" Jake asks warmly. Close up, he's even better looking than I'd assumed. Amazing what money can do, the gloss it can give you.

"Same thing that brought you here, I'd guess," Nico says. I notice the way he flexes his biceps just the littlest bit. His arms have a darker tan and are definitely bigger than Jake's, and I fight the urge to roll my eyes.

Boys.

"Oh, so you're also here looking for buried treasure?" Jake replies, his eyebrows raised over the frames of his sunglasses, before laughing and clapping a hand on Nico's shoulder. "Fucking with you, mate. We're just here for a good time off the beaten path."

"Same," Brittany says, stepping forward. She's changed into a brightly patterned pink-and-green bikini, and I see Jake give her an admiring look that somehow isn't sleazy, a quick head-to-toe glance that doesn't make you feel like you need a shower afterward.

Brittany's smile gets a little slyer, one hip cocked as she nods her head in the direction of his boat.

"Have you and your wife been here long?"

Subtle.

Jake glances over his shoulder. "Girlfriend," he corrects. "Eliza. And no, just a couple of days. You're lucky you got in when you did. Had some ugly weather the day we arrived."

Nico brightens, launching into a story about the storm we were caught in—probably the same nasty weather Jake mentioned—and bored by this obvious show of machismo, I head for the stern to get a better look at the island.

Amma is already standing there, arms folded tightly around her body, and as I get closer, I realize there are twin tracks of tears on her cheeks.

Alarmed, I reach out and lay a hand on her arm. "You okay?"

She startles, and reaches up to swipe at her damp cheeks. "Yeah, sorry. Just . . . guess I got kind of overwhelmed, you know? That we're finally here, but also it's the beginning of the end."

I definitely get feeling that way at the *end* of a vacation—wanting to soak in what you can even as you're already anticipating the impending return to reality. But it seems a little weird to cry when a trip like this is just beginning.

But Amma *is* a little weird. Brittany is easier to be around, not nearly as prickly. Once again, I wonder how they became friends, what keeps them together when they actually seem pretty different.

Instead, I smile at Amma and nod toward the island. "Think of it as the beginning of the beginning," I say. "The beginning of two weeks in this amazing place with no one around."

"No one except those two," Amma whispers quickly, as Jake approaches us.

"So, Nico here says your group might be amenable to a beach party tonight?"

Amma stiffens, and I worry she's going to say no. But then a switch seems to flip, and she gives Jake a million-watt smile, so convincing that for a moment, I wonder if I imagined her earlier discomfort. "Wouldn't miss it for the world."

# NINE

It takes us a little bit to get things situated. Nico wants to find the perfect spot to anchor, somewhere close enough to shore that we can easily swim to the beach, but not so shallow that we're scraping the hull. We eventually anchor just a few yards from the *Azure Sky*, the water around us so clear that I can see all the way to the sandy bottom.

By the time we're done, Jake and Eliza have already taken their dinghy—if the spiffy Zodiac can be called that—over to the beach.

Our own dinghy is still affixed to the starboard side of the boat, but we're anchored close enough to shore that I just strip off the T-shirt and shorts I'm wearing over my bathing suit and jump over the side, opting to swim to the island instead.

Warm water closes over my head, and my sunburned skin stings from the salt, but when I break the surface, I'm grinning so hard my face hurts. Even though my eyes smart, the island in front of me is the most beautiful thing I've ever seen, prettier than a dream, better than any of the fantasies I spun up in Mom's hospital room when all I wanted was to run to the ends of the earth.

I hear a splash to my right, and then Brittany's head bobs up next to me, followed by Amma's, then Nico's, all of us beaming. I feel a pleasant ache in my muscles as I start to swim. For a few days, we've been cooped up, and getting to stretch out like this feels even better than I expected.

I remember Nico warning us about sharks around the island, but not even that can kill my buzz as I pump my arms and legs, making my way toward the shimmering beach. It only takes a few minutes, then my toes touch the sandy bottom, and I'm there.

Meroe Island.

It's a pretty name, melodic when you say it out loud, making it easy to forget that it's named after a shipwreck.

After all the wrong turns, I finally took one that brought me to a real, live, deserted island, some honest-to-god *Blue Lagoon*– type shit.

It's already late afternoon, the light turning golden and soft. The shore curves away into the distance, and beyond it is what looks like a nearly impenetrable jungle of palms and other greenery.

Slicking my wet hair back from my face, I gesture at the jungle. "I think the airstrip Nico talked about is somewhere through there. If we ever want to check it out."

"Oh yeah, very high on my list of priorities," Amma replies, and the bite in her words irks me. She's clearly still pissed about Jake and Eliza.

But I'm used to handling negativity. I shrug and say, "You never know. After a week, you might get bored of watching perfect sunsets and swimming in turquoise seas. It happens."

Nico gives a mock growl as he charges me, his arms going around my waist, lifting me off my feet as I shriek. "Or we could play pirates," he teases, swinging me around. "Capturing that booty."

Rolling my eyes, I pull myself out of his arms, still smiling. "I actually can't believe it's taken you this long in our relationship to make that joke."

Up ahead on the beach, Jake has set up a ring of stones, filling it with branches and dried palm leaves, and as I approach, he pushes his sunglasses up his nose and grins at me.

"Is a bonfire on the beach too cliché for the first night?"

I smile back, shaking my head. "Just the right amount of cliché."

"Knew I liked you. Eliza, come meet Lux."

I'm actually a little surprised he remembered my name. It's unusual enough that most people need reminding, or they call me Liz, Lucy, Lex—something close, but not quite right. The fact that Jake clocked it so fast makes me like him more.

Eliza opens her arms to hug me. "Our new roommate!" she says, laughing as she squeezes me. I'm very aware that I'm salty and damp while she smells amazing—like this perfume I once smelled in a guest's room called California Reverie. I'd even spritzed some on my wrists, walking around the rest of the day taking surreptitious sniffs of my skin. It had made me feel like a totally different woman.

"Island-mate," I joke, and she laughs generously even though it's definitely not that funny.

"Honestly, I'm just thrilled you're here. I love this bastard, but the idea of several weeks alone with him on an island was too bleak to contemplate."

Her accent is pure BBC, vowels rich, consonants clipped, and when she reaches up to push her hair back from her face, diamond studs sparkle in her ears.

"Yes, your arrival has probably saved me from a late-night castration, and for that, you deserve a beer," Jake says.

I wonder if they always talk like this, each sentence a tennis ball lobbed, firing back and forth with the ease of sharp, smart people who know each other well.

Jake opens a giant cooler and pulls out a beer, and when he

hands it to me, I actually gasp at how cold it is. We have a fridge on the boat, but Nico said ice was a needless extravagance, so pretty much everything we've had to drink has been lukewarm. And I haven't had a beer since we left the mainland—no drinking on the open sea and all that.

"Your fella tells me you're out of Hawaii?" he asks.

"Maui, yeah," I reply, taking a sip and closing my eyes at how good, how *refreshing*, the beer is. "Well, San Diego for me originally, but we've been in Hawaii for a few months."

"We were thinking of Hawaii after this," Eliza says, wrapping both arms around Jake's waist, her fingers curled around the wrist of her opposite hand. He has an arm casually draped across her shoulders, his other hand holding his own beer. "Jake's been loads of times, but I never have."

"It's beautiful," I tell her, and she gestures to our surroundings. "As beautiful as this?"

I look back out at the sea again, at how the clear aqua bleeds into darker blue farther out, contrasting with the bright sapphire of the sky.

"I don't know if any place is as beautiful as this," I say, and I mean it.

Nico joins us, Brittany trailing just behind.

"Bonfire, nice," he says approvingly to Jake, who introduces him to Eliza, who gives Nico the same warm hug, the same bright smile.

"I'll go get dinner, shall I?" Eliza looks at our group over the rims of her sunglasses. "You'll eat with us, right? A proper celebration?"

Given that our plans for tonight were Spam and rice, I nod, maybe a little too eagerly.

She gives Jake a quick kiss before heading for the Zodiac, which they've dragged onto the sand.

"Need some help?" Brittany asks, and Eliza beckons with one arm.

"Wouldn't say no!"

Amma watches quietly, still standing in the shallows, her arms crossed. But then Nico is taking a beer from Jake, and we're lighting the fire, and I don't have time to wonder what her deal is.

———

WHEN ELIZA HAD OFFERED US dinner, I hadn't been expecting a feast.

Grilled fish; oysters, cold and briny; roasted potatoes; delicate spears of asparagus wrapped in bacon; and a dessert that appears to be made of strawberries and whatever it is that actual angels eat.

I haven't eaten this well in months, not since coming to Maui, really, and Eliza just keeps flitting around, offering more, opening some new container full of some new delight and constantly insisting that we take some, that they brought too much, that she gets "overly excited" in the kitchen.

And the wine . . .

Bottles and bottles, just as cold and crisp as the beer, and by the time the sun has set and it's grown dark on the island, I'm full and drunk, and beyond happy.

I'm *content*.

It's a sensation I haven't felt in a while. Years, maybe.

Jake stands, popping open a bottle of champagne. We all give a drunken shout when it froths from the neck of the bottle, as Jake sloppily fills our glasses.

Once we all have some champagne, he stands by the fire, shirt half-unbuttoned, hair mussed, and lifts his glass. "To Meroe Island," he intones, and we all raise our drinks. "To those unfortunate fuckers who crashed and died here—"

"Boooo!" Eliza says, reaching out with one long leg to kick his shin. "No sad shit!"

Jake catches her ankle easily, pulling her leg up and, in a surprisingly graceful move given how much he's had to drink, leans down to press a kiss against the top of her foot, their eyes meeting in a way that makes my cheeks suddenly flush hot.

"My beloved is right," he says, letting her foot fall back to the sand. "No sad shit. Only jubilation for new friends, and a hell of a first night together."

We all cheers to that.

All of us, except for Amma.

# BEFORE

Rome is better.

Maybe it's the heat, or the bustle of the busy streets. The fact that they're walking so much every day that they're exhausted when they fall into their beds at night. Or it could be that this time, they were smarter, and picked a hostel right in the middle of things, not far from the Spanish Steps, and the nights are never too quiet.

Or it could just be that the food is so, so good.

After the accident, during those first few black months (*in the before*), Brittany hadn't wanted to eat anything. Had barely been able to, and what she did eat had no taste, and sat heavy on her tongue until she invariably spit it out or threw it up. Her weight dropped, her eyes sank deeper into her face, and the shape of her skull emerged beneath her thinning hair. She'd taken a perverse comfort in watching herself almost disappear, fading into the background. It felt easier than going forward and trying to live in this new world.

Now when she looks in the mirror, she's still too thin, but it's not as scary anymore, and yesterday, when she took her first bite of basil gelato in the Piazza Navona, it had exploded on her tongue, creamy and rich, bright and fresh, and she'd felt like maybe she was getting better. Maybe life wouldn't always feel so hard, so pointless.

She feels that way now, sitting at a café with Amma, the sunshine hot on her bare shoulders as they sip cappuccinos and Amma scrolls through the pictures on her phone.

"This one is good," she says, holding it up for Brittany to see.

It's of the two of them in front of the Colosseum, and it *is* good. They're smiling, arms around each other, and Brittany thinks that if you saw that picture in a dorm room or on a fridge, you'd think, *Those girls are so lucky.*

No pity, no concern. Two pretty, happy friends, making the most of their youth and traveling the world together.

Every day of this trip, she feels a little closer to actually *being* that girl, the one she's pretending to be.

"Send that one to me," she says to Amma, and as soon as the text comes through, she sets it as her phone background.

Four weeks ago, before they left for Europe, the background was a picture of her family. All four of them, her mom and dad, and her younger brother, Brian. Smiling with the setting sun behind them, their faces a little sunburned because they had been on their annual beach trip to Florida.

The last vacation they'd taken.

Brittany used to look at that picture on her phone and wonder if it would've been better if she'd known it would be the last time. She had fought with Brian, who'd brought his PlayStation with him and spent hours screaming into his headset, those piercing whoops and battle cries that drove her insane. There had been too many slamming doors on that trip, and on the last night, Brittany sat on her bed, playing on her phone, and told her mom just to bring something back from dinner, because she didn't feel like going out.

Her mom had been disappointed, but had agreed.

That was the thing that still killed Brittany to remember, the way the corners of her mother's mouth had turned down, the soft sigh as she'd closed Brittany's door, her dark hair swinging just above her shoulders as she'd turned away.

After the accident, Brittany replayed that sigh over and over in her mind, just like she catalogued every missed and never returned phone call, every time she hadn't replied to a like or a comment on a Facebook post.

Sometimes she hates that past version of herself so much she wants to crawl out of her own skin.

But doing this, replacing the background on her phone, helps a little. It makes her feel like she's starting to build that new, future self that Dr. Amin keeps telling her about.

She looks at those smiling girls, and she almost believes she's one of them.

<hr>

BUT THE CRYING STARTS AGAIN on their fifth night in Rome.

It shocks her at first, the sobs that seem to well up in her chest out of nowhere, the sudden ache in her throat. That panicky feeling, her face too hot, her eyes stinging, her whole body shaking as she tries so hard to push the tears away.

*I thought I was getting better,* and the words are pitiful even in the silence of her own mind. *I thought this was over.*

But she's beginning to realize there isn't an over, not really. The waves can just keep on coming like this, and there's nothing she can do to stop them.

Amma doesn't cross the space between their beds this time, doesn't make those soothing noises that Brittany simultaneously hates and appreciates, so Brittany stays curled up into herself like a wounded animal, waiting for the sun to rise.

Once it does, they go back out, walk the streets, duck into shops, eat more overpriced pasta, and it's only as the sky turns to dusk, as they sit at another outdoor café, that Brittany utters the words that have been on the tip of her tongue all day.

"Maybe we should go home."

She knows Amma is thinking it, too: that they've had their moments of fun, but this isn't the escape they were after. Except, maybe it is, for Amma? Brittany can never really tell. She loves the other girl, loves her more dearly than she's ever loved any friend, but over and over again, she's reminded that they only have this one awful thing in common, and nothing else. She doesn't really know what Amma is like, regular Amma, in-the-before Amma. She could be suffering, too—just better at hiding it.

Now, she looks across the table at Brittany and gives a little shrug. "Maybe we should. My money is getting tight, and at least we got to see Paris and we've had nearly a week here in Rome. That's not nothing."

It's true. Brittany had always dreamed of visiting both cities, had hung a poster of the Eiffel Tower in her dorm room, for fuck's sake, and now she's also tasted gelato in the shadow of the Colosseum. Maybe it's enough.

She stirs her cappuccino, glances over at the table of people next to her, raggedy backpacks by their feet. They're a little sunburned, their clothes wrinkled and dull in the way things get when they're repeatedly cleaned in hostel sinks and never dry completely. One of the girls leans down to unbuckle her sandal, laughing when the straps fall away to reveal stripes of pale skin amongst a layer of dust. Brittany's accumulated that dust, too, walking through Rome, and she wishes she had that girl's easy laugh, wishes all of this wasn't so fucking hard for her for some reason.

And then she realizes the girl is staring directly at her, her sheaf of strawberry-blond hair pushed behind one ear as she grins and waves at Brittany.

Brittany nods back, but to her surprise, the girl actually gets up from her seat, crossing the crowded little café to come over to their table.

"Hiya!" she says brightly, and then she's offering her hand, a faded, fraying string bracelet around one slender wrist. "I'm Chloe."

A small moment. But that's how it starts.

Dear Mama/Pop/Sis:

Greetings from Paradise! Me and the boys landed a real sweet assignment and find ourselves on [CENSORED]. It's so pretty, I wish you all could see it. Like that book I made Pop read every night when I was twelve, *Robinson Crusoe*. There are palm trees everywhere, coconuts, too. One of the fellas, [CENSORED], even made a pet out of a monkey! We call him Barnum, and [CENSORED] trained him to take peanuts right out of our hands. It really passes the time, but it makes me miss home and Shep even more. He still doing good? I know he's getting old, but tell him he's gotta hang on til we're done whooping these guys!

Today, I went for a walk by myself for a bit just to get some quiet, and even though the guys say this place is spooky, I think it's peaceful. I guess there's some story about a [CENSORED] here back in [CENSORED] where some guys ended up killing each other for food, but luckily, we got a whole box of supplies, so things shouldn't get that bad for us. And looking out at all that ocean makes me think of being back home, seeing cornfields all the way to the horizon. I miss you all, but getting to see the world like this counts for something. You really get that every place is the same in a way. The guys say it's boring here, but I tell them they should come to our farm in the winter, see how quiet it gets!

So no, I don't mind being out here on [CENSORED]. It's not a bad place, just a lonely one, and there's nothing wrong with that.

Will write again soon.

Your son/brother, L.

—LETTER HOME FROM PFC LEONARD AMES (1923–MIA 1943, DECLARED DEAD 1950)

# NOW

# TEN

"What do you think their deal is?"

Last night had been fun. Almost too much fun, if my dry mouth and aching head are any indication. Despite the hangover, all I can think about this morning is all that food, all that wine. The diamonds in Eliza's ears.

"Jake and Eliza?" Brittany asks now, and I nod. We took the dinghy over to the beach with Amma, while Nico stayed behind on the boat.

Brittany shrugs. "They're rich, obviously," she says. "But they seem cool. And laid-back. Which is kind of surprising because I assumed most rich people were uptight."

So it isn't her money funding this trip. I'd wondered, because if they're willing to hand Nico $50,000, money is clearly coming from *somewhere*. And they've been traveling for, what? Months now?

Brittany flashes me a smile. "But then again, I don't really know any. Do you?"

*Nico.*

We don't really talk about Nico's family, the life he led before he chucked it all to go sailing. And Nico never really acts like a rich person. But every once in a while, I'm reminded that he and I grew up very differently.

Once, he'd come to pick me up from work at the Haleakala, driving up to the front of the hotel rather than the back entrance, and even though he'd been wearing his usual shorts and ripped T-shirt, the valet had immediately assumed he was a guest. Nico had told me about it later, laughing, but I'd wondered what it was about him that exuded that aura that he belonged.

Or maybe I was overthinking it.

Amma snorts. "Rich people are just people," she says. "Some are cool, some are assholes."

She's wearing a simple black bikini that emphasizes the pale smoothness of her skin, and she's not quite as tense as she seemed yesterday. But she's still in a mood, clearly.

"That's true," I tell her. "When I worked at the Haleakala, we saw *all* types, trust me."

Amma gives me a smile. "You must have seen some fucked-up shit, working at a resort like that."

"Oh, you would not even believe," I assure her, and then I launch into the sex toy story. By the time I'm done, all three of us are laughing, the sound echoing loudly along the empty stretch of beach.

I realize again just how quiet it is here. Last night, I'd lain on our cushioned table and listened to the surf crashing against the shore in the distance. That sound, that constant murmur in the background, had been there in Hawaii, too, of course, but never this close. Besides—out here, there are no other sounds vying for your attention. No traffic, no voices, no music. Just the wind and the surf, the call of birds, the gentle creaking of the palm trees.

Next to me, Brittany bumps my hip with hers. "This is everything we promised, right?"

I look out at the bright turquoise sea, stretching out in every direction, and nod. "And more," I assure her, reaching out to take her hand and squeeze it. It's the kind of easily affectionate thing I used to do with girls back home. I hadn't realized how much I missed having female friends.

Brittany squeezes back, and even Amma seems relaxed as we walk along the beach until we reach the blanket where Eliza and Jake are stretched out.

Eliza is on her stomach, her cheek resting on her folded arms, her back bare, while Jake has a towel bunched up behind his head, a paperback in one hand. The pages and the cover are curling up, waterlogged, no doubt, and I can't make out the title.

He lifts his head slightly as we approach, already smiling.

"G'day, neighbors," he says cheerfully as Eliza lifts her cheek from her arms.

"What are you three up to?" she asks, rolling over.

I'm not a prude, not by any means, but it's still a little startling how casual she is being topless in front of us, and I'm glad I have my sunglasses on so that I don't have to worry about where my eyes land.

"Just doing a little exploring," I answer.

"There's a great swimming spot just around this bend," Jake says, propping himself up on one elbow and pointing farther down the beach. "I can show you—"

"That's okay," Amma says quickly, and links her arm through mine. "You guys enjoy your morning."

She begins tugging me down the beach, and Brittany calls after us, "I'll catch up in a few!"

She turns back to Jake and Eliza, drawing a pattern in the sand with one toe, and only once we're out of earshot do I ask Amma, "Do you want to tell me what that was about?"

"What was what about?"

I stop, looking at her even though all I can really see is my face reflected in her sunglasses. "Your attitude around them. Do you not like Eliza and Jake?"

She sighs, pushing her hair behind her ears and turning to look out at the ocean for a second. "It's not that. It's just . . ." She gives an uncomfortable shrug. "Brittany basically loves everyone she meets right from the jump, and I like to take a little more time, you know? Ease in."

"Ah, so you're the cat and she's the golden retriever," I say, and she gives a startled burst of laughter.

"What?"

"In friendships or relationships, usually one person is the cat—guarded, a little standoffish—someone where you have to *work* for it. And then the other person is the golden retriever. Loves immediately and completely."

"Licks faces? Humps things?" Amma asks, grinning, and I look back down the beach to where I can just make out Brittany still standing there with Eliza and Jake.

"Doesn't look like it's gotten that far yet," I say, and Amma laughs again.

"So, I take it you're also a cat."

"Mm-hmm," I say, nodding. "And Nico was a born golden retriever." Now it's my turn to shrug. "It's why we work."

Amma nods, shading her eyes. "I can see that. I was saying to Brittany the other night that you two are such couple goals."

The thought gives me a little rush of pleasure. I've never really gotten to see me and Nico through anyone else's eyes, and I'm suddenly curious to learn everything Amma thinks of us.

"You think so?"

"Oh, totally," she replies, pushing her sunglasses back up her nose. Her skin is already starting to brown a little, her shoulders golden. Mine, I know, are already turning pink despite the layer of high-SPF I slathered on earlier. "Living in Hawaii, traveling the world together . . . that's the dream, right?"

Amma smiles when she says it, but there's something a little sad in it, and when she looks back out at the water, she says, "My boyfriend and I were going to do Europe like that. Maybe move on from there to Asia. He must've bought every travel guide he could find. Even got me one of those awful money belts for my birthday. You know, the kind that strap around your waist?" She gestures to her flat stomach, and I nod.

"I told him I'd die before I'd wear that, but honestly, it was kind of sweet, how excited he was. How prepared."

She laughs a little, shaking her head, and then presses her lips together, her chin wobbling slightly.

"Did you . . . break up?" I ask, gently because I feel like we're clearly straying into sensitive territory.

Amma's hand reaches up to brush at her cheek. "Basically," she says, then shakes her head again. "Anyway, it was probably a stupid idea anyway, and now I get to travel with Brittany, which is so much better."

Amma flashes me a bright smile, and I smile back even though I can still see the track on her cheek where a tear slipped out.

And then, before I can ask more, she's walking down the beach, gesturing for me to follow her.

We only go a few more yards before we find the place Jake must have been talking about. It's like the lagoon where the boats are anchored, but much smaller, a cove surrounded on three sides by sand, and we don't even pause before diving into the water.

When I break back through the surface, Amma laughs, splashing me with one hand.

"You just went full *Little Mermaid*," she teases, miming throwing back her hair. I smile and let myself float on my back. The sky is as blue as it was yesterday, with only a few fat, puffy clouds lazily moving across it.

Peace begins settling over me in a way I haven't experienced since Mom died. For the first time in years, I'm not worried about . . . anything. Not money or cancer, school or Nico. I can just float right here, *literally,* in the perfect present. I know it can't last—this sort of tranquility is meant to be temporary, and I've learned the hard way that it's smarter to always think about that next bend in the road, always be prepared for whatever is coming next. It's when you stop doing that that the worst seems to happen, after all.

But I promise myself that I'll try to savor it.

I feel Amma's hand brush mine, and when I look to my right, she's also floating next to me.

I wonder how long we can stay out here before Nico will begin to wonder about us. We didn't bring anything—no phones, no towels, and while I lathered up before heading out, I know I'll burn if we stay out too long.

"Oh, fuck!"

There's splashing, a hand grasping for my leg.

I lift my head, and there it is.

The fin is small, black one minute, gray the next, all depending on how the light hits it. And while it's nothing like the monster that loomed in my dreams after I saw *Jaws* for the first time, it's enough to send my heart into my throat, my stomach plummeting to somewhere near my knees.

There is something so sinister about that fin, slicing through the water like a blade, disrupting the tranquility of this perfect place.

I feel like I'm in a dream as I flip over and swim back to the beach, like the water has suddenly become glue, thick and viscous, slowing my movements even though I know I'm swimming as fast as I can, that the shore is so close. Still, my entire body is tense with fear, bracing for a sudden spike of pain, the numbing terror of knowing you're about to become food.

Amma is right next to me, and I'm struck by a sudden, dark thought.

*I don't have to beat the shark, I just have to beat her.*

Even as I reach the shallow water myself, scrambling to my feet in an awkward crawl, I can picture it in my mind: Amma and the shark both gaining on me, my foot connecting with Amma's jaw, her teeth clocking together, her blood ribboning out bright red in the clear water as the shark turns for her while I'm safe, I'm out, I'm *alive* . . .

The vision is fleeting, fading as Amma and I both stumble onto the beach, but when I look at her, I'm filled with the same weird thrill of horror and amazement as when you peer over the edge of a cliff and think, *What if I jumped right now?*

The relief that you didn't do it mixed with the giddy awfulness of knowing that *you could*.

We're both on shore now, and looking out at the water, the fin is no closer than it was. The shark is just turning lazy circles out at the mouth of the lagoon. It was never chasing us at all.

We collapse onto the sand, laughing in the way you do when you've just been scared shitless, but somehow come out of it okay.

"Oh my god," Amma gasps, wrapping an arm around her middle. "We were almost those girls!"

I raise a shaking hand to push my wet hair back from my face. "Which girls?"

She sits and wraps an arm around her knees.

"You know," she says. "The stupid ones in horror movies. The ones who are flitting about and joking around despite it being really obvious they're going to die in the opening scene."

"Okay, but that couldn't be us because we didn't have our tits hanging out," I remind her, and she laughs again.

"Solid point," Amma says, nodding at me with approval. "It would've been Eliza, then."

That makes both of us crack up, and out in the lagoon, I see the shark turn toward the open water. "Guess he got tired of our shit," I observe, and Amma stands up, picking up a handful of sand.

"Fuck off, shark!" she yells, throwing it into the water, and for whatever reason, that's the funniest thing I have ever heard, because I laugh so hard that tears stream down my cheeks, and Amma laughs, too, the two of us giggling in a way I haven't done in nearly three years. Ever since Mom died.

"I like you, Lux," Amma says once we settle down. "I mean, I knew when we met you that you were obviously cool, but now I really like you."

It's pathetic the way those words warm me, pathetic how much I've missed being accepted by other women, having this kind of easy camaraderie. It makes me think about how I felt just a few minutes ago, floating in all that clear water. Like I could just exist as someone in the present, no past, no worries about the future.

Fuck, that would be nice.

Amma smiles at me from behind her sunglasses. "And as we've discussed, I don't like people that easily," she says, "so it's a very high bar."

She's teasing, but I'm remembering what I felt in the water, that urge to kick her to save myself.

*You're a survivor,* Brittany had said after the storm. Maybe that's all it was, some deep human instinct of self-preservation.

But something about that image—Amma in the water, blood in her mouth—stays with me for the rest of the day.

# ELEVEN

We've been on Meroe for four days before we decide to tackle the jungle.

From the deck of the *Susannah*, the island is a paradise. Coconut palms rise up to the sky, the water laps against a white shore, and everything is postcard-perfect.

But the interior of the island is different.

I know Nico said that the island was used as a landing point during World War II, and that there's an old airstrip somewhere in there, but studying all these trees now, it's hard to believe. The island seems impenetrable and dark, and I don't know why we can't just do what we do every day—swim, walk on the beach, drink. That's a lot closer to my idea of a good time than hacking our way through jungle just to see some old war shit.

But Nico and Jake were super pumped about the whole thing, calling it "an adventure," so I'm trying—again—to be the cool girlfriend, who is up for anything. Sometimes I think if I can just keep pretending to be her enough, I'll eventually become her.

Brittany and Eliza are both wearing similar expressions of

resigned indulgence. Amma, on the other hand, has been right at Nico's side, asking a million questions: how long is the airstrip, when was it in use, did people actually live here, on and on, and Nico is, of course, eating it up even though most of his answers boil down to, "Um . . . I don't know."

Next to me, Eliza nudges my arm. "Should we be taking notes?" she asks in a low voice, nodding at Amma, and I snort.

"Some people are definitely acting like there's a test later," I whisper a little too loudly. Amma glances over at me sharply, even though I don't think she actually heard what I said.

But maybe she picked up on the tone, because she steps away from Nico, sulkily folding her arms across her body.

She runs hot and cold, that girl. Brittany and I had spent the day after the almost shark attack on the *Azure Sky*, and Amma hadn't joined us, hanging out on the *Susannah* instead. It didn't seem to bug Brittany, but I could hear them whispering in their cabin at night, and I wondered if they'd been arguing.

Not for the first time, I'm glad Jake and Eliza are here, too. Having extra people definitely helps defuse any possible tension.

The six of us stand there on the beach, looking into the jungle. Nico and Jake each hold machetes, both of which came from the *Azure Sky*. It had seemed like an insane amount of macho overkill at first, but now, as I stare into the thick vegetation just a few feet from shore, it makes sense.

"So, you guys are seriously going to hack through this shit like Rambo?" Brittany asks, one hand on her hip, her eyebrows raised.

"Only way to do it, love," Jake replies. He's not quite as well put-together today, trading his shorts and button-downs for an old T-shirt and a baggy pair of khakis, an ancient pair of sneakers on his feet.

The machete makes a whizzing noise as Nico swings it, thwacking into a thick vine with a sound that's both damp and meaty, making me shudder a little. "Fucking sick," he mutters, little-boy excitement gleaming in his eyes, and Eliza laughs.

"God, you are such a dude."

She over-enunciates, drawing out the vowel, *duuuuude,* and Nico laughs, too, shrugging.

"It's fun. You wanna try?"

He hands her the machete, and she wraps her fingers around the handle, testing the weight of it before swinging. Her stroke isn't nearly as hard as Nico's, and the blade gets stuck in the vine she was attempting to slice.

"Bugger me," she says, tugging, and Jake steps forward, adding his grip to hers as they pull the machete back.

"Harder than it looks, eh?"

As the blade pops out, Eliza staggers back a little, bumping her back into Jake's chest, and he uses the opportunity to duck his head and press a kiss to her neck.

"I'm sweaty!" Eliza objects, but he only grins and kisses her again, on the cheek this time.

"We're all sweaty," he reminds her, then gestures up to the sun overhead, already beating down on us even though it's barely nine in the morning. "And we're gonna get a lot sweatier before the day is out."

He's not lying. Jake and Nico take turns cutting through the underbrush, and I pull at stray vines and branches with my hands, Brittany, Amma, and Eliza all doing the same. It still seems like it takes us ages to make any real progress, and I'm just about to suggest we take a break, when suddenly, the vegetation opens up a little more, and we're in a clearing.

It's so humid in the jungle that I feel like I can't breathe, and the air that enters my lungs is thick and heavy. Underneath my rash guard, my skin has grown prickly and itchy, and even the backs of my knees are sweating.

But there's something beautiful here, too. Beautiful and wild and strange.

"It's so quiet," Amma says. There's a low drone of insects, and the rustling of the leaves overhead as the trees sway in the breeze, but other than that, there's no sound, not even the waves from the beach, as if the jungle has closed around us, sealing us in.

"It's like church," Brittany adds, then reaches for Amma's hand. "Like that church in Italy, remember?"

I see Amma's throat move as she swallows, the way she squeezes Brittany's hand, and I think back to that photo of them on Brittany's phone. In moments like this, it's easy to see why their friendship works even though they're so different. Shared experiences do that to people, and I wonder if when we leave Meroe, we'll have this kind of bond, too.

I like that idea.

Nico points up ahead with the tip of his machete. "Come on. That looks like a path."

It is a path—not a great one, and we definitely have to do more hacking through the jungle, but it's easier now, and after just a few minutes, the greenery clears again, leaving us in a vast open space, no trees overhead, the ocean pulsing against the shore just a few yards away.

We've reached the other side of the island. The surf is stronger here, the waves bigger outside the protected lagoon where we're harbored. When I step forward, my foot catches the edge of something.

I look down and see cracked asphalt, grass and vines pushing through the black cement. "Guess this is your airstrip!" I call to Nico, and he looks around, clearly a little disappointed.

"Man," he says, reaching back to ruffle the long hair at the back of his neck, his machete still in hand. "I thought it would be . . . I don't know. Not so fucked up, I guess."

Jake pushes his sunglasses up his nose with one finger, his other arm loosely looped around Eliza's waist. "That's the jungle for you, mate. Takes everything back in a flash."

He snaps his fingers in emphasis. There's something eerie about this part of the island, something unsettling. Maybe it's the reminder that this place has a history, a dark history, at that. That there were other people here once, and this isn't some paradise completely free from all the bullshit of the modern world. Or maybe it's just how loud, how violent the sea sounds here.

Suddenly, all I want to do is go back to our beach, our safe little harbor.

But Nico is already pushing at the vines along the airstrip with the tip of his machete, squatting down to take a closer look.

"You said they used this during World War II?" Amma asks, crouching down next to him.

"Yeah, it was a quick refueling station," Nico says, then gestures with his blade. "Kept tanks over there according to some of the pictures I saw."

"Where did you see pictures?" I call, and he squints at me.

"I looked it up before we came."

News to me, but Amma smiles at him, laying a hand on his arm. "That's so cool that you did some research."

There's nothing offside about the way she's touching him or her words, and I like Amma now, I genuinely do, but there's something about the way the two of them look, crouched there together, that makes my stomach twist, just the littlest bit. Maybe it's because I remember that moment before we left Maui, seeing the two of them on the deck of the *Susannah,* looking like they belonged there.

Or maybe it's because Amma looks like her, the real Susannah.

But whatever this feeling is, it's stupid and irrational, and I push it down.

"You okay?" Brittany asks in a low voice, appearing at my side.

"Yeah, fine," I say. "Just hot and tired and not that interested in World War II, I guess."

She can tell it's more than that, I think, but she just smiles and gives me a quick squeeze. Eliza walks over to me then, somehow still looking pretty and put-together despite the humidity. "Why exactly are we doing this instead of drinking on the beach?"

I shake my head. "Boys."

"True," she says with a nod, then puts an arm around me.

"Let's head back and leave them to it. I put a bottle of Pinot Grigio in the chiller before we left, and it is *screaming* for me."

I imagine the cold, crisp white wine sliding down my throat and almost begin salivating. I turn to tell the others that Eliza and I are heading back, when my foot bumps something hidden in the tall vegetation near the runway.

I look down, expecting to see an oversized rock.

Instead, teeth grin up at me, empty eye sockets searching the sky. A skull.

# TWELVE

Lux?" I hear Nico call, but I'm frozen in place, staring at the skull, those cracked teeth, those gaping holes that used to be eyes. When Nico reaches me, I clutch at his shirt, my entire body shaking.

"It's . . . it's a skull," I say, nearly panting, and Nico's eyes widen as he looks down.

"Holy fuck."

He lets go of me, and I nearly stumble, my knees quivering. Brittany is suddenly there on one side of me, Eliza on the other, both holding my elbows.

Nico gently lifts the skull with both hands.

"Jesus!" Brittany yelps, but Amma kneels down next to him.

"How long do you think it's been here?"

Jake is at Nico's other side now, his machete dangling from one hand. He lowers his sunglasses to squint at it. "Long time, I'd say. Look how weathered it is."

Nico brings it closer to his face, and my vision begins to swim.

"You said they used this place as a staging area during World War II, right?" Amma asks, close enough to Nico now that their shoulders touch. "I mean, someone could've gotten wounded and died here. Or sick. Maybe they were buried, but something dug it up."

The image immediately crawls through my brain—some jungle creature pawing at the dirt, unearthing a body, biting, tearing . . .

"Sweetie, drink some water, okay?"

Eliza is in front of me with a metal thermos, and even though the water is warm and there's a vague chemical aftertaste, I sip greedily, feeling some of my nausea recede.

Nico isn't even looking at me.

"Or, maybe they got *got*, you know?" he says to Jake. "Out here, you're in a fight with someone, who would even know if you just . . . finished them off?"

He turned back to the skull in his hand, his brown eyes bright. "God, that would be sick. If we found some guy who was murdered in the forties?"

I'm starting to feel a little less woozy now, and awkwardly aware that I'm the only one who was freaking out over this. I *was* the one who found it, but now that some of the shock is wearing off, I feel . . . silly. Like I totally overreacted.

Grinning, Nico holds the skull in one hand.

"Now *this* is some real adventure shit. Sailing to a deserted island, hacking through jungle, finding some old solider who got fragged." He turns the skull in his hands again. "It makes a cool story. When people see this thing in the *Susannah*, they're gonna be like, 'What the fuck?' and I can tell them—"

"I'm sorry, what did you just say?"

Nico turns to look at me then, his brows drawn together. "The skull. Hey." He walks forward, using his free hand to smooth my hair back from my face, but I remember those fingers on the bone just a minute ago, and there it is again, that sick, swaying sensation.

"You found it, babe," he goes on, still smiling. "Don't you want your own trophy on the boat?"

"It was a *person*," I say, and my voice is too loud. Overhead, a flock of birds takes to the sky, noisily squawking, and I'm suddenly aware that sweat is slithering down my spine, and my hair is still sticking to my cheeks. I probably look awful, and I wish I hadn't said anything, wish that I could just look at this thing like everyone else—as a cool artifact, a little bit of macabre excitement.

But maybe you can only react that way when death has never actually touched you, personally. In my mom's final months, you could actually see the shape of her bones underneath her skin. I think of those bones sitting on someone's fucking boat, like they're just a cool souvenir, the equivalent of a plastic tiki cup or a jar full of shells . . .

Next to me, I notice Brittany is also a little pale, and when she reaches down to take my hand, squeezing it in support, her grip is tight enough to hurt.

"Lux is right," she says. "You can't just take it from here."

"It's old as hell," Amma argues, folding her arms over her chest. "And it's just a skull. Whoever it was has been gone a long time, Britt. It's just . . . an object now. It's no longer a person."

"If Lux doesn't want it on the boat, it shouldn't go on the boat," Eliza says firmly, and my face flushes even hotter because now people are taking sides over this thing that I started.

Jake suddenly steps forward, taking the skull from Nico. "Look, mate," he says lightly, "probably bad luck to have bones on your boat, don't you reckon? I'll take it and bury it somewhere. But we should take some pics of it or something, document where we found it and all that."

For a second, I think Nico might argue with him or try to press the issue. If he does, I realize I have no idea how to react. I don't want to start a fight, but I also really, really don't want that thing on the boat. And more important, I don't want to have to explain myself. I want Nico to get it, to remember the things I've told him about my mom and understand why a human skull isn't exactly my idea of discovering buried treasure.

Instead, Nico nods at Jake. "Yeah, good point, man. Bad juju, probably."

We spend the next thirty minutes or so poking around the airstrip, but the fun has gone out of it, and before lunch, we're heading back to the beach. Jake and Eliza disappear off on their own for a while, and Brittany and Amma go swimming while I head back to the boat, saying I'm going to nap, but really, I just want to be alone.

It's nearly dinnertime before anyone else comes on board.

I'm sitting on the deck, letting my legs dangle over the side, when Nico approaches.

"You doing okay?" he asks, squatting down next to me.

I'm not, actually. I still feel shaken up, which in turn makes me feel stupid and silly. Nico and Jake are right—the skull had probably been there since the forties, it was nothing to be creeped out about.

But the bigger issue is that once again, something bothered me—*frightened* me—and Nico gave exactly zero fucks.

"Just a weird day," I say, and Nico sighs.

"This isn't Maui or the Haleakala," he says, running his hand through his hair. "It's a little wilder, a little weirder here. That's what makes it fun."

"Yeah, stumbling over dead people, super fun," I say, and he bumps my shoulder with his.

"Can you lighten up?"

He doesn't sound mad or irritated, just a little frustrated, but I still hate it. It's another one of those moments, those signs of the man he could have been—the man I sometimes worry he may actually be. I pull away from him, my fingers curling around the wooden edge of the boat.

"Why don't you go talk to Amma?" I suggest. "She seemed to be as psyched about that skull as you were."

He sits there for a moment, and I can tell that he can't decide how best to handle this, how to handle *me*. If he should just leave it alone, or try to argue his way out of this.

In the end, he gives a muttered, "Whatever," and heaves himself back to his feet. After a pause, I hear a splash, and when I twist to look over my shoulder, I see him swimming to the shore, his arms cutting smooth, sharp strokes through the sparkling water.

The sun is setting, and it's turned the sky a brilliant array of colors, from purple to orange, to the cotton candy pink of the clouds. The only sound is birdsong and the lap of the waves against the hull, and I close my eyes.

Nico is right. This place is wild and weird, and that's the appeal of it. It's why Brittany and Amma wanted to come here, why Jake and Eliza chose it. For the adventure.

And isn't that what I wanted?

Standing up, I glance back toward the *Azure Sky*. I can make out Jake and Eliza, puttering around the deck, and I know Brittany and Amma are still on the island. Nico has stopped swimming, treading water as he turns to look at me, and without letting myself think, I reach for the hem of my T-shirt, yanking it over my head. I shuck out of my shorts just as quickly, and then I'm diving into the ocean, naked and maybe just a little bit insane.

Nico's laugh when I come up makes it worth it, though.

He swims over to me, our bare legs bumping and tangling as he leans forward to press a clumsy, salty kiss to my lips.

I wrap an arm around his shoulders, his skin slick against mine, and kiss him back.

"I'm sorry." I breathe against his mouth when we part, and he smiles, bumps his forehead into mine.

"It's okay, babe," he says. "I know it's a different way of living out here. But it's good practice for when we take off, just the two of us."

There's a piercing whistle from the beach, and we turn in the water to see Brittany on the shore, laughing and giving us a thumbs-up. I laugh, too, sinking a little farther down into the water to cover my breasts, my boldness draining away now that things are okay with me and Nico.

Amma is next to Britt on the beach, her hands in her pockets.

I think about her shoulder against Nico's, and the way that her hand had brushed his as she'd reached out to touch the skull.

*Just a weird day,* I think again.

*Just a weird day.*

# THIRTEEN

That night we decide to hang out on the *Azure Sky*.

It feels cozy, the way you'd feel sitting around a campfire. The six of us are arranged on the deck, which is illuminated by little fairy lights that Eliza strung up, the boat gently rocking at anchor. Amma has plugged her phone into the speakers, and a low-key mix of acoustic coffeehouse stuff plays softly in the background.

Jake is on one of the low-seated chairs, Eliza on the deck between his legs, one arm draped over his thigh as he tells Nico about some boat race back in Sydney. Amma sits next to him, slowly peeling the label from her beer bottle.

Brittany kneels behind me, gently attempting to untangle my salt- and sea-ravaged hair, and I tip my head back to smile at her.

"No one has played with my hair since I was a kid," I tell her.

"It's totally selfishly motivated," she replies. "You have the best hair on this boat, and it's a crime to let it sit like this."

That makes me laugh as I take another sip of my drink. I'm more than a little drunk, and everything has gone soft and hazy. Jake made us daiquiris, but they're not the kind I'm used to—those bright pink frozen concoctions that came out of machines at the Haleakala. This is just fresh lime juice, some sugar, and really good rum, not a strawberry in sight. I'm on my third, and my face is starting to feel a little numb, but I can't seem to stop. The more I drink, the further away this afternoon feels. Like it happened to someone else.

Nico laughs at something Jake says, and I look over at him, warmth spreading in my chest that has nothing to do with the booze.

*I'm so glad he brought us here. I'm so glad we met Brittany and Amma and Eliza and Jake. I'm—*

"Alright, petal, your eyes are crossing," Jake says, leaning forward to take the half-empty glass from my hand. I surrender it without a fight, grinning at him.

"Did you just call me petal?"

"He calls every woman that," Eliza says, lightly pinching Jake's knee. "He thinks it's charming and, annoyingly, he's right."

"It is charming," I agree. "I mean, usually when dudes call me sweetie or babe or something, I hate it."

"I call you babe," Nico objects, and I wave a hand at him.

"I mean dudes I'm not dating. Random dudes."

Jakes raises his eyebrows. "Am I random?"

I'm probably too drunk to be having this conversation, my words pinging all over the place, and I shake my head. "No, we're friends now. I think," I say, and from behind me, Brittany chuckles.

"You are so wasted, Lux."

I really am. I haven't gotten drunk like this in a long time. Haven't really felt safe enough. When grief is still raw, drinking and drugs are a double-edged sword. They can numb you, make you feel the pain less, but they can also crack you wide open, leaving you vulnerable for a flood to come rushing back in when you least expect it. I'd learned that lesson the hard way in the months after Mom, when a couple of vodka and sodas in my apartment turned into four, turned into six, and next thing I knew, I was sick and crying on the bathroom floor.

There's no flood now. Instead, I look around at my new friends and wish my mom could've met them. Wish she could've seen this place, this slice of paradise that feels like something out of a dream.

"There," Brittany says from behind me, patting my hair. "All fixed and beautiful."

I reach back, and my hair actually feels smooth under my fingertips for the first time in forever, twisted in a low knot at the back of my neck.

"All gussied up and nowhere to show it off," Eliza says, smiling, and reaches for her phone.

"I can take a picture at least," she says. "Not that I can share it until we're back in civilization."

Jake tilts his beer bottle in her direction. "Alright, now here's a thought for you—is the place where things like Instagram and Twitter exist more or less civilized than this, God's own masterpiece of nature, hmm?"

"Ohhh," Brittany says, coming around from behind me to flop onto the deck. "You're one of those types. Too good for a well-chosen filter."

"Nah, he's just old," Eliza says, wrapping an arm around Jake's shin and looking up at him. "Turned thirty last month, now pretends he's never used an emoji in his life."

"I haven't," Jake insists, and Eliza rolls her eyes.

"Do you know," she goes on, lifting one finger in the air, "that this boat actually *came* with some ludicrously expensive Wi-Fi situation, and Jacob Arthur Kelly here had it *ripped the fuck out*? *That* is how committed this motherfucker is to being off the grid."

"I'm spending weeks in paradise with my lady, I cannot have her checking her Twitter or reading celebrity gossip," Jake replies, then he leans down to kiss Eliza's forehead. "That's not being thirty, that's just good sense."

They're so cute together, so perfectly matched, and suddenly I wish I was sitting next to Nico, that we could drape ourselves over each other with that same ease and comfort.

But it would look awkward now, trying to clamber over to him, like I was trying to prove something. And besides, Amma is already sitting there. They're not touching, they're not even all that close together, but I still get that same knot in my stomach, that same little burst of jealousy.

"Thirty, huh," Nico says, bracing himself on his hands as he stretches out his legs. "That makes you the elder statesman, I suppose. I'm twenty-six, Lux is twenty-four—"

"Twenty-five now, twenty-four when you met me," I correct him, and he nods.

"Right. And Brittany and Amma, you're what? Twenty-two?"

They both nod, and Eliza gives a mock shudder. "Oh my god, Jake, we're ancient! Does that makes us . . ." She pauses, her face twisting into a rictus of horror. *The responsible ones?*

"Christ, what a nightmare," he replies, then stands, slightly unsteady. "Alright, I need to do something hideously irresponsible right this second lest I start checking my retirement fund and reading the *Financial Times*."

With that, he reaches for the hem of his T-shirt, pulling it over his head in one easy motion before moving to the starboard side of the catamaran.

Before I can even clock what he's doing, his trunks are sliding down his legs, his skin both golden and pale in the moonlight, and he leaps overboard with a whoop, the splash loud in the quiet night.

"You bloody lunatic!" Eliza hollers after him, and I lean over the side of the boat to see him floating there, grinning up at us as he treads water.

"Come on!" he calls back. "What's the point of being on a deserted island if you don't do a bit of skinny-dipping?"

Then Jake looks over at me. "Lux, I know you're a fan," he adds, winking, and my face goes hot all of a sudden.

He'd seen that? But then, even though this island is miles from anything, even though there's no internet or cell phone service, definitely no social media, it's not actually private. Not with all six of us sticking so close together.

Brittany is already moving to the side of the boat, shucking off her clothes and giggling, and Amma stands up, too, but doesn't make any move to get undressed.

"Britt, come on," she says. "It's dark, and you don't know what's down there. It could be dangerous."

"Oh, because you suddenly care so much about people being reckless," Brittany replies. She's still smiling, but Amma flinches like Brittany had hit her, actually stepping back and nearly bumping into Nico.

"You okay?" I hear him ask her, and she nods even as Brittany, naked and beautiful in the moonlight, gives a shriek and jumps into the water.

"There's a girl!" Jake crows, and Eliza sighs, standing up and reaching for the ties of her sundress.

"If you can't beat 'em, join 'em," she says, and soon there's a third splash, more giggling, and shrieks from the water.

My brain feels hazy and unfocused as I watch their pale bodies cutting through the dark water, the moonlight dancing on the gentle waves. They're all smiling, joking around, as Eliza twines herself around Jake, his biceps flexing as he holds her there in the water. I think again about Jake watching me and Nico earlier, wondering if he liked it, if he looked at us the way I think I might be looking at him and Eliza now.

As though she senses my gaze, Eliza looks up. "Coming, Lux?" she calls, and I am just about to unbutton my shorts when I hear

Amma say, "I think I want to go back to the *Susannah*. I'm not feeling so great."

"Rum'll do that," Nico says, then glances over at me.

"You gonna swim or come back with us?"

I want to jump into that warm water with Jake, Eliza, and Brittany, I want to swim naked under the moon in this gorgeous place, but there's something about the idea of Nico and Amma alone on our boat that I don't like.

So I drop my hand from my waistband and turn away from the water, hearing Brittany call out, "Come on, Lux!"

"Maybe tomorrow!" I reply, and all three of them boo and hiss, Eliza giving me a thumbs-down, making me laugh.

The three of us head back to the *Susannah* in our tender, Amma going almost immediately to the cabin and shutting the door.

It's only when I'm settled in my bed with Nico, my head spinning, my mouth sticky and dry, that I remember that moment with her and Brittany, the pain—no, the near devastation—that had flashed across Amma's face.

*Oh, because you suddenly care so much about people being reckless?*

What had that meant? And why had it hurt Amma so much?

"Do you think there's something going on with Amma and Brittany?" I whisper, my voice so low I can hardly hear it.

But Nico is already asleep.

# BEFORE

Amma has heard the saying *three's a crowd* her whole life, but she's never experienced it for herself quite the way she does in Italy. Chloe slides into their life like she's always been there, like she was a part of this trip from the beginning.

From the first night they meet her in that café, Chloe is with them every step of the way, waiting outside their hostel or meeting them at some restaurant, and while Amma doesn't want to resent her, especially given how much Brittany seems to connect with her, it's getting harder and harder not to.

*Chloe says . . .*

It's how Britt opens every sentence.

Chloe says that restaurant has the best carbonara.

Chloe says the Spanish Steps are overrated.

Chloe says that part of the city has gotten really touristy.

*Chloe says, Chloe says.*

*Chloe* is suddenly the authority on everything, and Brittany can't stop parroting all of her opinions.

Even though it sometimes feels like Brittany is her closest friend, Amma reminds herself that she's only known her for a little over a year. Maybe this is just who Brittany is—maybe she's always looking for someone to follow. First it was Amma. Now, it's Chloe.

Amma understands the impulse, in a way—after everything that's happened to both of them, handing over the reins to someone else can feel easier.

But as they sit in a wine bar in the Trastevere neighborhood, Brittany laughing at some story Chloe is telling about her gap year in England, Amma tries to remind herself that Britt has been better since Chloe showed up. No more crying at night, no more talk of going home.

Which is why Amma had actually been relieved at first when Chloe had asked if she could tag along with them. The group she'd been with that first night had been a group of American grad students who were, according to Chloe, "getting really fucking boring," and at the time, Amma had thought there was something a little glamorous about being able to do that, to float between various groups of people, making new friends all along the way. No responsibility, no attachments.

No guilt.

Amma can't imagine what it would feel like to live without guilt. It's her permanent companion, has been since the moment she first looked up Brittany's Facebook, needing to see the girl whose life she'd ruined.

Learning they were both at the same school, that Brittany was only a year behind her at UMass, had made her stomach lurch, hard enough that she'd run to the bathroom and thrown up. It had felt too close, too . . . fated somehow. That she would be in Florida for spring break at the same time as this girl, a girl she might've seen walking across campus, a girl she might have bumped into in the bathroom at a party, drunkenly complimenting her lipstick or her hair.

Only later, when her head had cleared and her stomach had settled, had Amma understood. It *was* fate.

Fate giving her a chance to try and make this right somehow.

That's what led her to that counseling session at the church, what led her to sit down on a metal folding chair next to Brittany. Fate—and some bizarre notion of penance—had made her tell Brittany the biggest lie of her life.

At first, Amma had just wanted to see her. To hear her talk. And maybe there had been some sick part of her that felt compelled to hear Brittany's version of events. All Amma really knew was that she needed to actually *see* this person whose life was now as irrevocably altered as Amma's.

So that's why, even though there's *something* about Chloe—about her quick, wide smiles and her easy camaraderie with everyone she meets—that unsettles Amma, she will put up with their new friend and ignore the shit that irritates her. Like how Chloe had announced, the second they sat down, that she didn't have any cash, and could one of them cover her?

It's not the first time she's done this, and given how quickly they're going through their money, Amma is especially irritated, but Brittany quickly agrees, and now Amma is watching Chloe drink what are probably Brittany's last few euros.

She feels ready to leave, even though she's just had one glass of wine, when a group of guys comes in, taking the table next to them.

They're clearly Americans; the baseball caps give it away. In the month they've been traveling in Europe, Amma hasn't seen anyone from any other country wearing them.

Chloe leans forward, with that crooked smile of hers, red hair swinging. "I will bet the two of you twenty euros that those guys have the worst Instagram accounts you've ever seen."

Amma bites back what she really wants to say—*Do you even have twenty euros?*—but Brittany twists slightly in her chair to look at the trio. All three guys are sitting around a small metal table, their knees spread wide. They're also all wearing some variation of the same outfit—long khaki shorts, button-downs, the caps. All three wear aviator sunglasses and have giant glasses of beer sitting in front of them.

"That's a sucker's bet," Brittany says, shaking her head, and Chloe laughs, leaning back in her seat.

"Okay, but now I need to know if I'm right," she says, and then she stands and heads over to their table.

She puts her hand on the back of the chair of the alpha bro, the biggest of the three. He is wearing a fancy watch on one thick wrist, and several tattoos peep out from beneath his rolled-up sleeves.

"I swear I know you," Chloe says to the guy, her Aussie accent slipping into American so flawlessly that Amma raises her eyebrows in surprise.

"Did you go to Brown?" Chloe continues, and the guy shakes his head even as he pushes his sunglasses up to get a better look at her. Chloe is not a knockout, not in the same way Brittany is, but there's something about her that draws the eye, and Amma sees the way the guy's gaze slides over Chloe's body.

"USC," he replies, and Chloe giggles, cocking out one hip as she leans in a little closer. "Oh my god, duh."

She reaches out, playfully tapping the brim of his hat, where the USC logo is stitched in bright thread. The guy's smile widens. "But I do totally know you from somewhere," Chloe continues, and the guy shifts in his seat, somehow spreading his legs even wider.

"Why do they all do that?" Brittany mutters to Amma, tipping the contents of her wineglass down her throat. "It's so unattractive."

"You follow lacrosse?" the guy says to Chloe, his tone cocky. "Maybe that's it!"

Amma watches her and the dude put their heads together, phones emerging as they clearly exchange numbers or social media handles, maybe both. She wonders if Chloe has had more to drink than she realized because just as she gets up from her seat, Chloe stumbles a little, and drops her phone under the table. She's giggling as she retrieves it, while all three of the dudes take the opportunity to check out her ass.

"Classy," Amma murmurs, unsure whether she's trashing Chloe or the guys.

Once she's back in her seat, Chloe waggles her phone at them. "Check it."

In a few seconds, she has USC's profile pulled up, and surreptitiously shows it to Brittany and Amma. "What did I tell you?"

It's endless shots of the same guy posing next to fancy cars, his chin lifted, his gaze somewhere in the middle distance. He's shirtless in at least half of them, his skin golden and smooth, dark ink swirling up and down his massive biceps.

"What does he even do for a living?" Brittany asks. "I mean, shit, that's a Maybach he's standing in front of."

The waiter approaches, a bottle of wine in a cold bucket. "We didn't order that," Amma says, as Chloe twists to smile at the guys, waving in thanks.

Amma's face goes hot. Of course.

"Well, for one," Chloe says to Brittany as she fills her glass, "I can *guarantee* you he doesn't actually own that car. He's probably just doing a photo shoot at a lot. And two, all these guys are like this. This whole 'entrepreneur' thing. Call themselves CEOs of a company they made up themselves and which, surprise!——never turns a profit." She shakes her head. "These fuckers are everywhere. And they all look like that, and they all have social media accounts that look like this and say stupid shit like, 'You can't fly with lions if you swim with sheep.'"

That actually makes Amma laugh, but Brittany is still scrolling, frowning. "God, can't they see how douchey this is?"

"Douche calls to douche," Chloe answers with a shrug. "That's how they actually make money. They front like big guys, which sucks in other dudes who want to be big guys, too—then they run these, like, 'marketing workshops' for thousands of dollars. It's all a scam."

She glances back over at their table, and Amma sees a muscle move in her jaw. "And the worst part is, they get away with it."

The check arrives for the few glasses they ordered before the guys came in, and Brittany reaches for it.

"I've got it," Chloe says, taking the check and pulling out her wallet. Amma catches a glimpse inside her purse, and notices a wad of cash crammed in a side pocket.

"I thought you didn't have any cash," she says.

Chloe shrugs as she zips up her bag. "Found some."

# NOW

# FOURTEEN

I'm up early for some reason the next morning, drinking crappy instant coffee on the *Susannah*'s deck when Eliza motors over in the Zodiac. Despite all the daiquiris last night, she looks fresh and bright, her smile blinding in the early sunlight.

"Can I kidnap you?" she calls up, and I lift my plastic mug.

"Do you have better coffee?"

In response, she holds up a heavy-looking metal thermos, and I grin, putting my mug down.

"Consider me kidnapped, then."

Ducking my head into the cabin, I call out to Nico. "Babe? Eliza and I are going off to do a little exploring, okay?"

He grunts in acknowledgment, and I grab a pair of sunglasses and a towel, plus my beat-up sneakers, before hopping down the ladder into the waiting Zodiac.

Eliza grins at me, and then we're heading for the beach. We've gotten used to the convenience of swimming back and forth, leaving our phones behind. Jake even made us a little lean-to on the beach with a tarp where we can store towels and sunscreen.

It's funny how quickly this place has started to feel like home, even more than Maui did after months.

We stop in the shallows, getting out to drag the dinghy up the beach before Eliza points into the jungle. "You up for that again?"

I give a theatrical groan that makes her laugh, and she puts up her hands.

"Exactly zero skulls this time, I promise."

"Can you even make a promise like that here?"

She considers that, screwing up her face and tilting her head to the side. "You know what? Probably not!"

We follow the trail the guys hacked yesterday to the clearing, but this time, instead of pushing on the way we went, Eliza turns to the left. I follow her, already sweating, the heat and humidity of the jungle intense even though it's early in the day. But after just a few minutes, I hear the sound of rushing water, and I look at Eliza in surprise. There's a little smile playing around her lips, and she somehow still looks cool and put-together, her blond hair pulled up in a tight bun at the top of her head.

She winks, and pushes some branches back.

We've arrived at another small clearing, but this one contains a pool, fed by a waterfall. The scene is perfectly framed: the trees overhead keep it in shade, the water is clear, and there are patches of sand that are perfect for sitting.

"I found this the other day," she says. "Okay, technically Jake found it, and only because he was looking for an exotic place to shag, but still."

It's an easy scene to imagine, and I find myself blushing instantaneously: the two of them, beautiful, blond, and tan, slicked with water . . . the thought sends a sudden, surprising thrum of desire through me. Maybe it's just because Nico and I haven't had sex since before we left Maui. Clearly, I should bring him here and rectify that.

"How long have you two been together?" I ask, following Eliza to a sandy patch where we sit, watching the water flow into the pool.

"Oh god," she says on a sigh, tipping her head back. "Depends on how you look at it. Technically, about a month."

They have the easy comfort of people who've been together for ages, and my face must reveal my shock because Eliza laughs. "I know. We come across as very Old-Married. But I've actually known him since we were teenagers, so that's part of it. Timing was never right until recently. What about you and Nico?"

"Nearly a year now," I say. "We met in San Diego, then he sailed on to Maui and I followed."

"Romantic," she says, nodding approvingly, before looking back toward the pool, her arms around her knees. "It's funny, because you two seem so different, really."

I've never really considered what Nico and I look like to the outside world. We've more or less been in this little secluded bubble of two up until now.

"Do we?"

"Mmm," she nods. "He's so laid-back he's basically horizontal. Which isn't a bad thing!" Eliza holds up one hand, reassuring me. "God knows we need more men like that. But you seem so . . . I don't know. Tough. Steely."

I laugh self-consciously. "Seriously?"

She nods again. "Seriously. But it's weird, because sometimes you're like—"

Sitting up straight, she clenches her fists, her jaw, stares off into the distance like a woman on a mission, and I laugh, embarrassed and pleased at this version of me.

"Like a proper Valkyrie," she says, letting the pose drop. "But then, other times, you're all—"

A new pose. She curls her shoulders forward, ducks her head, looks up at me through her lashes, and I laugh again, but it's forced. Is that how I come across? So . . . meek? Timid?

Eliza shakes it off, sitting up straight again. "I have not even *begun* to figure you out yet, Lux McAllister," she concludes, and I am surprised to hear myself reply, "You and me both."

The words hang there, neither of us saying anything for a long time.

Eliza gestures toward the pool in front of us. "I know it looks pretty, but it's brackish. Totally undrinkable."

"I wonder if those shipwrecked sailors ever stumbled across it," I say, grateful for the change of subject. I imagine those men from long ago, sunburned and skinny, wearing the heavy blue wool coats of the British navy in this heat. "That would've been fucking awful, right? Coming ashore, discovering paradise, but it won't help you."

"Water, water everywhere, not a drop to drink," Eliza quotes as she nods. Then she elbows me. "But that's not us, thank Christ. Plenty of water back on board."

"And plenty of wine," I add, making her laugh.

"That, too."

She leans back on her elbows, toeing off her shoes and lifting her face to the sky. "So, tell me everything about yourself, Lux."

I mimic her posture. "Everything?"

"Well, the interesting bits."

I scoff. "There aren't many of those."

Eliza looks over at me, sliding her sunglasses down her nose. "I refuse to believe that. My god, woman, look at you! Living in Maui, sailing around the world with a scorchingly hot man . . . Brittany tells me you nearly went overboard in a storm on the way here and completely kept your cool." She shrugs. "That all sounds very fucking interesting to me."

The weirdest thing is, when she says it like that, I actually *feel* interesting. Like someone who has done shit.

And I really like that version of me.

Maybe it's the easy warmth in her voice, maybe it's the beauty of our surroundings, maybe I just really like Eliza, but I hear myself say, "My mom died. When I was in college."

I find myself telling her the whole story: about the divorce and my dad's new family, how I asked him for help when Mom was sick, and how he wouldn't give it.

"What a prick," she mutters, and the words are out before I can stop myself.

"I got him back."

Eliza turns to look at me, eyebrows raised, and I can't help but smile a little even as the memory brings back this queasy mix of excitement and shame.

"He came to her funeral, believe it or not. After all of that, he fucking showed up at the memorial service." I shake my head. "I couldn't believe it. He said he 'owed it to her.'"

Eliza snorts. "Seems like he owed her a shit-ton more than that."

"Exactly," I say. "He couldn't be there for her when she was sick, but he could fly all the way to San Diego once she was dead?" I shake my head, remembering Dad in his nice navy suit, his expression contrite, my whole body stiff as he'd gone to hug me. *I wanted to be here for you.*

"Of course," I go on, "he'd brought his new wife and his new kids. Had the decency not to bring them to the funeral home, but they were there. Might as well take in the world-famous zoo when you fly into town to pretend to care about your oldest kid, right?"

That's what had gotten me the most. I would've respected him more if he just hadn't shown up, but he wanted to have it both ways. Look like the Good Dad when it didn't matter anymore, and actually *be* the Good Dad to his new kids.

"So, what did you do?" Eliza asks, and I glance over at her.

I've never told anyone about this—not even Nico. I didn't think he'd understand.

"He wanted to take me out to dinner that last night he was there," I continue, "at this fancy place in the Gaslamp Quarter. I guess as some kind of sympathetic gesture? So I said I'd go, but then I showed up late. Waited for him to order his drink, get settled."

"I am already loving this story."

I smile, remembering the rush I'd felt when I walked in. "I went straight to his table, and just . . . let him have it. Told him what a shitty dad he was, how he thought he could start over with some new family, but they'd eventually work out how shitty he was, too."

Eliza is sitting up now, her arms around her knees. "If this ends with you throwing his own drink right in his face, I'm going to be *delighted*."

"It does, yes," I admit, my face flushing with the memory, remembering how the entire restaurant had fallen silent at that point, how the martini had made a splashing sound as it hit his forehead. "I also got escorted out and permanently banned from the restaurant, but honestly, I was fine with that. It's not like I was ever going back there again."

Later, I'd lain in bed thinking that I might have set myself on fire just to burn my dad, but it had felt worth it. The way his face had gone pale, the satisfaction of finally, finally saying everything I'd wanted to, of giving in to that side of myself that just wanted to fucking *do* something, no matter how impulsive.

I shrug, suddenly shy. "It sounds stupid, I'm sure."

"It doesn't." Her hand lands on mine, squeezing it. "It sounds brave."

I look over at her, smiling even as I feel my throat go tight. "Thanks."

"Told you," she goes on. "Tough. Steely. A fighter."

"Yeah, well, lately, I feel more like a drifter." I sigh. "Like I'm just clinging on to someone else's dream."

"Nothing wrong with a little drifting," she tells me, and then flashes me that bright white grin again. "Means you have options."

"Options," I repeat, and I like that. It feels more solid when she puts it that way. Like I'm not just drifting, but waiting. Waiting for the right thing, the right opportunity, the right dream to pursue.

If only I can figure out what it is.

We stay at the pool for another hour or so, and when we head back, the others are already gathered on the beach. It's become a routine now, all of us congregating there by midday, and it's like we're a little family on vacation or something.

But as Eliza and I approach, I realize no one is talking. They're all just staring at the horizon, frowning. I approach Brittany.

"What's going on?"

She points.

There, out at sea, is a sail.

Given that there were other people here when we showed up, it shouldn't surprise me that another boat might turn up. But it's still unnerving, seeing someone sail directly toward us—toward what has started to feel like our own private island.

We watch in silence as the boat makes its way through the shoals. It's not as nice as the *Azure Sky*, not even as nice as the *Susannah*. A solidly middle-of-the-road boat, and seeing it makes my heart sink.

"Shit," Brittany says at my side, shading her eyes against the sun. "I don't want to share."

There's something so plaintive in her voice that I laugh even though I'm disappointed, too.

"You're already sharing with Eliza and Jake," I remind her, and she glances over at me.

"But they're friends now," she says. "Friends with good booze, too. These people aren't friends. They're interlopers."

"Wanna defend the island?" I ask her. "Make booby traps, go full *Swiss Family Robinson*?"

I'm joking, obviously, but Brittany says, "Maybe we could go get that skull back at the airstrip. Put it on the beach, scare them into leaving."

When she sees my horrified expression, she laughs, bumping her hip against mine. "Oh my god, your face."

Before turning her gaze back to sea, she asks, "Speaking of, what were you and Eliza doing in the jungle?"

It's right there on the tip of my tongue to tell her all about the pool, that perfect hidden spot, but something stops me. "Oh, just walking around. Nothing special."

She nods as the boat motors over the breakers and into the harbor. From this distance, I spot a single figure, standing at the wheel.

"And then," Jake says with a sigh, "there were seven."

# BEFORE

Eliza is almost seventeen when it all comes crashing down.

Before that night in April, her life hadn't exactly been charmed. There was never enough money, her dad split before she even really knew him, and she and Mum had moved *so* many times. They'd lived in big cities like London and Manchester, and tiny villages with names that sound like something out of a storybook—but, for Eliza, they were still just a series of council flats and shitty schools.

She's glided by, Eliza has, because she's pretty, because she's quick, because she worked out that thing, that secret, that takes most people ages to learn—no one really wants you to be yourself. They only want themselves reflected back at them.

Eliza is very good at doing just that.

So while she never has the nicest clothes or the hottest brands, she always has friends, always finds herself at the center of things, and that's where she likes to be, where she feels the most in control.

By the time she's sixteen, things have settled. Her mum has a good job now, working as a housekeeper for a rich family just outside of London, while Eliza is firmly ensconced in the social hierarchy of her school: queen bee, a perfect golden girl despite her rather dingy semidetached house and her drugstore makeup. She's studying for her GSCEs, smart enough to get into a decent university, smart enough to ensure that the life that trapped her mother isn't going to trap her.

And then, of course, there's Jake.

———

SHE MEETS HIM ON A typically rainy afternoon. They've only got the one car, she and Mum, and Eliza needed to drive into the village to do some shopping after school. Mum let her use it, but only if Eliza agreed to pick her up from work that afternoon. Eliza is irritated that her shopping trip has been cut short, and then more irritated when her mum doesn't come out at the appointed time, even after she blows the horn.

Rain splatters on her, slithering down the back of her jacket as she jogs up to the front steps of the fancy brick house with its box hedges and its smart red door.

Eliza rings the bell, pissed off and wet, her hair already curling in the damp, and when the door opens, she's ready to snap at her mum or some other tight-arsed maid standing there.

She doesn't expect *him.*

Tall, with hair just a few shades darker than her own golden blond, and eyes that are almost painfully blue, Jake Kelly is, she'll eventually learn, both his family's pride and their black sheep, a Problem Child already kicked out of two boarding schools back in Australia, where the Kellys are from. This move to England is a sort of last resort, a chance to finally "straighten the boy out."

It won't take. Nothing ever will. But Eliza doesn't know that yet.

She only knows that he is the fittest boy she's ever seen, standing there in his school uniform with his tie undone, his jacket off. He's a year older than her, she knows, having heard her mum mention Mr. Kelly's son, how he goes to the posh boy's school in the next village over, how there are already "issues," and that Mr. Kelly is thinking of transferring him somewhere a bit stricter.

"Um, hi," she says, and he smiles at her appraisingly, leaning against the doorframe.

"G'day."

He does this, she'll eventually learn. Leans heavy on the Aussie thing with new people. He is charm and sunshine itself when it suits him.

It's a long time before Eliza figures out that it's all mostly surface, an act, as much as her queen bee thing is.

But all that is still to come. Right now, Eliza just returns his smile and says, "I'm here to pick up my mum? Beth?"

"Here I am, love. Sorry."

Her mum rushes toward the door, pulling on her coat, and Eliza notices that her hair is mussed, the pretty pink lipstick she was wearing that morning is gone, and she won't figure it out, not then, but it turns out cleaning is not the only thing Beth does for Mr. Kelly.

"See you around," Jake says to Eliza, and it feels like a promise and a threat all at once.

She likes that.

IT'S A SECRET AT FIRST, Eliza and Jake. She starts needing the car more regularly so that she has to pick Mum up from that big fancy house, starts turning up earlier so that she has to hang around and wait.

The first time Jake kisses her, it's in the car, parked in the driveway while the rain pours down outside, and he tastes like smoke and cinnamon gum, and Eliza falls hard, so hard that she doesn't notice what's going on with her mum. Her sudden distraction, the phone ringing at all hours, the way she always seems to be at the Kellys, even on Saturdays—none of it registers as strange. Eliza is in her own bubble of school and Jake, so she's genuinely shocked when, about a month after that first kiss, Jake says to her, "You know our parents are fucking, right?"

She and Jake are in his bed, his door locked, his music playing loudly, not that it really matters. Eliza's never seen anyone able to get away with as much as Jake manages to get away with.

Now she places a hand on his chest, pushing herself up to look in his eyes. "What are you talking about?"

Nodding, Jake skims a hand over her bare back. "In case you haven't noticed, she's always here, and this house is never all that clean, petal."

That makes sense, even as it curdles something in Eliza's stomach. There's something so . . . pathetic about it. Being the side piece to a rich guy, always at his beck and call.

But Eliza won't realize just how pathetic it is until that night in April when her mother doesn't come home.

At first, it doesn't really worry her—she likes having the house to herself, figures her mum is off with Mr. Kelly again. When the phone rings, she has no premonition of how much her life is about to change.

The first thing she hears is Mum sniffling. "Oh, baby," her mum says. "Oh baby, I am so sorry."

The story comes rushing out then. How she was just "popping down to London for the afternoon," and got stopped at Kings Cross, how the little carryall bag she brought with her just happened to be full of three kilos of cocaine, and now she's sitting in a jail in London, and she's calling Mr. Kelly to see if he can post bail, but he's not picking up, so she's not sure when she'll be home.

"Mum," Eliza says, her voice a croak, her whole body going hot and cold at the same time. "You have to tell them the drugs are his. Because they are, right? He made you take them to London?"

"Jack had nothing to do with this," her mum says, and Eliza scoffs even though she's crying.

"Right, because you just got three kilos of coke on your own, and then just decided to carry them with you to London. Mum, please!"

Her mum's voice is so soft when she answers, so tired. "It won't matter anyway."

It doesn't. Her mum never comes back from London, sentenced to ten years for trafficking with the intent to sell. She never once mentions Jack Kelly's name, pleads guilty, and is swallowed up by the system.

Her last night in the village, the night before her mum's sister will take her off to Essex, Eliza sees Jake one final time. After her mum's arrest, she's stayed away from him, him and his whole bloody family, but she knows they're going back to Australia soon, and she thinks about it all the time, him and his father—his fucking father—in some other big house, able to start over clean and fresh whenever they want or need.

She sits there in his car, her eyes stinging with how much she's cried, her tissues crumpled in her hand, and he lights a joint, offering her a hit.

She doesn't take it, the idea of drugs abhorrent to her now. She's vowed to never touch any of it again.

Jake only shrugs, sucking the blue smoke into his lungs, exhaling it into the car, and Eliza feels slightly dizzy.

"It's all just so unfair," she says now.

"Fucking way of it, isn't it?" Jake replies easily, and Eliza looks at him.

He's so handsome, caught in the orange glow of the streetlight, and she suddenly understands that men like Jake's father—men like Jake himself—will get away with this forever.

Eliza thought she had worked out the secret, but it's nothing compared to this secret brotherhood of men.

"I guess," she says, and what she thinks is, *But it doesn't have to be.*

*It won't be for me.*

A_Wandering_Heart: Anyone ever heard of #MeroeIsland? Apparently it's just a few days sail from Hawaii, and me and some friends were thinking of hitting it up after #HawaiianPro. Thoughts??

Shaka2379: @A_Wandering_Heart WOULD NOT. That place has bad vibes. Me and some buddies stopped by two years ago 2/10 DO NOT RECOMMEND.

A_Wandering_Heart: @Shaka2379 Lol, okay?? What do you mean "bad vibes?"

Shaka2379: @A_Wandering_Heart Idk just alot of people died there I guess, place feels off. We were gonna stay for like a week bailed after 2 days. IF U GO U KNO.

UrBoyRobbRoy: @Shaka2379 @A_Wandering_ Heart PUUUUSSSSSSIES. More for the rest of us!!! #GonnaEatThatLongPigSon #FuckinInfluencers

Twitter, March 2022

# NOW

# FIFTEEN

The other boat anchors behind the *Susannah* and the *Azure Sky*, and I take it as a good sign. Whoever is aboard, they're respectful and keeping their distance.

"Should we take the dinghy out to greet them?" Nico asks. His arm is slung around my shoulders, and I step a little closer to him.

"Welcoming party?" Jake asks. "Not a terrible idea."

"I'm not feeling all that welcoming, darling," Eliza replies. "Why don't you and Nico go? Put the fear of god in them just in case."

Jake snorts. "Ah yes, nothing more intimidating than one guy in salmon shorts, and another sporting a dinosaur bandana."

But a man has already jumped off the boat, and is swimming for shore.

"Well, at least he's observing the local customs," Amma jokes, but we're all too tense to laugh.

I can't help it—watching someone else approach the island that has now started to seem like "ours," I feel possessive.

I didn't know I had that streak in me, and it strikes me how much we revert back to the most basic human instincts when we leave civilization behind, even temporarily.

The man is a capable swimmer, and he quickly reaches the shore, staggering toward us with a big smile on his face.

He's ropy and skinny, his shorts hanging low on his hips, held up by a belt so old and fraying that at first glance, it looks like a stray piece of twine. His hair has been buzzed down to the scalp, pink skin showing through in some places where the sun obviously got him. But he's got an easy grin as he surveys us on the beach, his hands on his hips. He's not quite as tall as Jake, but a little taller than Nico. Still, I think I could knock him over with one good push.

"Paradise, huh!" he says, throwing his arms wide, and when we just stare at him, he drops his arms, stepping forward and extending a hand. "I'm Robbie." He's American, with a southern accent I can't quite place. "Hope it's cool I've turned up?"

Jake is the first to take his hand, with that winning smile I've seen before, but this time, it doesn't quite reach his eyes. I wonder if his easy friendliness has always just been an act and I'm only noticing it now.

"Jake Kelly. More the merrier, mate," he says, and Robbie's eyes grow wide, his smile even bigger.

"Ah, an Aussie, niiiiiiiiiice," he drawls, then takes in the rest of us. "And beautiful ladies. Man, this is even better than I'd hoped."

Great, he's fucking smarmy.

"I'm Lux," I tell him. "This is my boyfriend, Nico, and this is Brittany and Amma."

"And this is Eliza, my lovely lady," Jake says, looping an arm around Eliza's waist and pulling her forward. "So, Robbie. What brings you to Meroe?"

"I dunno," Robbie replies, leaning down to scratch at a bug bite on his shin. "Guess I just wanted to see some shit off the beaten path, you know?" That quick grin again, showing lots of teeth. "A friend stopped by here a few years ago on a sail, said it was cool as fuck, and I thought I'd check it out myself." He shrugs happily. "And gotta say, seems like he was right. This place is pretty fucking rad."

Nodding at Nico, he adds, "Sick bandana, man."

There's something about this guy that I immediately do not like. Something that makes me more than a little nervous. He reminds me of guys we got at the Cove sometimes, the ones who only ever ordered Pabst Blue Ribbon and had eyes that slid over our bare legs like slime.

"I sailed out of Papeete," he continues. "Heading for Hawaii eventually, I guess, but you know how it is."

Now he has Jake's and Nico's attention. "Tahiti?" Nico asks, stepping forward. "Fuck, man, that's a lot of sailing on your own."

Robbie throws his arms out again. "What is life if not to live it, right?"

I catch Eliza's eye, see the way the corner of her mouth kicks up just the littlest bit. Like me, she's not feeling this guy's entire . . . vibe, and I lean close to Brittany.

"Love a guy who sounds like an inspirational Insta account," I whisper.

She snorts, and I see Amma cut a sharp glance in our direction.

"So!" Robbie claps abruptly. "Y'all got anything to eat? Because I'm not gonna lie, I'm fucking starving."

❧

It's LIKE A REPEAT of our first night on Meroe. There's good food—Eliza and Brittany cooked together in the *Azure Sky*'s little kitchen—good wine, too much of both, but now there's this new person in our midst, shirtless and skinny, smelling like salt water and engine grease and too much time alone.

I really don't like him.

It feels unfair, like hating a kicked puppy or something, but as

I watch Robbie shovel Jake and Eliza's food into his mouth and down an entire bottle of sauvignon blanc, I wish we could go back to just a few hours ago, when it was just the six of us.

"This place has a really fucked-up history, right?" Robbie says. He's still holding the bottle of wine by its neck, his knuckles red and raw, and the firelight makes strange shadows under his cheekbones, his eyes. "Sailors eating each other and shit?"

"Sailors were wrecked here," I say, reaching into the cooler for a fresh bottle of wine. It's a little embarrassing how quickly I've gotten used to treating Jake and Eliza's provisions like they're ours. Sure, we've provided a jar of peanut butter and the occasional beer, but all the good shit is Jake and Eliza's. I have the fleeting thought that we should offer to pay for what we've been eating, before I remember that of the four of us on the *Susannah*, I'm certainly not the one with that kind of money.

Outside the circle of light provided by the bonfire, the night is dark, save for the stars and the occasional white flash of the surf as it breaks. I keep my eyes on Robbie's as I stick in the corkscrew. "I don't know about eating each other."

Robbie laughs, a phlegmy, thick sound. "Oh, if there was a shipwreck, there were cannibals. People do what they got to do to survive, you know?"

He looks around the fire, grinning. "Wouldn't you?"

"This is gross," Amma announces, getting up, but Robbie doesn't seem offended.

"Yeah, it is," he agrees, then shrugs. "That shit still happened, though."

"We can't know—" Brittany says, but to my surprise, Nico cuts her off.

"We do, actually. Dude's right. When the HMS *Meroe* wrecked here, there were thirty-two survivors. Only eight walked off this island. There was a trial and everything. The stuff about cannibalism didn't make it into the papers, but there's no doubt they wouldn't have made it without eating the ones that died." He grins, tearing apart a shrimp with his teeth. "Long pig. Apparently tastes just like barbecue."

My stomach churns, and I look at the still half-full plate of food in front of me. It was fish, grilled and savory and nothing at all like what Nico's talking about, but I know I can't stomach any more food tonight.

"But maybe they were just . . . I don't know, stronger or something. Tougher."

That makes Robbie laugh again, only this time, it sounds more menacing. "Oh, they were tougher," he agrees. "Place like this, it does things to people. Reveals who you really are, when you strip all the bullshit away."

He gives me that grin again, his teeth yellowed and slightly crooked.

"That's why they survived."

# SIXTEEN

I wake up too early the next morning, the light in the cabin a soft lilac as I gently disentangle myself from Nico, slipping on the still-damp swimsuit I have hanging on one of the kitchen cabinet doors.

The whole main cabin is a bit of a mess, I realize as I look around, and I wonder if I should come back later this afternoon and straighten up a bit. We spend so much time on the island lately that the *Susannah*, which was supposed to be our home base, is starting to feel more like a staging area. The place where we sleep and get dressed and occasionally grab food, but nothing more.

When I step out onto the deck, the sun is just rising, turning both the sky and water the prettiest shades of pink and orange, and I grin as I leap over the side of the boat, the water sliding over me, warm and salty.

The swim to shore takes just a few minutes, and I immediately head for the little lean-to Jake set up the other day. There are some books in there, courtesy of my collection, a few towels, and usually some protein bars—another one of the *Susannah*'s few contributions to the shared rations.

But as I walk up the slight rise to the edge of the trees, I see someone has already beaten me there.

"Morning!" Robbie calls. He's claimed one of Eliza's batik blankets, his arms around his skinny knees, one of the protein bars in his hand, spilling crumbs. There's also an open bottle of beer next to him, half-full.

"Tell you what, can't beat a breakfast beer and getting to watch a beautiful woman come out of the water."

He says it easily, his tone friendly, but I still don't like it, don't like the way his eyes skate over me, admiring.

But it's his first full day here, and maybe he's just one of those guys, the type that doesn't even realize they're being creepy. I make myself smile as I reply, "Can't say I've ever had a breakfast beer."

"Oh girl, best thing in the fucking world," he says, offering me a sip from his bottle. "Beer first thing in the morning sets the *tone*, you know. The motherfucking *tone* for your whole *day*."

I shake my head at the offered bottle.

"No, thanks."

"Your loss," he says cheerfully, taking another drink and then a bite of the protein bar. I notice there are two other empty wrappers discarded next to him and once again fight down my irritation.

Still, I hear the sharpness in my tone when I ask, "So how long are you planning on staying?"

He shrugs. "Dunno, man. Gonna see which way the wind blows, you know?"

Mouth full, he gestures with what's left of his—*our*—protein bar back at the jungle. "Or maybe I'll just find a place to camp out. Live the dream forever."

When he flashes his teeth at me this time, there's a chunk of dried blueberry stuck there, and I feel my stomach roll a little.

"What, live here?" I ask, reaching past him into the shelter for a bottle of water. It's warm and tastes like chemicals, but it still helps.

Robbie nods. "People have. Like, I read this one story about a dude who was stationed here in World War II. War ended, he didn't feel like going back. My buddy who stopped by here a couple of years ago said he found the dude's shack in the jungle. Dude was long gone, obviously. Fucker would be, like, ninety or something by now. But he did it. He did the damn thing!"

Another chortle, and Robbie leans back on his elbows. "Maybe I'll do the damn thing, too."

I think of spending our last week here with Robbie and have to fight to keep myself from grimacing.

"And he wasn't the only one," Robbie continues, looking at me. "Not the only one who said, 'to hell with it,' and set up permanent camp. The guy I knew who came here, Chipper, he said he was sure there was someone else living on the island. He kept hearing noises, and finding, like, traps in the trees and shit."

"No one could survive here that long," I say, even as I remember the skull at the airstrip, the concrete proof that people had lived, and died, on Meroe. "Not without replenishing supplies."

Robbie shrugs. "Easy-peasy, girlie. Sail back to Hawaii, reload. Then you come right back here, keep livin' the dream."

He spreads his arms wide like he did last night, taking in all of the island, and I look past him at the line of trees, the darkness of the jungle.

For the past week, it's felt like we've had this place all to ourselves, our own private paradise.

But Robbie is right. If you had a boat, you could stay here indefinitely.

The idea that Robbie might not be the only person we've been sharing the island with sends a shudder through me, and I'm grateful when I hear someone call, "Lux!"

It's Jake, making his way up the beach. Looking farther down the shoreline, I can see the dinghy pulled up on the sand.

He's wearing a pair of faded red trunks and some boat shoes, and as he approaches, I see his gaze slide to Robbie.

"Hey, there," he says, friendly enough, but the smile doesn't reach his eyes.

"Hey yourself!" Robbie calls back, then stands up, brushing the sand off his shorts. "Not creeping on your lady, promise," he says, and I look over at him sharply, trying to figure out if he's fucking with us.

"Not his lady," I say even as Jake says, "My girl's still on the boat."

Robbie looks back and forth between us, then chuckles, shaking his head. "Right, right, she's with the other guy, the dude with the—" He makes a gesture over his bicep, indicating, I guess, Nico's tattoo. "And your lady is blond. It's all coming back to me now."

Jake gives me a wink, and I feel myself flush a little. Just the suggestion of being "his girl" makes me feel . . . embarrassed? Self-conscious? It's like having a sex dream about a friend or a co-worker. You might not have been into them before, but suddenly they've reared up in your mind as an option.

"At least he thought I had excellent taste," Jake offers, making me laugh.

Then he jerks his head. "Come on, Lux," he says. "I want to show you something."

━━━◆━━━

JAKE TAKES ME FARTHER DOWN the beach, past the dinghy, and we round a corner into a small cove, the beach rising up in a small cliff over the water. It's only about five or six feet up, but we scramble, slipping and sliding, and when Jake reaches down to take my hand, I let him, his palm warm against mine.

The image of him and Eliza at the pool flashes through my mind again, and my entire body goes hot with it, making me stumble as we crest the little ridge.

"You okay?" he asks, glancing back at me, and I nod, making myself smile.

"Great, yeah."

There's another one of Eliza's blankets spread out there, set back against the tree line so that it's in natural shade, and another cooler, plus a stack of paperback books. "Eliza and I sensed that our original spot might get a little crowded, so we decided to go slightly farther afield," he says, spreading his hand out. "You like?"

"Very nice," I agree, looking around. "But where is Eliza?"

"Off on a walkabout," he replies, shoving his hands in his pockets. "Think she's getting a bit sick of me, to be honest."

He says it lightly, but I still frown.

"You guys okay?"

Jake waves me off. "Oh, fine. Just been cooped up together too long, I suppose."

I shade my eyes, looking down at the beach, and as I turn to the left, I can see Eliza far down the shore, her blond hair blowing in the wind. "She said you've known each other since you were teenagers."

"Mmm," he hums in agreement. "First love. Nearly knocked me off my bloody feet when I ran into her again a few months back. I was at this pub in Canberra, and there she was. Moving through the crowd, holding a pint, like some sort of goddess." He shakes his head, smiling at the memory. "Funny thing is, I didn't recognize her straight off. Just thought, 'Ah, that's a beautiful woman, I should probably go talk to her,' and then . . ."

"Then Eliza," I sum up and he laughs.

"Good summation of my whole life, really. 'Then Eliza.' Anyway, we picked right up where we'd left off, like no time had passed."

I look over at him and see he's watching Eliza, too. "And then you just . . . decided to travel the world together?"

"Something like that, yeah," he says, then looks back at me. "And you and our intrepid Mr. Johannsen?"

I briefly tell him about meeting Nico at the Cove, about the months in Maui, and he nods as I finish.

"Aren't we a pair of lucky sods, then? Meeting people to take us up on these glorious adventures."

Something about that surprises me. I don't know why, but I'd just assumed this had all been Jake's idea. He grins, nudging me with his elbow. "She's very persuasive, my Eliza. When she says, 'We should sail to a fucking deserted island,' well. You find yourself sailing to a fucking deserted island."

I can see that. Eliza has that kind of energy—she's the sort of person you want to please for whatever reason. Maybe it's because she presents you with a version of yourself that you desperately want to live up to.

Something sparkles in the sunlight, catching my eye, and I see that farther down the tree line, there's a line of empty beer and wine bottles set up.

Raising an eyebrow at Jake, I point. "You doing that frat guy thing of collecting empties?"

He laughs. "Not exactly."

There's a plain black box made of heavy plastic or maybe metal sitting next to the stack of books, and he goes over to it now, flipping it open.

Nestled inside is a gun.

My mouth goes dry.

I've never actually seen a gun up close before. Nico has a flare gun of course, locked in a bright orange-and-white box back in the cabin, but this is the real deal, a sleek, lethal thing of dark metal, and when Jake sees my face, he laughs again.

"Trust me, petal, you don't want to be out in the middle of

nowhere and not have one of these things. Although I am not using it for anything more interesting than shooting bottles."

He holds it up to me.

"Wanna try?"

I don't like guns, have never seen the need for one, but I look
over into the darkness of the trees, remembering what Robbie said
about someone living here.

"I guess?" I say. The next thing I know, it's in my hand, warm
and heavy, and Jake is standing behind me, showing me how high
to lift my arms, how to widen my stance.

"It has a hell of a kickback if you're not ready for it," he says,
"so be sure you're as steady as you can be. Eyes on the target, elbows loose. There's a girl."

He's right there at my back, his skin warm against mine, and
I'm suddenly very aware that he's shirtless and I'm just wearing
a one-piece. But there's nothing creepy in how he stands, and he
keeps a respectful distance as he helps me position my arms.

"Aim," he says, and I pick one of the biggest bottles, a bright
blue one I remember was filled with Riesling just a day or so ago.

I slide back the hammer, my heart pounding in my ears.

"Now picture it's someone you really hate, and fire," he says.

I laugh, but even as he says it, I suddenly see Robbie's face in
front of me, calling me girlie, that fucking blueberry in his teeth.

I pull the trigger.

# BEFORE

They don't go home after Rome after all. Instead, they move on to London, where the weather is cooler, the nights out are more raucous, and Brittany wonders why she ever thought she wanted to end this trip early.

Chloe had asked if it was cool if she came, too, as Brittany had hoped she would. Amma agreed—though Brittany saw the way her eyes hardened and her jaw tightened as she replied flatly, "That's a great idea."

They kick off their first night in London at a pub, of course. It has some stupid name—something clichéd and obvious like the Crowned Stag—and the walls are dark, covered in paintings of men in nice coats killing perfectly innocent animals. While Amma is at the bar, ordering more drinks, Chloe slips her hand into some guy's jacket, pulls out a wad of bills, and hands it to Brittany.

For a moment, Brittany is stunned.

You can't just *rob* people. This is pickpocketing, like they're orphans in Charles Dickens or some shit, but Chloe just winks at her, and before she can stop herself, Brittany stuffs the cash into her purse.

She lies awake in the hostel that night, waiting—for sirens or men with flashlights to burst in, to turn her purse upside down until the money falls out. She'll confess everything, she'll tell them she was stupid and made a huge mistake.

But it never happens. And the next morning, she treats Chloe and Amma both to a full English breakfast with those stolen pounds, and no one says shit to her, no one looks twice, and it feels . . . *good.* Harmless.

It's strange to have a secret with Chloe, instead of with Amma, but Amma wouldn't understand. Amma had lost her boyfriend, which hurt, Brittany knew, but it wasn't the same thing as having your whole family wiped out.

She'd never told Amma the full story. How some guy with the ridiculous name of Sterling Northcutt had had too much to drink on spring break, got behind the wheel of a massive Suburban he'd rented, and crossed the double line, plowing into the sensible Prius Brittany's father had bought the year before.

Someone had taken Brittany's family from her with their stupid, reckless choices. Someone who'd looked a lot like that USC asshole sitting at that bar in Trastevere, and the idea that Chloe might've hurt him, even a little bit, had filled her with a fierce sense of satisfaction.

*Fuck those guys,* she'd thought. *All of them. With too much money and too few responsibilities and no fucking conscience.*

The world gave those guys enough. What was the harm in taking some back?

Besides, if she could keep doing this, she might never have to go home. Never have to figure out how to live in the after.

<hr>

AFTER JUST A FEW DAYS in the UK, Chloe has a new plan.

"Australia?"

Brittany is sitting with Chloe in their room at the hostel. Amma has gone to use the little internet café near the train station, saying she had some emails to send, but Brittany knows she could've done that on her phone, and she wonders if her friend just needed a break.

Sometimes Brittany feels she needs a break from Amma. The longer this trip stretches on, the more she's reminded that Amma is not a beloved bestie from college like they've tried to pretend. Amma is just a person who also had a terrible thing happen to her, and now they're stuck together, even though they have nothing else in common.

Brittany doesn't have that much in common with Chloe, either, if she's honest, but Chloe is easier, more fun to be around.

Chloe is not a constant reminder of what happened.

And now, she wants Brittany to join her in Australia.

She reaches out, pushing Brittany's knee. "Don't you want to see it?"

Brittany does. She's loved Europe, but Australia would be a real adventure. Somewhere she'd never even dreamed of going.

"You've still got plenty of money, right?"

They haven't talked about Brittany's money before. Not how much of it she has, not how much of it she's spent. Eventually, Brittany knows, she'll have to tell Chloe about it. Her parents, the accident. The settlement from both insurance and Sterling Northcutt's family.

But for now, she just nods. "Yeah."

"Well, there you go!" says Chloe, grinning. "And if money becomes an issue, we can stay with my friends, or find other cheap hostels. I promise you, it can totally be done."

And then she reaches for her bag, pulling out a wad of paper bills. "And of course, there's always the bro circuit."

Brittany reaches over and takes Chloe's hand, the hand holding all those bills. They crunch slightly under her fingers, and she feels her heart lift at the idea that this can continue, that the idea of "home" could keep receding further and further into the distance.

"Let's go."

# NOW

# SEVENTEEN

Robbie has been here four days.

I keep expecting to wake up one morning and discover his boat is gone, that he's moved on to whatever is next for him. But no, every day, there it sits, the ridiculously named *Last Dance with Mary Jane*.

Every day, there *he* is.

The second day, the day Jake took me shooting, Robbie sat on a patch of sand and spent hours hacking away at a piece of driftwood with a bent and dull-looking pocketknife. That afternoon, he disappeared into the jungle, a beat-up black canvas bag slung over one shoulder.

The third day, he announced he was going fishing, and stood out in the shallows with a line tied to a Vienna sausage.

"Stupid bugger," Jake says from his spot on the beach, and Nico leans past him to see what Robbie is doing.

"Mate!" Jake calls out. "Don't eat anything you catch!"

"Why shouldn't he?" Nico asks, and Jake looks over at him.

"Bunch of 'em here are toxic as fuck. Kill you dead in a couple of hours if you eat 'em." His teeth flash in a quick smile. "Another one of Meroe's little treats. Surprised you didn't know."

Something flashes across Nico's face, gone before I can identify it.

But it doesn't matter because Robbie doesn't catch anything.

On the fourth day, the beach is empty when we all swim over, and I breathe an audible sigh of relief as we set up camp in our original lean-to.

"You must be completely shit at cards," Jake teases, as I situate myself on a blanket. He's wearing a pair of blue-and-white-striped trunks today, shorter and more fitted than the board shorts Nico usually wears, the hair on his legs golden and curling in the sunlight.

I blush. "What do you mean?"

"Everything you're thinking is clear on your face. For example, I can tell that you're intensely grateful our new friend hasn't made an appearance yet today."

"*Yet* is the key word there," Brittany says as she lies down next to me, adjusting her sunglasses. "My bet is he's not leaving before we do."

"Well, yeah. First night we rolled out an entire feast for him, what do you expect?"

That's Amma, sitting on Brittany's other side. She's pulled out the paperback that Jake had been reading when we first arrived, and I realize it's a spy thriller, silhouetted figures running across a dark blue background.

"We rolled out a feast for you, too," Eliza says with a slight edge in her voice. I can't blame her—Amma's never been anything but borderline rude to Eliza, no matter how nice Eliza is in return.

"Yeah, but we obviously weren't freeloading creeps," Amma replies.

"Bit harsh, that," Jake says mildly, looking back out to sea.

We all sit in slightly awkward silence before Eliza says, "Lux, darling, would you be an absolute legend and go back to the *Azure Sky*? Since our friend is not out and about today, I think I'll break open the good wine. You know where it is, right?"

I nod, getting up and dusting the sand off the backs of my legs. The *Azure Sky*'s dinghy is up on the beach, and I easily maneuver it back into the water, pointing it toward the catamaran. I wave at Nico as we pass.

As always, I'm struck by how clean everything is aboard the *Azure Sky*, how sleek and neat the deck is. The longer we're moored here, the more ragged the *Susannah* seems to become, her deck littered with damp towels, pairs of shoes, spare lines.

I slide open the door to the main cabin.

And freeze.

Robbie is standing there, his back to me, the lizard tattoo on his shoulder leering at me. He's got his hands on his hips as he looks at something by the sink, and the cabin is flooded by his scent. Sweat, salt, mildewed laundry . . .

"What are you doing?"

He whirls around, his expression totally closed off for just a split second before it once again dissolves into that goofy grin. "Lux!" he says. "Just checking shit out, you know. Seeing how the other half lives."

He runs a hand over the teak cabinets overhead, whistling through his teeth. "Gotta say, the other half lives right."

"You shouldn't be here," I say, my voice faltering, hating that I sound like a teacher or something, scolding a kid for being out of class.

His grin doesn't fade, but his eyes seem to harden as he says, "Are *you* supposed to be here? Pretty sure this isn't your boat."

"Right, but Eliza actually sent me over here to get something for her."

"Jake and Eliiiiiza," Robbie drawls, leaning one hip against the counter. "Good friends of yours, huh? Bosom buddies?"

My feet are itchy with the need to run, my skin tingling with cold sweat, but I stand my ground, arms folded over my chest, chin raised. "I'm just saying, don't come aboard someone's boat without permission."

"If you think me doing a little snooping is the worst crime happening around here, you got another think coming, baby girl."

"Don't call me that," I snap, feeling enraged and panicky. If I shouted, the others would probably hear me, but how quickly could they get here?

"Just trying to be a friend," he says with a shrug. "Or hell, maybe you already know how people like *that* have a boat like *this*."

"I think you need to leave," I say firmly.

His smile slips into something harder, crueler. "Meroe Island is cursed, you know that, right? You and your friends think you're having a good time, makin' content for Instagram or whatever it is the fuck y'all do, but it ain't the kind of place for that."

"You're the one who wants to stay on it," I remind him, thinking of that first night, his buddy that had stayed here for god knows how long.

"'Cause I get what kind of place this is. But you and your friends? This place is gonna snap you up." He brings his teeth together with a hard clack, startling me so that I nearly trip on the steps behind me.

That makes him laugh, and it's the pleasure that he's clearly taking from frightening me that makes me look toward the knife on the table next to me.

It's for shucking oysters—not particularly deadly—but I snatch it up anyway, surging forward until the tip hovers just beside Robbie's eye.

That laugh dies in his throat as he holds up both hands. "Alright now, baby girl."

"*I said* don't call me that."

I edge the knife closer, my breaths coming fast. We are in the middle of nowhere. There are no rules here, no police to call, no passport checks. If I killed this man, threw his body into the ocean, sunk his boat—who would ever know?

The realization is almost dizzying. I spent months on Maui dreaming of the freedom of the open seas, but I never really considered its darker side. Out here, we're untethered. Which means we can do anything.

*I* could do anything.

"Look, I didn't mean to scare you," Robbie says now, backing away.

I see his dark eyes flicking nervously between the knife and my expression.

He's afraid of me.

I lower the blade, nodding. "Good."

As I step back, he shakes his head. "Who knew you had that in you, girl? Tell me, which one of those fuckers would you eat first?"

He jerks his head toward the beach, toward Jake and Eliza and Nico and Amma and Brittany, and I'm sick to my stomach all of a sudden, wishing I were anywhere but here.

"Fuck you," I say, but it's weak, and he just laughs again.

"No shame, little girl, no shame. I'm just saying, when it comes to beating Meroe, I'd put my money on you every time."

With that, he pushes past me, heading up the stairs, and I hear a splash as he dives over the side.

I'm still shaking, and I almost drop the bottle of wine I pull out of the fridge. As I finally reemerge on the deck, I see Jake and Eliza standing on the shore, looking toward the boat. They must've seen Robbie on deck, and I lift a hand, letting them know everything is okay before climbing back down into the dinghy.

Robbie is still there, treading water and looking up at the sky, and when I motor past him, he actually smiles at me again, like nothing happened.

I look away, keeping my gaze on the beach.

Jake, Eliza, and Nico are waiting for me in the shallows.

"Why was that asshole on our boat?" Jake asks. He's got his sunglasses pushed up, his eyes as blue as the sky above, but his expression is furious. I've never seen him like this before, and I shake my head.

"He was snooping around."

"Motherfucker," Jake mutters, looking over at Eliza, and now that I'm back on the beach, now that I'm safe, I suddenly remember Robbie's words——*what those two must be doing to have a boat like that.*

It was bullshit, just a creep who was trying to fuck with me.

Jake turns, striding back to our lean-to. He fishes around in there for a second, and then he straightens up, heading back toward us. Sunlight flashing off metal.

The gun.

"Whoa, man," Nico says. He's still got one hand on my elbow, steadying me. "Isn't that a little intense?"

"I'm just going to talk to him," Jake says, but his mouth is set in a thin, hard line.

"Jake, for fuck's sake," Eliza says, and he looks over at her sharply.

"What? Do you want him snooping around in there, Eliza? Really think about that before you answer."

"I don't," she snaps back, "but I also think this macho shit is unnecessary and frankly a little embarrassing."

Jake scoffs at that. "Terribly sorry to embarrass you, darling. How will you ever cope?"

"Can you two cut it out?"

That's Amma now, her hands fisted at her sides, her gaze darting between the shore and the rest of us. "He's coming."

Robbie is making his way into the shallows now, water running off his skinny body, his cutoffs dark with it, and Brittany steps closer to me.

"Did he say anything to you?" she asks. "On the boat?"

I don't know why I don't tell her—or any of them—all the shit he said. Maybe I don't want this tense situation to escalate more than it already has. And it's not like he hurt me or anything. I held my own, and even now, I remember how it had felt, holding that knife on him. Seeing that littlest bit of fear in his eyes.

I don't want to tell them that part, either.

I shake my head. "Nothing important."

Robbie is in front of us now, his hands on his hips, that same grin he always wears on his face.

"Y'all having a party without me?" he asks, and Jake steps forward.

"What were you doing on my boat?" he asks, and Robbie's grin never slips. He just shrugs.

"Checking shit out. I thought this was a whole *mi casa es su casa* scene, you know?" He gestures at all of us, flinging one hand toward the lean-to.

"Well, it's not," Jake says, "and if I see you on my boat again—"

"You're gonna what? Go all *Crocodile Dundee* on me?"

He feints a quick series of punches in Jake's direction, startling all of us. Robbie just laughs, but Nico's voice is low and menacing as he says, "Come on, man."

Jake doesn't flinch. He raises the gun calmly, its barrel just a few inches from Robbie's forehead.

"Jake!" Eliza barks, and Brittany grabs my arm, pulling both of us even farther away from the scene.

Robbie is still smiling, but his eyes are very hard now. "Easy, man," he says. "This ain't *Lord of the Flies,* and I sure as fuck ain't Piggy."

"Think you've overstayed your welcome, mate," Jake says, his tone light, but his arm steady as he holds the gun on Robbie. Was it just a couple of days ago that I was holding that gun? That I was shooting empty wine bottles and laughing?

I don't feel like laughing now.

Amma is pale, and Nico still has one hand raised, like he plans to leap in and stop this at any moment, but Robbie and Jake stay focused on each other, Robbie's hands opening and closing at his sides, fingers flexing.

"That so?" he asks, then shakes his head, scrubbing one hand over his shorn hair. "Welp, in that case, guess I'll move on."

"Good idea."

Jake lowers the gun, and I think we all breathe a sigh of relief.

Robbie turns as if to go, and I can already picture him swimming back, pulling his ropy body up the ladder onto his boat and sailing away, leaving us the way we were.

But then he suddenly turns again, so quick he's moving before we can react, shouldering past Jake, hard enough to send him staggering back a couple of steps, and then Robbie is crashing through the jungle.

There's a sharp crack, loud enough and close enough that I actually shriek, my hands going up to my ears even as I hear Eliza say, "Jesus fucking Christ!"

*Jake shot him, he shot Robbie, he killed him, and we all just stood here and watched it,* my brain whimpers on a loop, but there's no scream and I can still hear Robbie moving through the trees even though the sounds are getting fainter.

And then it's quiet, leaving all of us staring at the spot where Robbie disappeared, into the jungle that's swallowed him up.

# EIGHTEEN

Where the fuck is he?"

I whisper the words in the darkness of the cabin, Nico curled up beside me. All afternoon, all evening, the six of us had waited on the beach, assuming Robbie would come back. His boat was still floating there, after all, near ours, and I've been lying here awake for hours, listening.

So far, nothing.

Jake is still on the beach, I know. Keeping watch. The thought should be comforting, but it's not, and even here on the *Susannah*, I feel jumpy and on edge. I still remember that hard look in Robbie's eyes, the snap of his teeth as he'd stepped closer to me.

"He could just be hiding out in the jungle, I guess?" I say even though Nico hasn't replied. "He talked about that, remember? Living here and shit?"

"Then let him, Lux. Who cares?" Nico says the words on a sigh, rolling over onto his back, and I shift so that I can look at him more clearly.

"I care!" I hiss. "He could just pop out of the trees at any time, totally catch us off guard. Who knows what the hell he would do?"

"Look, he's a fucking weirdo, no argument there," Nico says. "But he's harmless, Lux. He ran into the jungle with nothing on him but those ratty fucking shorts. Jake's the one with a fucking gun. Dude's probably just waiting for us to clear out so he can go back to his boat without getting shot."

"So it doesn't worry you at all that he got super weird with me, and is now *hiding somewhere on this island*?" I've always known Nico is laid-back, not the kind of guy to fret over things. But I'd told him what Robbie had said to me aboard the *Azure Sky*, told him how freaked out I was.

Now he reaches up, scrubbing a hand over his face. "I just think you're overestimating how dangerous that guy actually is, that's all."

Dropping his hand, he turns to look at me. "I mean, Amma was saying earlier that she thinks *she* could take the dude in a fight, and she weighs like ninety pounds."

I'd seen him and Amma talking earlier at the bow of the *Susannah*, Amma laughing at something Nico said, Nico grinning at her, and thought it was weird they were being so casual after what happened. Now I know they were joking about this, and the thought makes me bite my lip before I say something catty.

Nico reaches out then, his hand skimming down my arm. "I know it was scary, babe," he says. "And I'm sorry. But seriously, I don't want you lying awake at night, thinking this dude is the boogeyman."

"That's not what I'm doing," I insist, shaking his hand off. "And I don't appreciate your, 'Oh, I'm too cool to worry about things,' shit right now. Not about this."

I'm not sure I've ever been mad at Nico. Not really, honestly angry, but here we are, and I have no idea how he'll react.

He sighs, rolling over to face me, propping his head up in his hand. "Lux," he says, pushing my hair out of my face with his free hand. "Can we not do this?"

Before I can reply, he leans over, brushing his lips over mine, and even though I'm still mad, still worried, it's easy to respond, to open my mouth to him and let him really kiss me, his hand now coming up to slide up my rib cage, hot against my skin.

"We can't," I whisper when his hand moves to the waistband of the shorts I'm wearing to sleep in. "Brittany and Amma . . ."

Nico groans softly, dropping his forehead to mine. "We could be quiet," he whispers, smiling, and I shake my head.

"I'd feel too weird."

"And I feel weird that I haven't touched you in days," he murmurs, his nose tracing a ticklish path over my cheek.

A part of me realizes that this is some kind of attempt at distracting me, but since it's working, I don't really care.

"Not exactly how we planned our first big sail going, is it?" I ask as I scratch my nails gently over his collarbone.

"There will be other trips," he replies. "Private ones, just you and me. Tahiti." He kisses the tip of my nose. "Fiji." Another kiss. "Anywhere you want to go."

"I think that's a Beach Boys song," I whisper back, making him chuckle, and even though there's still that worry in the back of my mind, that constant buzz about Robbie and where he is, in this moment, I can forget all of that.

Just for a little bit.

"Well," I whisper, letting my hand rest on the back of his neck, "if you promise to be *really* quiet . . ."

"I'm not the one we have to worry about," he replies, his leg nudging my thighs apart as he pulls me closer.

Nico kisses me again, and I arch up against him, losing myself in the sensation of his skin on mine, the taste of his mouth, the scratch of his stubble.

I've just started moving my hand down his chest when there's a sound.

The door to the cabin creaks open, and I look over Nico's shoulder to see a silhouette there.

Amma.

"Sorry," she whispers in the darkness, her hand coming out to steady herself as she makes her way into the main cabin. "Needed some water."

I doubt she can see much in the darkness of the cabin, but I still scoot away from Nico with a barely suppressed sigh of irritation.

"No worries," he replies, cheerful as ever, and Amma makes her way over to the little fridge beneath the sink.

Once she's got her bottle and tiptoed her way back across to the cabin, Nico turns again to me, but I put a hand on his chest, shaking my head.

"Told you," I whisper. "Too weird."

He flops onto his back with a muttered, "Shit."

I take his hand, lacing his fingers through mine.

"Tomorrow," I say. "We'll find some time tomorrow."

BUT THE NEXT DAY, PRIVACY is hard to find. Jake and Eliza are already on the beach when we get there, and perhaps because they're still thinking about Robbie, Brittany and Amma are sticking close.

"Any sign of the dude?" Nico asks Jake, who shakes his head.

"Nothing. Probably camping out in the jungle, doing his *Robinson Crusoe* thing."

I look out at the trees past his shoulder, frowning.

"So, we're just not going to worry about him?" I ask, and Jake follows my gaze, lifting his chin slightly.

"Didn't say that. But short of sending out some kind of hunting party for him, I'm not sure what else there is to do."

He's smiling as he says it, but I remember the calm way he'd lifted that gun to Robbie's head yesterday, the crack of the shot as Robbie had darted into the trees.

What if Jake had hit him? Not killed him, but just clipped him. What if we'd heard Robbie scream, seen his blood on the sand? What the fuck would we have done then?

Wrapping my arms around myself, I turn away, but there's an itchy spot between my shoulder blades, like someone is watching me, and I know I'm going to feel that way until Robbie either shows up and leaves, or until *we* leave.

Which, I realize with a little surprise, is only a few days away now.

Like a lot of things on Meroe, time has started to feel . . . slippery. Pliant in a way it doesn't back home.

Brittany has joined us now, her purple one-piece bright against the blue water behind her. "A hunting party," she repeats, shaking her head but smiling. "God, can you imagine? All of us trekking through the jungle to kill Robbie? How very *Lost*."

Jake laughs, and even Nico smiles a bit, but the image is too clear to me, too easy to see. I can practically feel the sweat gathering behind my knees, between my breasts, on my lower back, can feel the prickle of fear but also the adrenaline I'd felt yesterday, pulling that fucking oyster knife on him.

*We should,* I almost say. *We should go find him before he comes back.*

I don't like that this is where my mind went. With a little wave to the others, I gesture down toward the water.

"Going for a swim."

I'm almost afraid Brittany will ask to join me, but instead, she moves farther up the beach toward Eliza. I watch as she flops under the tarp next to her, playfully throwing one arm around Eliza's neck and tugging her close, Eliza laughing as her sunglasses slip.

Brittany is like that, I've learned, easy with her body and her affection, but I hadn't realized she and Eliza had already bonded so much.

I glance over at Amma to see if she noticed, but she's talking to Nico, their heads close together, and I turn away, almost running into the water.

It's as warm as always, which is nice, but I feel like I could use the bracing shock of cold water. Something to clear my head.

I swim in aimless circles for a bit before finally getting out, heading for the pile of towels we keep up near the tree line.

I've just grabbed one when I hear, "Are we cool?"

I stop and turn to see Amma bracing one hand against the trunk of a palm tree, her sunglasses pushed on top of her head, holding her hair back from her face. She's not as pretty as Brittany, but she's definitely striking, her skin gone very tan, a constellation of freckles spattered over the bridge of her nose.

"What?"

She shrugs, crossing her arms. "I don't know. I'm just getting a vibe. Like I've pissed you off somehow." Holding up a hand, she adds, "And I realized after I got back in bed last night that I might've interrupted something with you and Nico, which is awkward as fuck."

"Oh, it's no big deal," I say, waving her off even as my face heats a little at the memory. "Hazard of boat life."

"Seriously," she replies, smiling. "I know you'll be happy to have him to yourself when all this is over."

I don't say anything, and again, she rushes into the silence. "Sorry, I hope it doesn't bug you that I've been spending time with Nico. Brittany is doing her golden retriever thing with Eliza and Jake, and it's just . . . it's nice to have someone new to talk to. He's a good listener."

I think about the night Nico and I met, that way he has of focusing on you and only you. Still, something about all of this is weird. Amma's smile is too bright, her posture a little too stiff.

"He actually reminds me a lot of the guy I was telling you about. The boyfriend I was going to travel with."

The wind is blowing through the palm trees overhead, their leaves sighing and swaying, casting shifting shadows on Amma's face.

"Your ex-boyfriend, right," I say.

Amma swallows hard, looking away for a second before turning back to me and saying, "So, there's something I should tell you. Britt and I weren't totally honest about how we met," she tells me, her eyes not meeting mine. "About it being in college."

I'm not sure how to respond to that. Why would they lie about something so minor?

"We met in a counseling group," she goes on, then looks over at me. "Grief counseling. Brittany's whole family was killed in a drunk driving accident. Mom, dad, little brother. All . . . three of them."

Her voice goes tight, chin wobbling a bit before she clears her throat and goes on. "And I'd lost my boyfriend."

"Oh," I say. Suddenly her tears when she was talking about him that first day make more sense.

"We tell people the college story because . . . well, we don't want to be *those* girls, you know? The sad, tragic ones. The ones who needed grief counseling."

Now *that* I can completely understand. I've spent the past few years trying not to be that girl.

"Anyway," she goes on, waving a hand. "I just . . . figured you should know all that. I figured you'd get it."

"I do," I say, and suddenly all my catty thoughts about Amma, that twisting in my stomach when I'd see her with Nico, fills me with shame.

Stepping forward, I lay a hand on her arm. "And I'm so sorry."

"Thanks. It's been . . . awful, but we're here now. And Brittany's happy. Traveling like this was her idea, her way of using the money from insurance and the settlement to do something she thought her family would've appreciated. They were big on experiences, getting out there, living life."

"And your boyfriend," I add. "It's what he wanted to do, too, right? So, you're doing a good thing, too."

She nods, but the movement is jerky. "Right. Okay, well, that's probably enough sharing and caring for today. I may devote the rest of the morning to getting day drunk."

"Never a bad idea."

She turns to go, but then stops, pointing at something in the trees. "Wait, what the fuck is that?"

It takes me a second to see what she's staring at, but then I make out a shape, hanging in the branches, something that's not just a vine curling in on itself.

I only take a couple of steps into the trees, but it's like that first day we went exploring—everything immediately seems quieter, the air instantly thicker, even though I can still see Amma just behind me, the sea and sky beyond her.

There is a rope hanging from the tree. Skinny, worn rope that feels scratchy in my hand when I reach out and touch it, following the loop it makes up to a knot.

I tug at the dangling bit of the rope, and the loop hanging from the branch tightens like a noose.

It's some kind of trap, probably to catch birds, maybe even the odd lizard.

*Robbie's buddy.*

Robbie had said his friend was sure that someone had still been living on the island, subsisting off the jungle and what supplies they picked up on sails. Was this trap left over from that guy, whoever he was?

Or, I wondered, my eyes scanning the darkness of the jungle beyond, was it new?

# NINETEEN

The next day, we all go to the pool Eliza brought me to.

None of us mention Robbie or the trap I'd found yesterday, but I know we're all thinking about it. It's nice to do something different, to be distracted by a change of scenery.

Now, I sit with Brittany on the edge of the pool, watching Nico and Amma swim. Jake and Eliza are sharing their own bit of sand, Eliza leaning back between his legs.

"What do you think it would be like to live here?" Brittany says. "I mean, yes, it's paradise and all, but wouldn't it get boring after a while? Lonely? Besides, how many sunsets can you really look at?"

That's how I'd started to feel in Maui, but I wasn't sure it was how I would feel here. In Maui, there had been responsibilities and jobs, real life intruding every day. Here?

Here you were just . . . free.

"I'd definitely get bored," Brittany says now. "I know that sounds entitled, but it's like . . . this is a place you come to forget, you know? Or disappear." Another shake of her head, dark hair spilling over her shoulders. "And I'm not sure I want to do either of those things—not forever, at least."

"Me, neither," I say, but I'm not sure if I actually mean it.

Brittany looks back over at me, but before she can say anything else, there's a shriek from the pool.

Amma is hanging upside down over Nico's shoulder, her skin pale against his bronzed chest, her bikini bottom riding precariously low as Nico ducks underneath the water again, pulling her with him. I can feel Brittany's eyes on me as we watch them horse around.

"Where's Jake?" I ask when Eliza comes and sits next to us.

She gestures back through the jungle. "He forgot his stupid book, couldn't possibly enjoy the afternoon without it, apparently. What were you two talking about?"

"Whether we could live here, on this island," Brittany answers, pushing her sunglasses up her nose with one finger. "We decided we definitely couldn't."

"Same," Eliza says, settling back on the sand. "Love a sunset, love a beach, but there's so much of the world to see. And honestly, I'm starting to miss cities." She takes a deep breath. "Not even a hint of exhaust fumes. How is a woman supposed to live on fresh air alone?"

Nico and Amma begin climbing out of the pool, and I watch from the corner of my eye as Nico drapes a towel over her shoulders.

"Where are you headed after this?" I ask, and Eliza shrugs.

"Not sure yet. Jake wants to go to Fiji, maybe Bora Bora, but I'm hoping I can convince him that Bangkok will be a nice change of pace from all these white-sand beaches."

I feel a pang of envy. I'll just be heading back to Maui, until Nico decides what we do next.

Eliza glances over and nudges me. "Wanna come with?"

I give a startled laugh even as the idea sends a flare of excitement through me. "To Bangkok?"

She nods, her blond hair coming loose from its sloppy topknot. "Why not? We like you, you're fun. You clearly want to travel."

"I do," I say, and then there's all the other stuff I should say, about how Nico and I have our own plans, but none of it comes out, not a word.

"Then come!" she says, and I look up to see Nico watching us as he scrubs at his sun-bleached hair with a towel. Did he overhear Eliza's invitation?

And more important, did he hear me not turn it down?

~

IT'S EVENING BY THE TIME we make our way back to the beach, and as I look out at the lagoon, it takes me a second to realize something is missing.

There are only two boats at anchor now.

The *Last Dance with Mary Jane* is gone.

Relief floods through me as I gesture toward the lagoon. "Guess he cleared out while we were gone?"

Nico squints out at the water, shading his eyes with one hand. "Guess so."

"Thank sweet fuck," Jake mutters, then grins at us. "I'd say that's cause for celebration. Come over. Let's pop some bottles, and toast to the end of that little fucker."

"Sounds good to me," Nico replies, his arm slipping around my waist.

It's hot, both of us are sweaty, and I'm still thinking of him and Amma in the pool, his arms around *her*. I slide away from him.

He doesn't say anything, but I feel his eyes on me as I climb into our dinghy, Brittany and Amma following.

The sun is slowly sinking below the horizon, and all of us are a little waterlogged as we come aboard the *Susannah*.

I'm the first to descend into the cabin, already craving a cold bottle of water from our tiny fridge.

But when I reach the bottom stair, something crunches underfoot.

There's a bit of gray plastic under my shoe. It takes me a moment to process that it's our radio—or rather, what's left of the radio. Shattered plastic, bent metal, loose wiring.

"What the fuck," I breathe.

"Lux?"

Nico is coming down the stairs behind me, and he quickly takes in the destruction.

"Do we have a backup?" I ask as he brushes past me to survey the mess.

"No," he says, tersely. "This was it."

He's quiet for a moment, then quickly brings his fist down on the counter.

"Motherfucker!" he roars, and I instinctively jump back, my heel crunching yet another piece of plastic.

"It had to be Robbie, right? I *told* you we needed to be worried about him!" I feel panic rising in my chest and my mind starts spinning.

"Is this really the time to play I-told-you-so?"

I stare at Nico. "That's not what I'm doing. I'm trying to remind you that sometimes I'm actually right about shit, and maybe you should've listened to me instead of acting like I was fucking crazy."

"Well, clearly you weren't crazy, and he is, okay? Are you happy now?"

"No!" I'm shrieking now, but I can't stop myself. "I'm not *happy*." Robbie was *here*, in our boat, among our things. He'd been watching and waiting for a chance to enact some kind of petty revenge.

"Nico!"

We hear Jake shouting, and we rush up to the deck. Brittany and Amma look between us and Jake on the deck of the *Azure Sky,* his hands cupped around his mouth.

Like Nico, he's scowling, his shoulders tense, and I know without even asking that Robbie got their stuff, too.

"How bad?" I call over.

"Fucking mess," Jake calls back, then waves at us with one arm. "Come on over, let's talk."

The four of us pile back into the dinghy, Nico's movements jerky and rough, and then we're all on the deck of the *Azure Sky.* The happy drowsiness of the afternoon has completely vanished, all of us standing stiffly, arms crossed, looking around. He could still be out there somewhere. Hiding out on the other side of the island. Waiting for us in the jungle.

And now we have no way of getting help. No contact at all with the outside world. We don't have a radio, and neither does the *Azure Sky.*

All of us are completely cut off.

"We have to leave," I say, and all five heads turn in my direction.

It sucks to cut the trip short under these circumstances, but it's obvious to me that we can't stay, not when Robbie could still be lurking, and is clearly dangerous and destructive.

"Lux, calm down," Nico says, placing a hand on my shoulder.

I recoil. "Calm down? Seriously?"

He frowns. "I'm just saying that panicking isn't going to help us right now."

"She's not panicking," Eliza says, coming to wrap an arm around me. "She's being sensible. We don't have radios, for fuck's sake, and clearly this guy is more unhinged than we thought if he's willing to do something like this."

"I get that," Nico says. "But Lux always does this. Acts like the fucking sky is falling."

The words are like a punch to my gut. "What are you talking about?"

"And besides," he goes on, shoving a hand through his hair. "It's not safe to be on open water with no radio. If we get into trouble, we're fucked."

"We're fucked *now*," I remind him, but he shakes his head.

"Let me think of something, okay? Maybe I can fix them, or—"

I can't stop the incredulous laugh that bursts out of me. "What, with coconuts or some shit? I like *Gilligan's Island,* too, Nico, but get real."

"Lux is right, mate."

Jake has his arms crossed, his expression unreadable behind his mirrored sunglasses. "Radios are fucked. There's no fixing that. But I have a satellite phone. Not the most reliable thing on the planet, but if I can get it up and running, I can try to get in touch with any boats in the area. See if anyone is headed this way, if they might have a backup radio or two that they can spare."

He shrugs. "It's not much, but I think it's our best option right now."

"Right, because you always know what's best," Nico says. There's a sinister expression on his face, one I've never seen before, almost a sneer.

Jake matches it with a confident grin. "In this case, reckon I do."

Before they can get into it, Amma steps forward, laying a hand on Nico's arm. "We should check the island, see if we can find him. Because maybe he's not even here, right? He could've done this as one last 'fuck you,' and then taken off."

She turns to Jake, cool as can be. "You have a gun, right?"

He nods, feet planted solidly on the deck. "It's not a bad idea.

There's only one other place to anchor here, over on the east side of the island. Let's go see if his boat's there. If it is, well. We'll deal with that. If not, then we can assume Amma's right, and he did this before leaving, just to fuck with us one last time."

Jake looks to Nico. "You in?"

Nico nods, not looking at me, and then Amma says, "I want to come, too."

I wait for someone to tell her that's a stupid idea, but no one does, and before I know it, the three of them are in the Zodiac, motoring to the other side of the island.

"Are you alright?" Eliza asks, squeezing me, and I shake my head. I'm scared and pissed off.

*She always acts like the fucking sky is falling.*

Like I've been some nag holding him back this entire time, a total drag, instead of the other way around. *I'm* the one who got the *Susannah* fixed for him. *I'm* the one who cleaned hotel rooms so we could pay rent—even though he could have solved both of those problems with a single phone call, if he was man enough to swallow his pride.

"Come on," Eliza says. "Let's go have a drink."

We do, sitting on the quiet, dark deck waiting, until finally, about two hours later, we hear the quiet hum of the Zodiac's motor.

I see it pull over to the *Susannah* first, watch Amma and Nico climb aboard, and then Jake is heading back toward us.

"Nothing!" he calls up almost immediately. "No boat, no asshole. Think Amma's theory was right. This was one last 'fuck you' before he went crawling back to wherever he came from."

It should be a relief, but I still feel anxious, scanning the shoreline like Robbie will come flying out of the jungle at any minute.

"Want me to take you back over?" Jake asks, and I look over my shoulder at Brittany, who has, somehow, managed to fall asleep on the deck and is now slowly coming awake, rising out of the little cocoon of towels she'd made.

"I'm ready," she says, already grabbing her shoes, but I shake my head.

"Do you mind if I stay here tonight?"

If Jake is surprised, he doesn't show it. "Fine by me."

"You sure?" Brittany asks, stopping beside me. Her eyes are sleepy, her hair messy, and she smells faintly like the red wine we had earlier. "I can stay with you if you want?"

It might be nice, but that would leave Amma and Nico alone on the boat together. I definitely don't want that. I shake my head.

"No, go on. I'll be over in the morning. I just . . ."

I trail off, and she nods, leaning in to hug me. "You need a break. Got it."

I watch her climb over the side and into the Zodiac, then sit out on the deck long after Jake comes back. There's another cabin below, but I decide to stay out there, lying on the deck, watching the stars overhead.

I don't think I'll sleep, but somehow, I do. I wake up just as the sun has begun to rise, turning the sky overhead a soft violet-pink.

Quietly, I slip over the side of the boat, and swim for the *Susannah*.

The door to the cabin is open, probably to get more air, and I move quietly down the steps, thinking I'll curl into bed with Nico after all, thinking that maybe, we can just move past this.

But Nico isn't on the table.

I see Brittany's dark hair spilling out from the blanket, and it feels like everything inside me has gone very still.

My footsteps are almost noiseless as I make my way to the cabin, my blood thrumming in my ears, my hands shaking as I push open the cabin door.

Nico is lying on his back, his feet pointed at the door, his bare skin very tan against the white sheet beneath him.

Amma is draped over him, her skin shining with sweat, a blue bead bracelet around her ankle.

It's the only thing she's wearing.

Hey Man.

Hope this gets thru, internet is kinda shit here but what can you do, right? Back in Teahupo'o, not sure for how long. Fucking surfers, can only take so much of those assholes. Riggs is in Uturoa right now, so I might try to meet up with him there. He says it's not as crowded or touristy, but I gotta tell you, Robs, after Meroe? Everything seems pretty fucking crowded and touristy. I was only gonna stay like three days because I figured any more than that, you end up talking to a volleyball, but I was there for like a week, 8 days? HAHA, oh shit, I just looked at what day it is today, and Jesus, dude, I was there for eighteen days, that is fucking CRAZY. ISLAND TIME!

Anyway u gotta go. Beg, borrow, steal, make it haaaapppppen, brother, because it's on this whole other level out there. By day three or something like that, I was like "fuck it with this ramen" and started fishing, started hunting. Caught this big-ass lizard and roasted it over a fire, caveman-style. (Tasted like ass but whatever.)

Only thing—if you go keep your mind CLEAR man because that place fuuuucks with you enough as it is. Seems like it would be awesome to get high on a deserted island but trust me, Robs, IT IS NOT AWESOME. I did it one night and ended up in some *Apocalypse Now* shit, stomping through the jungle with a goddamn KNIFE thinking there was someone out there. Kept hearing weird noises and not jungle noises like—person noises? If you feel me? Footsteps and shit, breathing. I'm telling you, it was WILD. I ended up finding this shack, left over from WWII probably, and I remembered a buddy of mine said a dude used to live on Meroe. Guess this was his house and it was SICK. I really thought about sticking around but I figured it was only a matter of time before some assholes showed up playing Gilligan.

Still Meroe is cool as hell. WEIRD as hell, so keep your head on a swivel, dude, but go. Trust.

Let me know how the fuck you are/where the fuck you are
(I won't tell Riggs, I know there's some shit that went down there)
(fuck man am I the last friend you DON'T have shit with?)

Later—

C

*Email sent December 3, 2019, from Christopher "Chipper" Davidson*

# TWENTY

I don't know why I head for the airstrip.

Maybe it's just that I don't want to deal with anyone, and I know that no one will think to look for me there.

Nico and Amma. Amma and Nico. I keep seeing them, their bodies curled around each other, keep remembering all those moments of them talking and laughing, and how I'd told myself I was being stupid.

*Good luck,* Susannah had said.

Turns out, I'd needed that warning.

Tears are streaming down my face now, mingling with my sweat, but I keep pushing through the foliage.

I've gone several more yards before I realize that nothing looks familiar. Or rather, it all looks *too* familiar—there's a sameness to the jungle that makes it easy to get confused.

I stop, take a deep breath, and look around.

It's just like it was the other day, steamy and hot, smelling thick and green, but everything feels closer now, like the air and vegetation are pressing in on me. I turn back in the other direction, but when I do, the leaves seem thicker still, the ground underfoot trickier.

I'm not panicked, not yet, but my heart is definitely beating faster as I keep going, hoping to find the right path at any minute.

But the jungle only gets denser, the heat more oppressive, and I can hear my own sharp breaths, sawing in and out of my lungs as I try to move as fast as I can.

I hear birds calling overhead, and when I look up, there are flashes of blue sky.

And then suddenly, the jungle thins, and I breathe a sigh of relief, thinking I've found the way to the airstrip after all.

But no. It's just another clearing, another place where the vegetation has clearly been hacked back by human hands. And directly in front of me, there's a building.

It's small, barely six feet across, and made of metal that's rusting in places. In place of a door there's simply an empty opening, framed by crawling vines. The interior beyond is completely dark.

It must've belonged to the navy when they were here, probably some kind of storage shed, but I immediately think of the trap in the trees, and Robbie's buddy, who swore someone was living on the island. The sudden shot of fear tastes acrid in my mouth, and cold sweat springs up under my arms and behind my knees.

"Hello?" I call tentatively, feeling both stupid and terrified as I do.

There's no answer, of course, and I move a little closer, ducking my head inside the shelter.

It's almost too dark to see anything—the thick cover of the jungle prevents most light from getting through—but there, in the corner, I can see . . . something.

A lump, a darker spot among the shadows. Too small to be a person. A bag maybe? Or just a bunch of debris?

I'm just about to step farther inside when there's movement near my foot, and as I look down, something green slithers past.

Rearing back, I nearly step on the tail of the snake, shrieking in spite of myself, but it's already disappeared under the side of the shack.

There's no sound other than my own heart pounding in my ears. I have to get out of here.

WHEN I STUMBLE BACK ONTO the beach, it's empty, and I see both dinghies are gone. Maybe they've all gone looking for me, but I don't really care, not right now.

My legs are shaking as I pull myself aboard the *Susannah*, stomach in knots, and I hope against hope that Nico and Amma aren't on board. I'm not ready to face either of them yet.

The deck is empty, thank god, and when I go below, it's clear I'm alone. Nico and Amma must have gone off somewhere together, and that thought is both a relief and another knife to my chest as I step into the cabin.

It's warm and damp in there, and I can't bring myself to get anywhere near the bed. I feel like I can still smell sex and Amma's sunscreen, and I'm afraid I'll see her long dark hair on the pillow that used to be mine. Instead, I perch on the edge of the berth, my fingers curled around the mattress.

It's okay, I tell myself. It's just a few more days, and then we'll go back to Hawaii.

But what will I do after that?

For the first time, I consider whether Nico and I could get past this. I hate how much the possibility fills me with relief, but I can't help it—it seems so much easier that way. Like these two weeks were just some weird little blip, a dream, and if we just ignore it, we could go back to the way things were.

Except, this trip has also revealed to me that *the way things were* involved Nico calling all the shots, living exactly how he wanted, while I drifted along in his currents.

I look around the tiny room. The curtain I made for our porthole is slightly crooked at the hem, cheerful yellow flowers gently staining the light that filters through the fabric. I realize how pathetic my attempts at making a life with Nico now seem. The *Susannah* was always Nico's. *Will* always be his.

I was just along for the ride.

And I'm sick of it.

I'd come back to the boat with the idea of gathering some of my things, and decamping to the beach for these last few nights. But with the dinghy gone, there's no way to do that, so instead, I wander up to the deck again.

Nico is standing there.

He's got his hands in his pockets, his head down. By his posture, I can tell that he knows he's been caught, and I don't have time to wonder how he figured it out.

"Lux—" he starts, but I cut him off.

"Don't. Don't do this."

"Don't you think we should at least talk about it?" he asks, and I feel tears sting my eyes.

"Is there anything to talk about? Really?"

Nico stares at me. His skin has grown even darker since we've been here. He's so tan he glows, and it hurts, how beautiful he is. Even now. Especially now. "So, you're breaking up with me on a deserted island. That's actually happening."

"You fucked someone else," I say, my voice low. I don't know where the others are right now, and the coziness that had seemed so fun our first few days here is now stifling. I feel like there's no way to have a private conversation, no way someone isn't overhearing everything we say.

"And I'm so sorry," Nico says. He actually looks it, which is the hardest part.

Then he adds, "But it's not like you haven't been really moody lately, Lux. I feel like every time I want to talk to you, you're with Eliza and Brittany. And then you got so pissed over that guy—"

"Because he was scary, Nico! Because it seemed like you didn't care about protecting me! Because we should've headed home then and there, but we didn't, and now our radios are fucked and *you* fucked someone else, and now we're stuck here. You can't blame me for being angry about that."

He shakes his head, his hair falling over his brow as he looks away from me. "I know it was uncool—" he starts, and I scoff loudly.

"'Uncool'—yeah, that's one word for it."

Glaring, he juts out his jaw. "This is what I mean. You've been a bitch ever since we got here, okay? So yeah, I'm an asshole and I slept with someone, but to be honest, Lux, I didn't think you'd care. I mean, you're going off with Jake and Eliza, right?"

I stare at him. "What?"

His arms are folded across his chest. "I heard Eliza invite you to leave with them. And the thing is, Lux, I didn't hear you say no. You were thinking about it, weren't you?"

I fall silent.

"So yeah, can't really blame me for feeling like, 'Hey, maybe Lux was never actually into me. Maybe it was the boat and the chance to do absolutely fuck-all with her life!'"

"That's not fair," I say, and now we're not even trying to be quiet, our voices ringing through the open air.

"You were a dick to me after Robbie," I go on. "I was pissed. And yeah, it was nice to have Eliza make that offer. But just because you didn't hear me say no doesn't mean I said yes. And it's definitely not an excuse to go off and fuck some girl you've known for like a week on *our* boat."

"*My* boat, Lux," he says. "*My* fucking boat."

And there it is.

There never really was an "us" in the true sense of things, not for Nico. But suspecting something in the darkest corners of your mind and hearing it said out loud are two different things.

"Your fucking boat," I echo, nodding. "And I'm getting off of it right now, don't worry."

"Lux," he says again, but I've stopped listening. I leave my sad little bag of things on the deck, and dive over the side, swimming for the *Azure Sky.*

I see Brittany on a striped blanket on the beach, stretched out underneath the sun. She's got her sunglasses on, a book open, and I bet she has her earbuds in, so I don't even bother waving to her or trying to call to her. Instead, I pull myself up and onto the *Azure Sky.*

Eliza had said I was welcome to sail with them any time I wanted, and I wonder if that's still an option now. Maybe I don't have to go back to Hawaii with Nico after all.

Robbie said that the island was cursed, and for the first time, I'm starting to believe there's some truth to that. Those dead sailors back in the 1800s, the overgrown airstrip, the skull, the abandoned building I found this morning . . . for a place full of natural beauty, it also seems full of horrible history.

I'm craving another drink, but the cooler on deck is empty, so I slide open the cabin door and stick my head in. "Eliza?" I call, even though I know she's not down there. Still, it feels a little strange to be creeping around the boat on my own.

Unlike our cabin on the *Susannah,* the interior of the *Azure Sky* is bright and open, with white furnishings, chrome accents, and shiny teak floors. I let myself imagine what it would be like to sail to Bangkok on a boat like this.

I open the stainless-steel refrigerator and pull out a twelve-pack, thinking that I might as well refill the deck cooler for Eliza while I'm at it. But my hands are sweating, and one of the bottles slips through my fingers, crashing onto the floor in a spray of broken amber glass and foam.

"Fuck," I mutter, stepping back from the spreading pool as the smell of yeast and hops fills the cabin.

I look around for a towel, anything to clean up the mess, but the whole minimalist thing they have going on means there's nothing at hand except for more metal and glass, and that's not exactly helpful right now.

I open the cabinet underneath the sink and there, next to a bottle of Windex, I find a neat pile of white towels.

There's also a lumpy black bag, its zipper partially opened.

*Wonder what all they got on that boat,* I hear Robbie say, remembering his crooked smile and hard eyes.

Robbie's bag. The one he'd thrown on shore that day. It had been black like this. Canvas, the zipper broken.

I feel like Bluebeard's wife as I pull it out into the light.

As soon as it's in my lap, I breathe a sigh of relief. It's not the same bag. This one is too new, branded with the Tumi logo, and when I try the zipper, it slides open just fine.

God, this place is making me paranoid.

I'm closing up the bag again when I notice an oddly shaped piece of plastic protruding.

Whatever is in the bag is heavy, and I have to use both hands to pull it out.

It's cash.

A *lot* of cash. Stacks of it, tightly bound together, and wrapped in plastic. American dollars, euros, British pounds, the colorful face of the queen smiling genteelly up at me.

My heart is pounding as I shove the money back in the bag, only to realize there are more plastic-wrapped parcels inside. One is cash, but two are thicker, heavier, and I realize, in numb disbe-lief, that they're bricks of hash.

So: not just cash, but drugs, too.

Nico had asked Jake and Eliza what they did, how they made a living, and Jake had been vague enough that I'd just assumed he was another rich kid with inherited wealth—he didn't have to actually make money, it just existed for him. And after hearing that they grew up together, I figured Eliza was the same.

But clearly, there's more to it than that.

Is that why they're here, on this deserted island? Are they run-ning from the law?

Suddenly, I realize just how little I actually know about Jake or Eliza, or Brittany or Amma for that matter—or fuck it, maybe even Nico. These people are basically all strangers to me, and I am alone with them in the middle of the Pacific Ocean. My head feels like it's stuffed with cotton, and my mouth has gone dry, and all I can think is I have to put all this shit back, exactly as I found it, quickly shoving it into the bag like the canvas will burn me.

That's when I hear footsteps on the stairs leading into the galley.

I turn to see Eliza standing there, looking down at me.

Smiling.

"So," she says, folding her arms, sun-bronzed and beautiful and remarkably calm. "Now you know our little secret."

# TWENTY-ONE

"You're gonna be cool about this, right?" Eliza asks after a long pause, and I nod almost automatically.

This is something Eliza is good at, I realize: phrasing a statement as a question, so that your only option is to agree with her.

Stepping forward, she leans down and takes the bag from me. "It's not that big of a deal," she goes on. "It's just some pot. We don't deal in the scarier stuff, you know? Just the fun shit."

She flashes that sparkling smile, and I nod robotically.

"Right, hash is nothing, really," I hear myself say, wondering if there's more hidden on the boat, and where.

Eliza can clearly read my mind. "I know, it looks like a lot, and yes, we'd be completely and utterly fucked if we got caught with it, but you know how it is—big risk, big reward."

"Totally," I say, nodding even more manically, and Eliza laughs, coming over to hug me.

"Oh, Luxy," she says. "Don't tell the others, but you're my favorite."

And it's so stupid and silly, but my whole body seems to flush with pleasure. How does she do it, make you feel like her approval is so important, so vital?

Then she looks right at me. "But something's wrong, isn't it, love?"

Before I can stop myself, it pours out of me. "I caught Nico and Amma. In bed."

Her brows draw tight together, a trio of wrinkles appearing above her nose. "Oh, Luxy," she says. "Oh, fuck."

Tears spill down my cheeks and I let her envelop me again.

"What a pair of cocks," she says, and that actually makes me laugh a little, pulling back as I swipe at my cheeks.

"Such cocks, yeah," I agree. "I swear to god, it's this place. Being on the edge of civilization, away from everything and everyone. I think it makes people insane."

Eliza nods. "What are you going to do now? Did you confront them?"

I shake my head. "No. In the moment, I was a complete coward and basically ran away."

"I understand that," Eliza says. "But maybe you'd feel better if it were all out in the open?"

I think about confronting Amma, but nothing about that scene appeals to me. "Right now, I just want to forget it," I tell her, and she squeezes my shoulders.

"Fair enough. Stay over here with us for a bit, hmm? We've got plenty of room."

I know it's not a permanent solution, but for now, it's enough. I nod. "I'd love to."

AS MUCH AS I'D LOVE to hide out on the *Azure Sky* for the rest of the trip, I know that I can't, and besides, I'm not the one who did anything wrong. It's not fair that I should have to give up the island just because Amma and Nico decided to be assholes. Still, as I swim for the beach later that afternoon, my stomach is in knots. I can see Brittany sitting on a towel, watching me approach, while Jake is farther up on the beach, underneath the tarp with a book. Nico and Amma are, thank god, nowhere to be seen.

As soon as I make my way onto the sand, Brittany is there, her fingers twisted together, the corner of her mouth turned down in an exaggerated frown. "Lux," she says, then sighs. "Shit."

I wring the water out of my hair, nodding and giving something that tries to be a laugh. "Yeah, shit indeed. Guess you already know."

"Amma told me."

She steps closer to me, her hand landing on my arm. We both smell like salt water and wet towels, a sharper, earthier scent underneath. We've all stopped bathing as much, going in and out of the sea enough times to feel clean even though we're not, not really. How did that happen so fast?

"I'm so sorry," she says, and then her words start tumbling out. "If I had had any idea that kind of thing was going to happen, I would've stopped it, I promise. I mean, Amma hasn't seemed even remotely interested in any guys while we were traveling, so I *never* thought—"

"Brittany."

I cover her hand with my own, and she laces our fingers together as she looks at me.

"It's not your fault," I tell her. "It's just . . . one of those things. Throw some hot people together, add stress and lots of alcohol . . ."

"That's not an excuse," Brittany says, and I'm surprised at how fierce she sounds. "It was a fucked-up thing to do to a friend."

It feels good, hearing her defend me like that, but I shake my head. "Come on, Britt. You know me and Amma aren't friends. Not really."

I'd liked her, sure, but I wasn't stupid—these kinds of trips didn't form lifelong bonds. I was just the girlfriend of the guy

Amma and Brittany had hired, and within a year, they'd forget my name, I bet.

But then Brittany squeezes my hand. "*We're* friends, though. Right?"

Again, there's this seriousness in her face, in her words, that surprises me, and I smile at her in spite of my confusion. "Yeah," I tell her. "Of course, we are."

"Good," she says, then pulls me in for a quick hug. "So it's official, I'm Team Lux on this, and they can both fuck off."

I laugh even as my throat tightens. "Okay, well, you just met me a couple weeks ago, and you've known Amma for a lot longer, so maybe don't throw her over completely. Even though I appreciate it."

When she pulls back, Brittany shakes her head. "Too late. I already told her once we get back to Hawaii, we're done."

"Because she slept with my boyfriend?"

Her gaze drifts past my shoulder, and I turn to see Amma on the deck of the *Susannah*, watching us.

"Because of a lot of things," Brittany says, and I wonder what *that* means.

Before I can ask, Jake walks over to us, his hands in his pockets, sand clinging to his calves. He looks so casual, so relaxed, and I suddenly remember with a jolt that Nico and Amma are not the only shock I've had today.

The money, the drugs. None of it really jibes with the man I see standing before me now in salmon swim trunks, his mirrored aviators reflecting the blue-green water and white sand.

"Everything alright?" he asks, and I nod, throwing Brittany a look. I'm sure Eliza will tell him what's going on, but I can't have this conversation with anyone else today.

How is it that you can be this far from anything resembling civilization, and still feel this watched, this scrutinized?

"Well, here's a bit of both good and bad news," Jake goes on, ducking his head so that he can look at us over the tops of his sunglasses. "Managed to get someone on the satellite phone this morning. There's a yacht headed this way out of Honolulu next week that can bring us a set of extra radios."

"Next week?"

We were supposed to leave Meroe in just a few days, had everything gone to plan. But now Jake was saying it was going to take even longer.

"Should add about ten days to the stay, yup," Jake agrees, looking back out at the water. "But not exactly any skin off our noses, is it? Maybe want to tighten up some of the rations a bit, go down to three bottles of wine a night instead of five."

His teeth flash white. "And it's not like Eliza and I had any set schedule for leaving, really. Look at it as God's way of saying he wants us to have a good time a little longer."

Ten more days.

Ten more days on this island with the man I loved and the woman he's cheated on me with.

Ten more days with Eliza and Jake and their secrets.

"Works for me," Brittany says, and I nod, too, even as I look around at the sand and the sea and the jungle behind us, wondering how a place that's so open, so free, could feel like such a trap.

# BEFORE

Eliza has never believed in fate. Some mystical force, pulling you where you're supposed to be, so that everything clicks together with perfect symmetry? No way. Besides, that kind of thinking takes power out of your hands, in her opinion, so fuck that.

But still, when she looks across a crowded pub and sees Jake Kelly standing there, a pint in one hand, surrounded as always by a pack of acolytes, she has to wonder if the universe isn't finally—*for fucking once*—doing her a favor.

Lord knows it owes her something.

After her mum, after Jake and all that, Eliza spent years drifting. A year of uni, then a new guy, one who had Jake's blue eyes and easy charm, but not his cash, not that gold-plated sense of self that Jake had somehow possessed even at seventeen.

That guy—Tom—lasted nearly two years, and then she was moving on again, settling in London with some girls she met through an online ad, and working at a bank.

When that had gotten too dull to be borne, she'd found a job bartending on a cruise ship. She usually worked the Spanish route, Southampton to Mallorca and all that, sunburned tourists paying too much for tequila sunrises that she'd always made with her brightest and fakest smile.

It wasn't a bad life. Eliza liked the travel, and the tips were good. It just wasn't what she'd envisioned for herself when she was younger.

Sure, she was going to gorgeous places, but she was doing it as staff when what she wanted was to be the person being waited on, the girl who ordered the drinks, not the girl who made them.

But eventually, she made enough money from that job to travel on her own for a bit, getting off the boat in the Canary Islands and never getting back on.

She covered most of southern Europe, ended up in Istanbul for a period, all while drifting into different groups of people, different friends. And with people like that—people you meet on the road—there's no real past and no real future. It can all just be a glorious present where Eliza can be anyone she wants. She doesn't have to tell people that her mum is in prison, doesn't have to confess to the wasted years on wasted men and wasted opportunities.

She can reinvent herself every time she ends up in a new place, and the freedom of that is heady.

But it's not nearly as heady as this moment, as she makes her way across the pub to Jake Kelly.

He doesn't recognize her at first. She can tell from the way that his eyes move over her that he's interested, but it's in a distracted sort of way, just a man seeing an attractive woman, doing whatever calculus it is men do as they decide if they're going to pursue or not.

And then . . .

His eyes widen, and the expression on his face fills Eliza with a sudden rush of triumph.

"Holy shit," he breathes as she comes close, and she smiles at him, placing a hand on his shoulder and going up on her tiptoes to kiss his cheek.

"Hiya, Jake."

He sets his beer on the bar behind him so quickly that some of it sloshes over the side, and then his hands are on her waist, his grin genuine as he looks down at her. His teenage lankiness has turned into something more solid, his chest broader, his face sharper. Unfair, really, that he should still be this beautiful, and that she should still feel her face grow hot when he looks at her, that she should immediately feel like a sixteen-year-old again, craving his reflected glow.

"How on earth have I gone over ten years without this face in my life?" he asks, smiling, and just like that, it's over, she's done for. Lost again in that easy smile and those blue eyes, and he doesn't even have to ask her to go home with him.

She just goes.

---

HOME IS A BOAT.

It makes her laugh at first when he takes her there. She can't seem to escape ships these days, but that's fine by her. She loves the water, and had even taken sailing lessons during her time on the cruise ship. Besides, the *Azure Sky* is not just any boat.

It's gorgeous, sleek and luxurious, and she sees Jake's pride in it as he shows her around.

"Where are you going to take her?" she asks, and he slides his arms around her waist from behind, kissing a spot behind her ear and raising goose bumps.

"Anywhere I fucking please," he replies, then nods toward a map opened up on the table in the galley.

"Thinking about this one spot. Meroe Island. Supposed to be quite the experience. Ancestor of mine got stranded there back in the 1800s. Poor bugger got eaten, if memory serves."

"By sharks?" Eliza asks, and Jake presses a gentle bite to the place where her neck meets her shoulder.

"By his mates," he replies, and she turns in his arms, looping her arms around his neck.

"And you want to go there *why*?"

That grin again, those dimples. "For the fun of it, darling. And speaking of fun . . ."

Eliza lets him lead her to the cabin, lay her down on the wide bed, and strip off her dress. It had bothered her for years, the way she still thought about those afternoons in Jake's bed as a teenager, how no man she'd slept with since had affected her quite the way he had.

She'd chalked it up to first love and adolescent hormones, but on this night, here on the *Azure Sky*, she learns she was wrong. It's just—Jake. Whatever sparked between them before is immediately rekindled again, and even though she has friends she knows are waiting on her, she falls asleep in his arms thinking she might never leave.

HER SECOND NIGHT ON THE boat, she finds the drugs.

Eliza wasn't snooping, not really. She was looking for a bloody wineglass, the ones they'd used the night before still dirty in the sink because god forbid Jake Kelly wash a glass, and she's certainly not doing it for him.

She opens a cabinet and sees stacks of something wrapped in plastic, and for a moment, her brain doesn't quite understand what they are, these solid bricks covered in cling film.

When she realizes what she's looking at, a strange thing happens inside of her. Her skin feels cold even as rage—a rage stronger than any she's ever felt—boils up in her stomach.

She's still squatting there in front of the cabinet when Jake comes out of the cabin, wearing just his boxer briefs and a robe, a cigarette dangling from his mouth.

"Ah," he says seeing her, and shrugs. "Family business continues apace."

He says it cheerfully, with that same grin—and that, in the end, is what dooms him.

For Jake, this is nothing more than A Thing That He Does. A way to make money—extra money, because for all he's joking, this is not his *actual* family business. That's real estate. This is simply a side hustle that allows him to buy fancy boats and never wear a suit unless he wants to.

This—the thing that destroyed her mother's life and, in many ways, her own—is just, for Jake Kelly, a bit of fun.

And it always will be.

No lesson learned from her mum's prison sentence. No remorse. The Kelly men just trundled on their way.

*He never even asked about her.*

Eliza realizes that now. The last time she'd seen Jake, her mum had just been sentenced to prison, but not once in the last two days has he asked about her. Where she is, how she is.

Like she never even existed.

Rising on shaking legs, Eliza turns to him, and schools her face very carefully into a bland expression. "Good to know," she says, and her voice doesn't crack even the tiniest bit.

He comes closer, kisses her cheek, and she smiles up at him. But inside, her mind is whirling and whirling, and something too hazy to be called a plan begins to form.

ELIZA DOESN'T SPEND THE NEXT night on the *Azure Sky*, or the night after that. She rejoins the friends she's been hanging out with, spending her time with them in various museums and shops and pubs and restaurants, and all the while, she's thinking—about Jake and that boat and his plans and those hidden bags under the sink. By the time her phone rings on the third day, the plan is not so hazy anymore.

She looks down at her mobile, smiling at the number that pops up.

She doesn't answer.

She doesn't answer Jake's second call or his third, either. She lets him wait five days before finally, she decides to pick up.

"Are you trying to torture me?" he asks as soon as she answers, and Eliza smiles, excusing herself from her friends and wandering into the back hallway of the pub where they've been drinking.

"A little," she admits, and she hears Jake laugh on the other end, imagines him sitting there on the deck of that gorgeous catamaran, tan and golden and gorgeous.

"Well, it's working," he replies. "I can't stop thinking about you. Haven't even washed my sheets, that's how pathetic I've become."

"Aww, Jake. Not used to being the one left in the morning, are you?"

"You're bloody well right I'm not," he answers, and then pauses. "Can I see you tonight?"

Eliza glances over her shoulder, back into the pub. "I'm busy tonight."

He groans. "Of course you are. Tomorrow?"

"Can't think that far ahead," she tells him, leaning against the wall, remembering all those afternoons she'd waited for *his* call, all the canceled plans just in case he'd want to see her that day. "Honestly, I'm not even sure I'm going to stay in Australia that much longer. Might be time to move on, have some new adventures."

Immediately, she begins to worry. Has she pushed it too far? Was that too obvious?

She holds her breath.

But then Jake says, "Lucky for you, this guy loves a good adventure. Remember that island I was telling you about? Meroe? Feels like the perfect time to head out that way. You, me, sand, surf. Whaddya say?"

"Jake," Eliza purrs, even as her heart pounds harder, her blood fizzing like champagne. "Are you asking me to sail away with you?"

"No," he says. "I'm *begging* you."

And Eliza laughs.

They sail out two days later.

And, of course, the big news this year was our trip to Hawaii! The weather was lovely the whole time—we really lucked out there! Hope you're all prepared to look at about a thousand pictures of dolphins next time we see you, because Dave and I sure did take a bunch, lol.

We did have one little "spooky" thing happen on our trip, though. We had sailed out to this place called Meroe Island. Dave wanted to check out an old WWII airstrip that's there, and I thought it might be neat to see a real live deserted island.

But when we got there, there was a boat already anchored. I know Dave was ready to be Robinson Crusoe, and he sure was disappointed! We hailed them, both on the radio, then just the old-fashioned way, shouting over the side, but there was no response. Thought that was a little funny, but then we figured maybe they were off exploring on the island.

Sure enough, I spotted somebody on the beach a few minutes later, but they disappeared back into the trees before I really had a chance to get a good look at them.

Now, y'all know I am not superstitious, but something about that quiet boat and that person darting into the jungle . . . it just gave me a bad feeling. It was the prettiest little island, but I told Dave there are lots of pretty little islands that don't make me feel like I'm about to crawl out of my skin. And the funny thing is, Dave actually agreed with me! Said the place gave him the creeps, so we just sailed on. Not sorry we did!

—Mullins Family Christmas Card, December 2016

# NOW

# TWENTY-TWO

It's our fifteenth day on the island.

If everything had gone like it was supposed to, we would have left yesterday, but instead, we're all still here.

Waiting.

I'm still on the *Azure Sky*, and so is Brittany. Nico and Amma are still on the *Susannah*, and it's like the six of us split into our own separate universes, barely interacting anymore. If our group is on the beach, Nico and Amma stay on the boat. If we're on board the *Azure Sky*, they're on the beach.

I don't know if anything is still going on between Nico and Amma. But I do know that Nico hasn't even tried to fight for me. And all I want now is just to leave this island behind: escape the heat and humidity, which have become like living things, pressing down on me. Escape the claustrophobia and the weird tension, and the constant, thrumming dread.

I'm starting to dream of cooler places. The air-conditioned chill of a movie theater. A brisk walk on the beach in December. The teeth-aching buzz from drinking a frozen cocktail too fast. Even as I wade into the clear blue water off the shore, I'm still sweating, the water the same temperature as a warm bath.

I take a deep breath through my nose and catch that now-familiar mix of salt water and slowly rotting vegetation. Despite the SPF 50 I religiously apply every few hours, the sun is searing my shoulders, the glare off the water already giving me a dull headache.

"I feel as though you're thinking entirely too deep thoughts for a morning like this."

Jake is approaching me, two beers dangling from one hand.

I'm still a little hungover from last night—the drinking sure hasn't slowed down since our group fractured—but I take the bottle he offers. The first sip hits my tongue, yeasty and sour, and my stomach rolls a little.

"I was just thinking that paradise isn't exactly what I'd expected."

I can see my reflection in Jake's sunglasses. My shoulders are freckled and peeling, and my hair is a tangled and salty mess, held back from my face with one of Nico's bandanas. Even though we've been living in the exact same conditions, Amma somehow didn't let herself become this feral.

Jake smiles at me, tipping the beer to his mouth. "Very few things are what they say on the tin, Lux," he tells me, then flashes me a grin. "Except me."

"Ah, so the feckless rich guy thing isn't just an act?"

He tilts his head back and laughs, and I try not to let my eyes linger on the smooth expanse of his throat, the way his hair curls against his earlobes.

Nico is technically hotter, but Jake is . . . magnetic. In the same genre of pretty rich boy, but he wears it differently. The fact that he's older than Nico is part of it, but it's something else—Nico has tried so hard to deny who he is, where he comes from. Jake just *owns* it, and that confidence and swagger is appealing—not nearly the turnoff I expected it to be.

"Come on," he says, gesturing back toward the beach. "Let's do a little exploring."

I know it's a bad idea, going off alone together when I'm feeling this way.

I follow him anyway.

WE WALK FOR A WHILE, following the curve of the shore. We don't talk much, but I'm very aware of how close we're standing, of the way the back of his hand brushes against mine every so often.

I finish the beer quickly, and it goes to my head more than one drink usually does. By the time we stop to sit down in the sand, the lagoon and what I think of as "our beach" feel far away. Like we've found our own little island, free from everyone else.

The trees aren't quite so thick here, and the sandy part of the beach is narrower, a little crescent of sand around the blue, blue waters of the lagoon. There's something liberating about looking out and only seeing open ocean, no sign of the *Susannah* or the *Azure Sky* on the horizon. For now, I can pretend that we're the only two people here.

Leaning back on his elbows, Jake nods out toward the sea. "It used to freak me out, you know. Open water like that."

"Sailing seems like a weird hobby to pick up then," I offer, and his grin makes the dimple in his cheek deepen. I wonder if he's practiced that smile, if he's studied it in the mirror and known the effect it would have on women.

"Touché," he acknowledges, then turns his attention back to the water. "But I was raised a Kelly, you see, and all the Kelly men sail."

I thought again of Nico, learning to sail at some prep school in Oregon, and wondered how two guys could be so similar, and yet also so different.

"What else do Kelly men do?" I ask, and he tilts his head back.

"They go to poncey schools, both at home and abroad. I went to a couple in Australia, then dear old dad sent me to England, ostensibly to straighten me out, but it didn't really take."

"Ah, so you were the prep school bad boy, got it," I reply, and he looks over at me with a grin.

"Never that bad, not truly."

"What a shame." My face is flushed, and I feel almost dizzy with my own recklessness. I know what I'm doing, what *we're* doing. Whatever it is, it's dangerous and stupid, and I'm going ahead with it anyway.

"So, tell me," he goes on, turning to face me. "What do the McAllister women do?"

"Fuck things up?" I say lightly, but he's studying me, and my skin feels too tight, and I look back out at the sea.

I decide to tell the truth. "We trust the wrong men," I say. "My dad . . . I guess he wasn't a bad guy, exactly. Just a careless one."

He doesn't reply, but I sense him listening. "He left when I was eleven, but he kept, like, *trying* the dad thing. For a little while at least. But then he had other kids, so I guess he didn't need to be *my* dad anymore."

I sigh. "It's not that he didn't care about me, or even that he didn't *want* to care, I think. He just . . . couldn't. Wasn't capable of it."

I think of Nico with his charming smile and capable hands, with his big dreams that are always, always *his* dreams. *You can come along, sure.*

But that's all it is. An empty offer, and an even emptier promise.

Jake lays his hand on top of mine. "Is it rude if I say that your dad sounds like a real cunt?"

That startles a laugh out of me, and I shake my head, looking at him. He's moved closer, and I know what's about to happen.

I wonder if we've been heading toward this since the first day we met.

His hand is gritty on my face from the sand, and when he rubs a thumb over my lips, I taste salt water. My heart is pounding, stomach swooping, and I know this is stupid, I know it's a mistake, I know it will just make everything worse.

But I don't care.

Not right now, with the sun beating down, the two of us like Adam and Eve, alone together in this little stretch of paradise, a solitary Eden.

"You should tell me to stop," Jake murmurs, his gaze on my mouth.

"I should," I agree, and he lifts his eyes to mine. They're almost as blue as the sea beyond us, the sky overhead.

"Are you?"

I answer by leaning in, closing the gap between us.

His lips are dry, but soft, and when his hand tangles in my hair, I feel a bolt of lust shoot through me, so strong that my mouth opens even more, his tongue pushing against mine as his fingers tighten, and my hand presses the damp hot skin of his bare chest.

In this moment, it doesn't feel like a mistake. It feels like it might be another adventure, one that's solely mine. For the first time in months, I'm doing what *I* want, not what Nico wants.

Besides—what Nico wants is Amma, apparently, so fuck him.

I deserve this.

It's different with Jake.

My mind won't let me say *better*, because even now, even after all that's happened, I feel disloyal somehow. I hate that Nico still takes up enough space in my heart for me to feel a little bad about this.

But Nico's the only guy I've been with for a long time, so I can't help but compare the two.

Jake's touch is firmer, more confident. He talks to me throughout, asking what I want, if I like this, if he can do that. And I'm saying *yes* so much that it just starts to blend into a chant, *yes yes yes* until I'm shaking and my fingers are gripping his hair, damp with sweat at the nape of his neck, and there's no Nico and no Eliza, nothing except the two of us here on this shady patch of sand with the Pacific behind us and coconut palms overhead.

Afterward, we lie side by side, staring up at the sunlight filtering through the fronds. "I feel like I'm in a music video."

He laughs, his arm tightening around me. "I have no idea if that's a compliment or not."

"Oh, it is," I reply. "Or I mean it to be."

A part of me wonders if I should tell him about Nico and Amma. But if I do, he might think this was just about revenge.

It *was* a little bit about revenge, don't get me wrong. But that wasn't all of it. This wasn't some even-up-the-score kind of thing—Nico fucked Amma, so I fucked Jake.

Except now that it's over, and I'm starting to come back to myself—remembering where I am, where *we* are—something like regret is sinking in.

Not so much for betraying Nico, but shit, I like Eliza.

What happens now?

I turn to Jake, about to ask him, but he must sense the question because he just taps the tip of my nose. "Our secret," he murmurs.

"Sure," I say, relieved and yet also, inexplicably, disappointed. "Our secret."

Just one more to add to the pile.

We get dressed, brushing sand off ourselves and each other, and Jake leans in to nuzzle my temple, to kiss my neck, and it makes me smile even as regret keeps settling in heavier and heavier. It's like the night after Mom's funeral, the adrenaline wearing off to leave this kind of sick sensation behind, this sense that I walked right up to the edge of a cliff and instead of backing up, I threw myself over.

*It's the island,* I tell myself. *Nothing is real here. Nothing matters.*

"Let's try to cut through here," Jake says, leading me off the beach and toward the tree line, and I hang back, looking skeptically up at the jungle.

"Did you hide a machete in those shorts?" I ask, and he flashes me a wink over his shoulder.

"Oh, the quips I could make to that. But no, it's just not as thick on this side."

"How do you know that?" I ask, but he's already heading in, and I follow, relieved to be out of the harsh glare of the sun.

Jake is right—the foliage is thinner in this part, the ground easier to maneuver, and we walk in silence, light filtering through the leaves, the air thick.

Every step I take brings me closer to having to face Eliza, so I'm not exactly in a rush.

Jake doesn't seem to be in a hurry, either, and when we see a vine of bright pink flowers, he snaps one off, and tucks it behind my ear, making me blush.

When he slips his hand into mine, I take it, letting him lead me deeper and deeper into the jungle.

I hear running water after a minute, and my sense of direction, completely confused by the sameness of everything, wonders if we've somehow come across what I've started to think of as our pool.

But when the trees part, I see we've come to a different clearing, one that's darker and more secluded than our little oasis. There's a waterfall here, too, but the water is sluggish, trickling down into a much smaller pool. There's a heavy, sickly sweet scent hanging in the air.

There's also something pale at the edge of the pool, and my brain struggles to make sense of the shape at first, thinking almost dazedly, *A foot, why does that look like someone's foot?*

It isn't until I hear Jake mutter, "Fucking asshole," that I realize what I'm looking at is Robbie's body.

# TWENTY-THREE

I've never seen a dead body before, not like this.

I was with Mom when she died, but that was sterile and serene, surrounded by the beep of monitors, the antiseptic smell of the hospital.

This is nothing like that.

I hang back, my hand clapped over my mouth as Jake approaches.

"What happened to him?" I manage to say, and he sighs, ruffling his hair.

"Not sure. He's facedown in the water. I don't see anything . . . obvious. There are a million ways to die out here, though."

He crouches down, tugging his shirt over his nose, and nudges at something lying there on the ground.

It's Robbie's black canvas bag, and when Jake picks it up and starts riffling through it, I hear myself say, "Don't!"

He looks up, confused. "It just seems wrong," I say. "Going through his stuff."

"He's dead, Lux. He'll deal," he replies, and then he makes a noise, a kind of grunt as he pulls something out of the bag.

It's a knife, a truly terrifying blade like something out of a slasher movie. It's curved with a jagged edge, the handle made of something that looks like bone, and when it hits the ground just a few feet in front of me, I fight the urge to kick it away.

But then he pulls out something else.

"His passport?" I ask, recognizing the small navy folder.

"No," he says, flipping through it, then rising to his feet. "Yours."

I blink, my skin suddenly cold despite the heat.

"What?"

"Yours," Jake says, opening the cover and slapping it against his palm. "He must've taken it when he broke the radios."

It had never occurred to me to check my things when we discovered the broken radios—it seemed so obvious that Robbie had come aboard for one reason and one reason only. Now I'm realizing that I haven't opened my purse, which I'd shoved under a cabinet on the *Susannah*, since we got here. All it held was my cell phone, my passport, and some cash—not exactly things I'd needed the past two weeks. I hadn't even opened it up when I'd brought it on board the *Azure Sky*, just tucked it away underneath my berth mattress for safekeeping.

"Why?" I ask now, folding my arms tightly around me. "Why would he have taken just mine?"

Jake shrugs. "You said you had a weird moment with him. Maybe he wanted to punish you? Would've made sailing back into Hawaii a real pain, let me tell you that."

Maybe. Or maybe . . .

I look again at that knife, thinking of Robbie out here in the jungle with it.

The knife, and my picture.

Waiting.

Plotting?

Jake is probably right—it was probably just to fuck with me, just to make my life a little more difficult after our confrontation on the boat, but I think about all the times I felt like someone was watching from the jungle, and I shiver.

Scanning the clearing, it's obvious Robbie had been staying here. There's a shirt draped over a branch, the remnants of a little fire, and when I approach it, I notice tiny bones strewn across the ground.

"The fish," I say, and Jake walks over, kicking at the ash and bones.

"Oh, that stupid fucker." He sighs. "We told him, didn't we? Bloody well told him."

It seems clear now. Robbie was always trying to catch fish, and he finally had, but the wrong ones. It's easy to imagine him, sick, poisoned, crawling over to that pool, drinking the brackish water in desperation—so weak he'd fallen facedown into the water, unable to lift his head.

An accident. A stupid, shitty accident.

But a reminder of how quickly this place turns on people.

How it eats them up.

"We have to tell someone," I say, and Jake nods.

"Right, we'll let the others know we found him."

"Not just them," I reply, frowning. "Like. We have to let . . . I don't know, the coast guard or something know? People might be looking for him."

"Lux, no one is looking for this sad bastard, I promise you that. Not our problem."

The words are so cold that I almost take a step back. "We can't just leave him here." Jake sighs, reaching up to rub the back of his neck as he looks around. "Well, I'm not carrying him back to our beach, are you?"

"Don't be a dick," I snap, and he holds both hands out, walking toward me.

"Hey," he says softly. "I'm sorry. But . . ."

He holds my shoulders, looking down into my eyes. "Lux, the guy was a creep, and possibly dangerous. You were right to worry he wasn't really gone. But it's not our fault he went and poisoned himself, and I'd be lying if I said we weren't almost certainly better off for it. Surely you can see that."

Part of me wants to recoil at Jake's words, but the thing is . . . he's right.

In a way, hadn't this been what I wanted? That first morning after Robbie disappeared, when Jake had joked about getting a "hunting party" together, hadn't something about that idea appealed to me, made me feel safer?

I feel myself nodding in agreement and let Jake pull me in, hugging me close.

"We'll tell the others," he repeats, "and when the ship gets here with the radios, we'll let them know. There's really nothing more we can do until then. Nothing more we *should* do."

He's right, and I know it.

"And the ship gets here when?" I ask. "Like, just a few more days now, right? A week?"

Jake still smells like salt and sea and me, and he rests his chin on the top of my head. "No more than a week. Maybe a couple of days longer, depending on how their sail goes, but soon."

Soon.

Soon, there will be other people here. Soon, we can leave. Soon, Meroe Island will just be a memory, a weird story from my crazy twenties that I can tell at bars and around campfires.

I know I'll never tell this part, though. Not me and Jake and this stolen afternoon, and not Robbie, lying on the jungle floor, my eyes drawn to his body over and over again as we turn to leave, watching until the jungle closes back around him.

# TWENTY-FOUR

Brittany and Eliza are on the beach when we get back, and seeing Eliza makes my stomach churn with guilt. After finding Robbie's body, I'd almost forgotten the shame I'd felt about Jake, and now, as she smiles brightly and waves, it all comes crashing back.

I've never been the kind of girl who went after someone else's boyfriend. I've never cheated in my life. And I *like* Eliza. A lot.

"There you two are!" she calls out. "Brittany and I were about to go searching."

Jesus, what if they had? What if they'd come across us when we were . . .

The idea makes my mouth go dry, my knees suddenly watery. How fucking stupid and selfish I'd been. How reckless.

"Where are Nico and Amma?" Jake asks, and Brittany sits up, sand clinging to her bare back.

"What's going on?"

"Need to have something of a group meeting," Jake replies, and Eliza stands, her smile fading.

"Jake, what's happened?"

"Robbie," is all he says, and then, thank god, Nico and Amma wander up before we have to go looking for them.

"Something up?" Nico asks, his eyes darting over to me.

We haven't talked in days, and I honestly thought I'd miss him more, even though he'd hurt me. But the longer we've gone without speaking, the more I've begun to realize that Nico and I never really talked that much in the first place. Not about important things, or stuff that really mattered. Everything was vague, these rosy-tinted dreams with no concrete details that allowed us to project whatever we wanted onto each other, without ever needing to confront who we actually were, as a couple. Turns out, we weren't right for one another. We never had been.

Amma is just behind him, her face hidden by her huge sunglasses, her lower lip caught between her teeth as she crosses her arms tightly over her torso. I can't see her eyes, but I know she's looking at me.

"Robbie's dead," I say, the words falling out of my mouth like stones.

Jake glances over at me, eyebrows raised. "No beating around the bush for Miss McAllister," he says, even as Brittany says, "What?" and Eliza sucks in a breath.

Nico rubs the back of his neck the way he does when he's nervous. "Jesus, seriously?"

"He was camping in the jungle," I go on, still seeing his body lying there, the bottom of that one shoe. "Like I'd thought. Looks like he caught some of those fish out in the lagoon. The really colorful ones?"

"The poisonous ones," Jake adds. "So yeah. Thus goeth Robbie."

"Fuck," Nico says on an exhale. "What are we going to do about it?"

"The ship with the radios gets here in the next week or so," Jake says, shrugging. "We'll let them know. I didn't find any ID in his stuff, and fuck knows where he's anchored his boat. We'll let someone else worry about that."

"Well," Eliza says, hands on her hips. "I wish I could say I was sorry about it, but the guy was a certified wanker."

She sounds like she's mimicking Jake as she says it, her normally crisp inflections sliding into the wider vowels of his Aussie accent for a second.

"How did you two find him?"

Amma is definitely looking at me now, and I make myself meet her gaze.

"We were just checking out the jungle," I say, willing myself not to blush, for my eyes not to slide guiltily to Eliza.

"A man can only take so much sun and sand before he has to go adventuring," Jake agrees, nodding, and he's so casual, so light, giving nothing away.

"God, you poor thing," Eliza clucks, coming forward to chafe her hands up and down my arms. "That must've been awful to see."

I don't deserve her sympathy right now, but I take it anyway.

"It was, yeah. But like you said, he wasn't a good dude, and like *Jake* said, we've . . . we've done all we can do, really."

"Do you know what we need?" Eliza says, wrapping her arms around me from the back. "We need a party."

"Because a guy died?" Amma speaks for the first time, and her voice is icy. Eliza shakes her head, her hair brushing over my shoulders.

"Nothing that morbid, love. It's just that . . . look, can we all admit it's been a shitty few days? We've all been off in our own little worlds, there's been all this tension, and we've still got a week or so to wait here. We can't keep going like this. So, I say we loosen up a bit, hmm?"

Leaning forward, she playfully presses a kiss to my cheek. "Lux? Party?"

It feels wrong and macabre, but it's not like anything else sounds better. Besides, it is really appealing to imagine recreating those first few days on Meroe, before Robbie showed up, before everything got so fucked.

A reset.

"I don't know that a bonfire and a few bottles of wine can help that much," Amma says now, still looking over at me.

"Oh darling," Eliza says, winking at me. "We've got something much better than wine."

THAT NIGHT, WE BUILD A huge bonfire, so big that as I stand next to it, watching the flames crawl up toward the sky, I'm actually a little afraid.

I imagine an ember, a spark, catching the leaves overhead, fire leaping from branch to branch, all of Meroe Island instantly aflame.

The image is so clear that I can almost see it, which is when I know that I am really fucked up.

I stay away from drugs for the most part, but after a day where my nerves felt like they had been scraped over barbed wire, oblivion had sounded nice. The thick, sweet smell of hash hangs over all of us, and my limbs are heavy with it as I flop onto the sand next to Brittany.

Or who I think is Brittany.

But it's Amma, her eyes dark and shining in the firelight.

"You," I say, studying her, and her eyes seem even shinier all of a sudden, like she might start crying.

"I'm sorry," she says. "About Nico. I . . . I told you he reminded me of Sterling, and I was telling him about everything, and it just happened, and—"

"Sterling?" I giggle. "Your dead boyfriend was named Sterling?"

I don't know why that's suddenly so funny to me, but it is,

Amma and Sterling, like something out of a WASP fever dream, and I fall back on the sand, helpless with laughter.

"You clearly have some kind of rich boy fetish," I tease her, once I catch my breath. She gives a little sheepish laugh and lies down next to me.

"This is weird," she says, and then raises her voice, shouting, "This is weird!"

That makes me laugh even more, and I look up at the sky, too, the stars tilting and swirling around us. "Everything here is weird!" I yell back, and then I feel like I'm laughing too hard, like at any moment, it will give way to tears.

I don't want to cry, so I stand up, pulling Amma to her feet, too, our hands sweaty as we clasp each other, turning in a slow circle.

Can't I forgive her? Haven't I done the same thing to Eliza? And how can it matter when we're here in this place where nothing is real?

Across the fire, Nico sits alone, and Jake is sitting there with Eliza, and it's just like our first night all over again—except I had been with Nico, and Jake was just the cute guy with the nice girlfriend, and how did it all get so fucked up so fast?

Amma pulls away from me, giggling, collapsing onto the sand, and suddenly Eliza is there, too—how did she move so fast? Wasn't she just sitting with Jake? But no, now Brittany is standing in the shadows, while Nico takes another hit from the joint Jake is holding.

Time is both slowing down and speeding up, and I'm happy and sad all at once. I take the joint Eliza offers, sucking more of that thick, sweet smoke into my lungs, the hash and the pot blending to make everything hazy.

I stumble back from the fire, my eyelids heavy as languor slips through me. Everything is heavy now, and I lie back down, the sand cool against my hot skin.

*I smoked too much,* I think distantly, feeling tired and strange all of a sudden, my arm too heavy to lift, my heels digging holes into the sand.

The sky is still spinning.

I look over to my right, and even that feels like too much effort, like my head has been replaced with a heavy stone, lolling on my neck.

Nico is there at the edge of the jungle, his body limned in firelight. I'm not mad at him anymore, and I want to tell him that, but I can't open my mouth, can't do anything but lie there as Nico splits into two people, two shadows.

Two Nicos.

That will make things easier. Amma can have one, and I can have the other.

The thought makes me laugh, or it would if I weren't suddenly feeling so sleepy.

The two Nicos hover on the edge of my vision, but I see now that one of them is smaller, skinnier.

Not two Nicos. Nico and Brittany.

I blink. No, not Brittany. It must be Amma because they're kissing now, the shadows blending into one.

In the firelight, Amma's hair looks darker, and I see Nico's hands come up, like he might push her away.

But they only flutter there for a moment, and then he's holding her, and they're still kissing, and I shut my eyes, not wanting to see.

When I open them again, both Nico and Amma are gone.

# BEFORE

Amma peels the label off a bottle of beer in a bar in Canberra, and wonders how she let shit go this far.

Chloe and Brittany are sitting at another table, a booth near the back, with a bunch of dudes in striped shirts and fraying khakis, and Amma knows it's going to be another night of watching the two of them flirt and preen and laugh, and in the morning, there will be rolls of cash in their bags that they'll insist they got from an ATM, or a watch that must've fallen in there or some other stupid shit like that, and they'll give each other those knowing looks because aren't they clever, aren't they smart, and isn't Amma just so trusting and naive?

She should go home.

She almost did, back in London. When Brittany had suggested following Chloe to Australia, she thought it sounded insane and stupid, and she could've said so. Just put an end to it all.

But she and Brittany had embarked on this thing together, and she didn't feel right, just leaving her with Chloe.

Chloe with her bright smile and hard eyes and fast fingers.

It was almost admirable, really. How good she was at sucking people in, making people trust her. And, as Amma kept reminding herself, it wasn't like these guys couldn't afford the losses. She understood where Chloe was coming from.

She just didn't want to be a part of it.

But she also couldn't abandon Brittany. Amma owes her. More than Brittany knows.

She can still see herself, giggling, the funnel lifted high as beer slid down the tube, the Florida breeze salty and warm, blowing her hair back from her face, her skin still tingling pleasantly from all the sun that day.

So many beers, poured down so many throats, and then an empty cooler, Amma pouting, winding her arms around her boyfriend's neck.

"Babe, you're not gonna let a girl go beerless on spring break, are you?"

Drunk, god he was *so* drunk, his brown eyes struggling to focus on her face, and she knew it, she *knew* how wasted he was, and she still asked him to go out for more beer anyway.

And he did.

And the family of three (*four, family of four, the other one sitting in her room at their beach rental, pouting, not knowing that everything was about to be taken from her in one blinding smash*) never saw him coming until it was too late.

So now here she is, in this shitty bar in this boring city, flat and green and filled with government buildings, boring suburbs. This wasn't the adventure she'd planned.

It isn't the adventure Brittany had planned, either, but she sure seemed to be having the time of her life, her face flushed with excitement that all these guys in their nice suits thought was for them.

Brittany and Chloe are getting up now, waving to the dudes, and Brittany signals to Amma that they're leaving.

She still hasn't finished her beer, but she sets it on the table anyway.

There will be another bar now, another club, until Chloe decides they're done for the night. That's always how it works.

But just as they step outside, a hand catches Chloe's arm, pulling her up short.

Amma freezes, the excitement in her veins dying a quick death as the guy, some law student in a nice suit and expensive glasses, glares down at Chloe.

"My watch," he says, his voice tight, and Amma sees Brittany's eyes go wide.

Chloe is just staring at the guy, giving a disbelieving laugh as she pulls her arm from his. "I don't have your fucking watch, mate," she says, but then he's reaching into the bag at her shoulder, and even as she squawks in outrage, he pulls out a gold Rolex, his mouth pressed in a hard line.

Chloe falters only for a flash. Amma actually sees it, the moment her mask slips, and the moment that follows, where she quickly regains the armor that gets her through life.

"My bag was on the floor, dickhead. Your watch probably fell into it."

"Sure," he says, and Amma holds her breath, wondering what will happen next.

Her heart is pounding. She's gotten used to them just . . . getting away with it. These little thefts that have felt so harmless.

They feel a lot less harmless now with people looking at them, scowling, with Steve the bartender picking up the phone behind the bar.

But then Chloe smiles at the guy, presses in closer. "Hey," she all but purrs. "Tell you what. I'll buy you a drink to make up for my bag being in the way of your watch, okay?"

It shouldn't work. The guy looked pissed just a minute ago, but to Amma's astonishment, that stern expression slowly gives way to a reluctant smile.

"Cheeky," he mutters, and Chloe shrugs.

And then he nods. "Fine, then. Least you can do for calling me a dickhead."

He goes back into the bar. Before following him, Chloe gives Brittany a tiny shake of her head. "I'll catch up with you, yeah?" she says.

Chloe doesn't return to the hostel until well after midnight.

Amma is waiting for her, sitting upright on her bed, longing for home with a kind of visceral ache she hasn't felt in forever.

"We could've gotten arrested," she hisses, keeping her voice low. "And Brittany and I could've gotten kicked out of the country or had our passports taken, or—"

"Okay, but none of that shit happened, did it?" Chloe says, cutting her off. She's sullen in the dim light, already moving to open a window, a pack of cigarettes in hand.

"Not this time," Amma replies, trying to keep her voice down even as anger spikes through her. "And only because we were lucky."

"No, Amma," Chloe says, her lighter flicking in the dark. "You know who's lucky? Those fucking assholes at the bar tonight. Those *other* fucking assholes in Italy. All these fucking assholes wandering around with their Rolexes and their fancy cars, who get to just waltz off from any fucking disaster they leave in their wake. *That's* who's lucky. You think Brady back there would've missed his watch for very long? No, he would've gone and bought another one, and forgot he ever even owned that first one. Shit like that is disposable to him."

Amma doesn't say anything, but she thinks about a pool party, three years back. A ruined watch, forgotten on a wrist, his laugh when she'd pointed it out. *Wanted a new one anyway.*

Chloe sucks on the cigarette, the tip glowing bright red before she exhales a cloud of smoke. "*We* are disposable to people like that."

For the first time, Amma realizes that Chloe is not just in this for a good time. She's angry. Furious, even.

And that worries her more than when she'd assumed Chloe was just reckless, just the kind of person who took what she wanted and damn the rest of it. Wasn't that why she was traveling around everywhere, going wherever the day took her?

Brittany has woken up, and she's perched on the edge of her bed, watching as Chloe crosses the room to take Amma's hand.

"Don't we deserve something?" Chloe's grip is cold and tight, and her nails dig into Amma's skin. She can't pretend she's not intrigued, that she doesn't feel that way, too, sometimes. The unfairness of how much Amma has lost, how much was taken from her, makes her want to scream at the injustice of the world. How can one mistake—yes, one big mistake, but still just that, an *accident*, a single bad moment of judgment in a lifetime of good choices—end everything?

But that doesn't mean they can just steal from strangers.

Amma yanks her hand away. "That's just an excuse," she says. "Bad shit happens to everyone every day. Life is unfair. But that doesn't mean we just get to do whatever the hell we want."

"Well, maybe it should," Chloe says quietly. Amma watches her gaze go to Brittany—Brittany, who's watching them both with those big eyes—and Amma knows that she's lost the argument.

The next morning, Amma goes out to grab a coffee, but when she passes the bar they were at last night, she sees a line of police tape across the door. A small crowd has gathered, peering inside.

Her entire body goes cold, and she almost steps forward to ask a bystander what's going on.

But she doesn't.

She keeps walking, her pulse racing, her stomach knotted, until she's back at the hostel. In the lobby, she pulls out her phone and googles the name of the bar.

There's a local news story, and her eyes skim the article, picking up key phrases.

*Brady Hendrix, law student, twenty-three, overdose* . . .

Sad, obviously. Tragic, even.

Not criminal, necessarily. An accident, most likely.

It can happen to anyone.

But Amma's hands are shaking as she walks back to the room. She keeps seeing Chloe's smile as she'd followed Brady back into the bar.

Brittany and Chloe aren't there when Amma returns, but Chloe's bag is sitting open on her bed.

Even as she paws through Chloe's things, Amma wonders what exactly she expects to find—the watch, a wallet, some sign that Chloe had stolen from Brady Hendrix after all?

*It still wouldn't mean she had anything to do with him dying,* Amma tells herself, but something deep and primal feels that if she sees that watch, she'll know for sure.

But there's nothing—no Rolex, no phone, not even the rolls of cash Amma has grown accustomed to seeing Chloe and Brittany flash proudly.

"What are you doing?"

Chloe stands there in the doorway, a paper cup of coffee in one hand, Brittany just behind her, and Amma takes her hand out of Chloe's bag.

"Nothing," she says, then adds, "looking for a tampon."

Chloe's mouth curls into a smile. "Well, now we finally know why you've been such a bitch lately," she jokes, and Amma sees the way she and Brittany share a look, hears the significance of *we.*

She can feel the circle closing. Amma is on the outside now.

# NOW

# TWENTY-FIVE

I wake up on the beach the next morning and for a second, I think I must be dying.

I can barely remember the night before—a haze of smoke and fire—and though I'd only smoked hash once before in my life, I didn't remember it making me feel this wretched. I'd sell my soul right now for a bottle of water, and I slowly stand, brushing stray sand from the backs of my legs before turning toward the lagoon.

The sun has just come up, painting the sky a rosy pink, and the water is still, glassy.

It's so beautiful that it takes me a moment to realize there's something wrong with what I'm seeing.

To my left, the *Azure Sky* floats contentedly in her usual spot.

But she's the only ship in the lagoon.

The *Susannah* is missing.

BRITTANY IS CURLED UP IN a mound of blankets behind me, and when I shake her awake, her eyes are a little swollen, her lips dry and flaky.

"What?" she mutters, and I point wordlessly toward the water. She stares blankly before realizing what has sent my stomach plummeting.

"Where is the *Susannah*?" She sits up, wide awake now. "And where's Amma?"

It all comes back to me. The party last night. Nico had been kissing Amma. My drug-addled brain had initially thought it was Brittany, but given who Nico's been fucking, it was definitely Amma.

And now the boat is gone, and Brittany and I are alone on the beach.

The other day, I'd thought the island was starting to feel claustrophobic. Now, looking out at that wide expanse of water, I feel impossibly small. If Nico has left us behind . . .

No.

No, he wouldn't do that. Nico is a lot of things, and I've only recently realized how shitty some of those things are, but he's not *that* kind of asshole. He wouldn't just abandon me, leave me alone with these strangers, and take off with some new girl on some new adventure.

Would he?

"We need to tell Jake and Eliza," I say, and head for the shoreline.

I'm still in my shorts and T-shirt from last night, but I don't care, throwing myself into the ocean and swimming for their boat. It's just a few yards away, and the water is so warm and still that it makes for a quick swim.

Hoisting myself up on the deck, I push wet hair out of my eyes and look back toward where the *Susannah* usually is, still struck by its absence.

"Lux?"

I turn.

Amma is on the deck, half-sprawled on one of the benches along the bow. She looks a little worse for wear, her hair a tangled mess, her eyes red as she blinks at me.

Relief floods through me.

*Nico didn't take Amma with him.*

The door separating the cabin from the deck slides open, and Jake and Eliza emerge, sleepy and rumpled, yet somehow still golden and beautiful.

"What's going on?" Eliza asks.

I gesture out to the lagoon. "Nico's gone. Or at least, the boat's gone."

By now, Brittany is on deck, wringing out her wet hair, and all five of us stand at the port side of the *Azure Sky*, looking at the open water.

"What? How? I didn't even hear anything last night," Jake says in confusion. "Although, I guess we were all pretty out of it."

He turns to Amma. "When did you last see Nico?"

I'm unprepared for how much this stings. For how quickly Amma has become The One Who Would Know Where Nico Is, because clearly, I sure as fuck don't.

"On the beach last night. The moon was pretty, and I was, you know. *Super* high, so I swam out. Got kind of confused and climbed up here, went to sleep." She shrugs. "It's all kind of a blur, honestly."

I look back to where the *Susannah* should be, like I can somehow will it to reappear. Last night *was* a blur, and we were all fucked up. Is that how Nico was able to sail away with *no one* hearing him?

I stand there, hands gripping my hair, and my stomach somersaulting. Jake steps forward, taking my arm. "Hey, hey, hey," he says in a soothing voice. "Don't panic, okay? He's probably just gone for a sail. Maybe he wanted some time alone on the water to clear his head."

"This is not a fucking Jimmy Buffett song, it's real," I snap. "And if something happens to him out there—"

Jake's Cool Guy thing is irritating. Yesterday, I'd found his laid-back charm refreshing and more than a little sexy. Today, I just wish someone would panic with me a little bit.

But no one is going to.

Brittany is tugging at the ends of her damp hair while Eliza has her arms folded over her chest, simply watching this all play out.

Amma scrubs her hands over her face before reaching into a canvas bag at her feet. She pulls out her phone and I feel this immediate, instinctual surge of relief. Yes, we'll call his phone, we'll call *someone*—

"Fuck," she mutters.

Brittany looks over and rolls her eyes. "You know there's no signal here."

Giving a frustrated sound, Amma tosses her phone onto a stack of striped towels on the deck. "I know, but I just thought . . . I don't know, I thought I'd try."

My throat closes up, sweat prickling along my spine. Being off the grid, fully disconnected—it had felt so freeing at first, but it feels like a trap now, like there are jaws closing around us. No radios to contact the outside world, no way to even contact each other if we get separated . . .

We're on our own.

And while that thought had once filled me with something close to elation, now there's only panic.

Amma runs her hands through her hair, looking around, and then she's over the side of the boat, her long arms cutting smooth strokes back to the beach.

The fuck?

"Lux, listen," Jake says now, stepping forward again but keeping his hands to himself. "If he's not back in a few hours, we'll worry. But for now, let's just relax and assume he woke up feeling as fucking rank as the rest of us, and thought getting an ocean breeze would help."

It's perfectly rational, but the mood on the island has been uneasy ever since Robbie showed up, like there's a storm about to break, and I just wish it would already. I wish I had an excuse to scream and lose my shit.

Instead, I nod. I'll keep it together a little longer. I'll wait.

I SWIM TO THE BEACH, hoping to catch Amma, but she's already disappeared.

I sit on the sand and let it trail through my fingers as I watch the horizon. Jake is right, Nico probably just needed to stretch his legs, so to speak. Maybe even get his head straight about me and Amma. The island *does* feel small, cramped. Like it's closing in on us.

Even now, as I look back over my shoulder, I swear the jungle feels closer than it did yesterday. I turn my attention back to the lagoon, trying to ignore the feeling that something—or someone?—is watching me from the trees.

*He's on the other side of the island,* I tell myself. *He'll be back any minute now.*

The water laps against the shore. When we first got here, I found that sound so peaceful, so comforting. Now, it grates on my nerves.

The day wears on. Brittany comes to bring me some water and extra sunscreen, sits with me for a bit, then eventually heads back to Jake and Eliza's boat.

Soon, the sun is setting, turning the sky that same blaze of brilliant orange and pink that enchanted me my first night here.

Seeing it now makes my stomach twist in knots. Sunset means night is almost here, and if Nico isn't back by the time it's dark . . .

I still can't comprehend that he left me here. But then again, I never would have thought he would cheat on me, right under my nose. The truth is, I have no idea what Nico might be capable of. The Nico I met in San Diego, the Nico who promised to show me the world, he wouldn't do this.

But Nicholas Johannsen III? Who the fuck knows?

My mind flashes back to Susannah, standing on that dock, her eyes red. *Good luck.* Alongside the immediate fear of *how the fuck will I get off this island,* there's a deeper anxiety that I can't shake—that I had been willing to put my faith in a man I never really knew. Never really cared to know. Like everything else in my life, I just let it—let *Nico*—happen to me. He was cute, he liked me, he offered me an escape. And I took it, ignoring so much shit that I shouldn't have, and now I'm here, on this island in the middle of nowhere, no boat, no clothes, no way of contacting the outside world.

No Nico.

I had been looking for an escape, and now I am quite literally trapped.

I'm still sitting on the beach when the sun sinks below the horizon. My eyes strain for that flash of green Nico always told me you could see if you looked carefully. But there's nothing. Another empty promise.

The sky fades from pinkish-orange to lavender to deep purple until finally the sky is navy blue, the stars so bright they stand out like sequins on an evening gown.

I don't realize I'm crying until I taste the salt on my lips.

# TWENTY-SIX

I swim back to the boat, no longer caring what might be lurking in the dark water.

I hear Jake and Eliza talking and laughing, the hiss and clink of beers being opened.

Nico has been missing the entire day, and these assholes sit here acting like everything is fine, like it's just another night in paradise.

When I haul myself onto the deck, Eliza looks over at me, eyes going wide.

"Jesus, Lux," she says. "Are you alright?"

Pushing my wet hair out of my face, I glare at her. "What do you fucking think? Nico isn't back," I say, shaking my head. "And I don't know where the fuck Amma is, either. Have you guys just been . . . sitting here all fucking day?"

Jake sighs, putting his beer down and crossing the deck to embrace me. I jerk away from him, nearly stumbling.

"Why is no one worried?" I shout. "Why do none of you give a fuck? Nico is *gone*. The *boat* is gone. Robbie fucking died out there, and Amma is just—what, spending the night in the jungle?"

Standing on the deck of the *Azure Sky*, it's hard to remember that first night here, just over two weeks ago, when I'd let myself believe I'd found something like a home with these people.

What had felt cozy then feels oppressive now, the water dark around us, locking us in.

Nico could be in that water.

Brittany emerges from the cabin, a cartoonish expression of concern on her face.

"What's going on?"

"Lux is upset about Nico," Eliza says, her tone just shy of patronizing.

I feel like I've stepped into some kind of twilight zone. Why is everyone acting like I'm blowing this way out of proportion? Even Brittany, who only makes a sympathetic clucking noise as she comes up on the deck, her arms outstretched. "Lux," she says, as if I'm a child throwing a tantrum. "Would it be all that strange if he had just gone back to Maui?"

I gape at her. "Um, yes? He's my *boyfriend*. He wouldn't just leave me on a deserted island? Besides, you're the one who *paid him* to take you here and back."

She drops her arms, tilting her head to one side. "Yeah, but—is Nico really the kind of guy you can count on?"

*You didn't think he'd sleep with Amma, but he did.*

*You didn't think he'd give you a fucked-up lifeline during a storm, but he did.*

*You didn't know him at all, did you?*

*And he didn't know you.*

"Lux," Eliza says, moving closer, a cloud of her perfume enveloping me. Her expression is gentle, her voice soft. "Did it ever occur to you that maybe he found out about you and Jake?"

My heart seems to stop beating in my chest, and the skin that was burning up just a minute ago goes icy.

"W-what?"

I look to Jake, whose face is unreadable, then to Brittany.

There's no shock, no surprise.

She knew, too.

They all knew.

My gaze swings back to Jake, but Eliza is already shaking her head. "Jake didn't say anything. I'm just not a fucking idiot, you know? 'Exploring the jungle.' Please. Anyone could have picked up on"—she lifts her hands, making an elegant gesture between me and Jake—"the vibes, as it were. And honestly, Lux, I'm not upset. These things happen." She gives a shrug. "Why should any of us cut ourselves off from experiences?" She reaches up and brushes my hair back from my face. "But not everyone is so enlightened, are they?"

A plaintive cry of *I want to go home* swells up in my throat like I'm a little girl. How did I ever think these people—these beautiful, glittering, fake people—were my friends?

The boat rocks gently on the dark water, and the stars are thick overhead, glistening against all that black, and I'm trapped in a nightmare I cannot wake up from.

But the realization that Nico might have known what happened with Jake changes everything.

Eliza is smiling in a way that chills me. "Is it *really* so hard to imagine that Nico might have decided to leave once he knew you'd cheated on him?"

"He didn't."

We all whip around to see Amma, pulling herself up the swim ladder, water streaming off her. She's pale, her hair is tangled, and there's something in her eyes that seems wild and angry.

"His boat is on the other side of the fucking island," she says, and my world tilts all over again.

"He's not on it, though," she continues, still shivering. "*And* the dinghy is there."

"Then where is he?" I ask, panic making my voice thin and

reedy, eyes still wildly scanning the beach, as if he's going to emerge from the jungle and start waving to us.

"What did you do to him?" Amma's voice is steady and cold. I whip around, assuming that the question is directed at Jake.

But Amma's gaze is fixed on Eliza.

"What did you do?" she screams, and then she's launching herself across the deck.

Chaos erupts. Amma is shouting and crying, Eliza is fending off her flailing fists, Jake is trying to break them apart, while Brittany hangs back, sobbing, "Stop, Amma, stop!" over and over again.

I manage to get ahold of Amma, pressing my thumb into the delicate joint at her wrist. "Amma, Jesus Christ, *stop*," I cry. "Eliza wouldn't do anything to Nico."

Amma drops her grip on Eliza, and whirls around to face me.

"You stupid bitch," she snarls. "You think these people are your *friends*? You think you have any fucking clue what's going on here?"

"Oh, because you're one to talk about friends, aren't you?" Brittany yells, her eyes wild, and then she looks at me.

"I know that Amma told you. About where we met. About my family."

Brittany's voice goes tight, her words thick and watery, and I nod, confused.

"And her poor, dead boyfriend, right?"

The fight goes out of Amma. Her shoulders sink, and she seems to stagger a little.

"You knew," she says, her voice suddenly flat. "I knew you knew. Or you'd find out before I could explain, but Brittany—"

"Well, Lux," Brittany continues as if Amma hadn't spoken, "here's a fun fact for you. Her boyfriend isn't dead. Just in prison. Do you want to tell her why, Amma?"

The night seems to be spinning around us, the boat rocking under our feet, sky and water dark, and Eliza is holding Brittany's arm, and Amma is reaching out for Brittany just as Jake comes forward, always the peacemaker, his arms out.

Amma must think he's reaching for her because she thrashes wildly, and her elbow catches me hard in the face.

Pain explodes around my nose, and my vision spangles with stars, then goes dark. I feel a rush of blood pouring down my face.

I can't be sure what happens next.

The yelling continues, and I'm backing away, but Amma is still advancing on me, and I'm slipping in drops of my own blood, Amma is reaching for me, I'm pulling back . . .

She slams into me. Does she stumble? Was she trying to tackle me? Was she pushed? I'll never know. But the two of us are suddenly falling through space, and then the water closes over my head, as salty and warm as the blood still gushing from my nose.

It's dark, and I'm in pain, the salt water stings everything. Amma's hands are still grasping for me, and then she has ahold of me, and my brain is screaming for air, for freedom.

Suddenly, that day with the shark—the image of my foot connecting with her jaw, saving me, dooming her—flashes through my mind.

It wasn't just a fantasy.

It was a premonition.

Amma's hands are still on me, preventing me from breaking the surface, and I kick and shove, and there's a hollow, clanging sound.

Amma's hands fall from me.

There are shouts from above, someone calling my name, but in my pain and panic, I just swim.

*Back to shore. Get back to shore, find Nico's boat, find out what happened, go, go, go . . .*

My muscles burn, my lungs are on fire, and the shore seems impossible to reach. Until, suddenly, I'm there, on my hands and knees in the sand, panting, gagging.

I try to crawl farther, but my body gives out, and I collapse, the world spinning into darkness.

When I open my eyes again, the sky is a soft pink, still navy at the edges, the sun not yet over the horizon.

Morning. No one has come for me, and when I lift my head, all I see is empty water.

The *Azure Sky* is gone.

I'm completely alone.

There's crusted blood under my nose, around my mouth, on my chin, and I sit up in disgust, swiping at it, wincing at the soreness, panic already beating a frantic tattoo in my blood.

*I'm alone, they left me, they left me, I'm alone on this island and there's no water, there's no food, I'm alone.*

I stand and wade into the shallows, cupping my hands to splash my face, my whole body shaking as I try to breathe, try to *think*.

Out of the corner of my eye, I see something pale next to me, lying on the shore.

A hand, palm up, fingers curled.

I follow that hand up a long, slender arm to the sleeve of a black T-shirt.

Amma is lying in the water, looking up at the sky, her eyes wide and horribly, horribly blank.

Dead.

# BEFORE

"I'm sorry, darling, but it seemed best to tell you the truth."

Brittany sits on a bench with Chloe in a park. They're still in Canberra, and even though it would be spring back home, it's autumn here. The leaves are turning, the sun is still warm, but the breeze has grown cool. She stares at the phone Chloe has handed her, her eyes fixed on the picture.

It's from two years ago.

It's Amma smiling wide, on someone's Facebook page. She's a little thinner than she is now, and her hair is shorter, barely brushing her shoulders.

Her arms are wrapped around a boy whose face is so familiar to Brittany, a face she saw in a courtroom, a face she still sees in her nightmares.

Sterling Northcutt.

The man—*no, the boy, the boy, hadn't the judge kept calling him a boy? Oh, this fine upstanding boy, never did anything wrong before, never ever until he got super fucking loaded one night, got behind the wheel of a car, and wiped out Brittany's entire life*—who killed her family.

"I don't understand," Brittany says, her body still numb, her heart slowing to half its normal speed as she looks at Amma, her best friend—the *one* person who actually understood how alone Brittany felt—with her arms wrapped around the man who ruined her life.

*Amelia-Marie and Sterling, CUUUUTIES IN LUUUUUUV,*

the caption reads, and Brittany keeps looking at that name, Amelia-Marie, wondering if maybe there's a mistake, knowing that there's not.

*Amma.*

"You said you met her in a grief group, right?" Chloe asks, and Brittany nods, remembering the room with its smell of burnt coffee. How Amma had picked the empty chair next to her; how, when Brittany had told the story of what had happened to her, Amma hadn't said anything—had simply nodded, reached over, and taken her hand. At the time, Brittany had been grateful that Amma hadn't pushed her for more details, hadn't asked any follow-up questions. Now, Brittany realizes, Amma had already known everything there was to tell.

There had been tears streaming down Amma's face during that first session, and seeing her break down, Brittany had felt a wave of relief. How nice it had been, to have a stranger share her grief. How good it felt, to no longer be so alone.

"She must have been, like, stalking you or something," Chloe goes on. "She lied about having a dead boyfriend to get close to you? It's just, incredibly fucked up. And not only that, she's loaded."

More pictures, more links.

Amma at her fancy Catholic school, photos from her mother's Facebook page of Amma all dressed up on a horse—a fucking horse!—and another of Amma when she was younger, standing in front of the Eiffel Tower with her parents and two older girls.

Oddly enough, that's the one that takes Brittany's breath away.

"She said . . . she said she'd never been to Paris."

Chloe puts an arm around her. "Jesus, what a lying bitch."

Brittany shakes her head, her eyes welling with tears. "She lied to me about *all* of it. About her family, about her background. About where she's lived and traveled. Why?"

"People are weird." Chloe sighs. "Maybe it was some kind of

atonement or something? Like, 'Sorry my boyfriend killed your family, let me make it up to you by being your friend'?"

The words make Brittany wince, and her stomach clench. Had Amma been there in that courtroom? Had she seen Brittany? She must have. All of this had to have started on that awful day.

"Or maybe she was just curious about you, you know?" Chloe adds. "In any case, it's pretty fucked up. And it's a pretty complicated lie to commit to."

It's more than fucked up. It's a betrayal that Brittany almost can't fathom, and she's suddenly so angry, so fucking *furious* . . .

"How did you find out?" she asks.

Chloe just shrugs.

"Something about her whole vibe just didn't feel right, you know? So, I looked her up. Found it all in a couple of minutes."

Of course. Of course, all those answers were right there, but Brittany had never even thought to google her, had believed Amma when she said she didn't really do social media, that after what happened to her boyfriend, she tried to minimize her internet presence as much as possible. And Brittany had just . . . trusted her.

She had fucking trusted her.

"But I guess the question now is," Chloe goes on, "what are we going to do about it?"

Brittany doesn't know the answer to that. Confront Amma? Show her what she's discovered?

She can picture it. *Morning, Amelia-Marie,* she'll say snidely.

But that's not enough. It would shock her, maybe upset her.

But it won't hurt her.

Brittany shakes her head. "I have to think about it," she finally replies.

"Of course," Chloe says, dropping her lighter in her bag. As she does, Brittany catches a flash of gold, sees the band of a watch lying there, and it seems familiar—but honestly, she's seen so many fucking watches, chains, even rings lately, that she can't be sure.

⸺⸺

CHLOE ISN'T THERE WHEN THEY wake up the next morning.

For a long time, Brittany refuses to believe she's gone for good.

"She's just gone to get coffee," she says to Amma. "She'll be back."

But the day drags on, the two of them sitting in their bunks, playing on their phones, and Chloe's bed stays empty.

There's no note, no text. Nothing left behind at all, like Chloe simply vanished in the night.

Like maybe Chloe had never really existed.

Amma would like that, Brittany thinks, her thoughts turning darker the longer Chloe is gone.

Chloe was her true friend in all this. Chloe, who was actually fun, who had kept them traveling, kept them from returning home where everything would be bleak and sad.

Chloe, who'd actually brought Brittany into the *after.*

Chloe, who was actually honest with her, as opposed to Amma, who'd lied over and over again.

The third day that Chloe's been gone, Amma sits up in her bunk. There are shadows underneath her eyes, and her hair is tangled around her face. She looks as rough as Brittany has ever seen her, and that fills her with a petty sort of joy.

"Look," Amma says, sighing, "I think she's probably taken off. I mean, this is where she's from, right? Maybe she went home. Back to Sydney or wherever."

Brittany wants to argue that Chloe wouldn't just bail on them without saying goodbye, but instead, she nods. "Maybe."

"And I gotta be honest with you, I'm feeling ready to go home, too." Amma offers her a tiny smile. "Or at least, my bank account is ready for me to go home."

*Except that you're rich,* Brittany thinks. *Except that when you go home, there are people waiting for you. You still have a family. And Sterling may be in jail, but he'll be out one day.*

That's the part Brittany finds the hardest to wrap her mind around. All these months of sharing their grief, of leaning on one another, of *understanding* one another, and it was all bullshit? Amma had *people* to go back to. Amma had sisters, a mother, a father. The worst thing that had happened to her was that her boyfriend was in jail.

And she'd let Brittany believe that they were the same. Now her impatience made sense. Her barely concealed exasperation when Brittany would lose whole nights crying.

It hurts so much to think about, that for a second, Brittany feels like she can't breathe, like there's something stabbing her in her chest.

Amma was never really her friend.

But Chloe had been, and now she was gone.

"Fine," Brittany says now, getting off her bunk and pulling her bag toward her. "We can go home."

"We've had a good time, right?" Amma offers.

"The best time," Brittany says, ignoring the tightness in her throat as she paws through her bag for clean clothes. Buying a ticket home is going to completely wipe her out, but there's still that roll of cash Chloe gave her the other night, and maybe she can exchange it for US currency at the airport—

Her hand brushes something, and she frowns, staring into her bag.

It's a phone.

Not her phone. That's still plugged in beside her bunk. This is a new phone, and she wonders if she picked it up by accident or if it had fallen into her bag somehow.

She turns it over, and sees a text message on the screen.

*Surprise, gorgeous!*

Chloe.

Her back still to Amma, Brittany studies the phone, reading the series of texts Chloe has sent, something joyful and dark unfurling in her heart.

Chloe didn't abandon her with Amma.

*What do you say, love?* Chloe's last text reads. *Meet you in the Pacific?* ☺

Their adventures aren't over—they're just beginning.

Dropping the phone back in her bag, Brittany turns to Amma with a smile. "What if we did one quick detour before heading home?"

# NOW

# TWENTY-SEVEN

I stumble away from the beach in horror. The fight last night feels like a blur now, like something that happened to someone else. The screaming, the falling overboard, the salt water in my mouth . . . it could be a dream if it weren't for Amma's body, making it so fucking real.

I don't know where I'm going as I weave my way up from the shore. The jungle path we cleared is several yards to the left of me, the vegetation here almost impenetrable, but I throw myself toward it anyway, like a little kid looking for a place to hide after she's done something bad.

I'm not wearing shoes, and the vines cut at the soles of my feet as I try to push my way through, sweat still pouring off me even though my teeth are chattering.

A thorn pierces my palm, and the pain is so sharp and stunning that tears immediately spring to my eyes. But don't I deserve the pain? Hadn't Amma hurt when she'd realized she couldn't breathe, her lungs screaming for air?

Blood smears the vines as I push deeper into the jungle.

It's darker in here, and I keep pushing myself back, back, back, away from Amma, away from the others finding out what I've done, away from all of it.

Light filters eerily through the trees here, casting long, strange shadows. I cradle my stinging hand, wrapping it in the hem of my T-shirt as I look around, trying to get my bearings.

Amma had said that the *Susannah* was on the other side of the island. Cutting through the jungle is only about two miles, and I can easily do that. If I can get to the boat, even if Nico isn't on it, then at least I'll have a way to get the fuck out of here. I could wait for the ship with the radios, but how will I explain to whoever shows up that there are two dead bodies on this island, and only me, all alone?

The heat in the island's interior is always intense, where the breeze off the sea can't reach. The vines that snake across the ground are fibrous and rough, like trying to walk over sandpaper, and it doesn't take long for my feet to start bleeding. My hand throbs, and I take deep breaths through my nose, trying to concentrate on anything but the pain and the fear.

I feel like I've been walking for ages, but when I look over my shoulder, I can still see the spot where I crashed in, the branches broken and bent. I can even make out a glimpse of white sand and blue sky.

*Get to the boat, get to the boat,* my mind keeps telling me. I have to get the fuck off this island. Something is deadly wrong with Meroe.

Still, Amma's words last night—the boat is on the other side of the island, but Nico isn't on it—snap at the corners of my mind. *Where the fuck did Nico go?*

I stop short. The jungle seems oddly quiet: the birds are no longer calling, the wind isn't sawing through the trees, and I become aware of another sound, a low buzzing.

And as soon as I make out the noise, I become aware of something else—a scent just underneath the saltwater and green earth scents. Something darker, sweeter, sicker.

Decay. Rot.

*Amma is lying on the beach, her skin already greenish, her features distorted . . .*

But no, she's too far away. It's not her corpse that I'm smelling. It's something else, something closer.

And then I see it.

Under a clump of ferns, the bottom of one shoe.

A Teva sandal.

Even in the oppressive heat, my body goes cold as I make my way toward Nico.

He's lying facedown, and I'm grateful for that.

I'm too numb to cry as I stare at his body, and the thick black cloud of flies hovering above his head. His hair has turned dark and tacky, matted with blood, and I can't look any closer to see what happened to him. I'm still so cold, shivering so violently it hurts, and my mind is racing so fast, trying to make sense of what I'm seeing.

*He fell. He hit his head and died here. Like Robbie. He fell, and it was an accident. A horrible accident.*

Except.

A machete lies just a few feet from Nico's body, no doubt tossed there once it had done its job.

I recognize the blue tape around the handle—I remember seeing it in Jake's hands as he hacked a path through the jungle—that day that feels like it was years ago, a lifetime ago.

It's Jake's machete, and it killed Nico.

He'd had it on the beach the night of the party, too. I'd seen him use it to cut down branches for the fire.

What happened? Had they argued? Had Nico confronted Jake about me? Or had it been something else?

All it would take was one hard blow, and then it would be over. Nico never would have seen it coming.

Like so much about Nico's life, even his death would have caught him by surprise.

I pick up the machete.

There are flies on the blade, too, Nico's blood still staining it, and I steel myself, wiping it on a nearby tree to clean it as best I can. It may have killed Nico, but it's going to save me.

# TWENTY-EIGHT

I have to move faster.

*You're a survivor, Lux,* Brittany had said after the storm on the boat, and I hope to god she's right.

I know I'm tougher than I let myself believe. I held that knife on Robbie, and if it had come down to me or him, I know I would've killed him.

But I didn't want to then, and I don't want to now. I want to get to the *Susannah* and get out of here.

I want to forget that Meroe Island ever existed.

As I walk, sweat drenches me, stinging my eyes, making the little cuts and scratches on my arms, my shins, my hands, burn. But I keep moving, and as I walk, I think of those sailors again, left to die and rot in what should've been an Eden.

I think of the skull we found and wonder where it came from. Who it belonged to.

The more I walk, the hotter I get, my head swimming. I haven't had any water to drink in ages, and now my body is losing fluid by the gallon, it feels like. My stomach cramps, my brain feels foggy, and I think I hear footsteps behind me.

I whirl around, the machete lifted, but there's nothing—just leaves, more trees, more jungle.

Robbie's words about someone living out here are pounding through my brain.

But he had just been fucking with me. There's no one else here, and that's almost scarier. No stranger killed Nico, there's no boogeyman hiding in the jungle: it had to be either Jake, Brittany, or Eliza.

It was one of the people I trusted—one of the people I called a friend.

It would be easier to believe almost anything else, but I don't have that luxury anymore. I can't close my eyes to what's happening around me, and I push on and on, thinking, *Just let me get to the other side, let me find the* Susannah . . .

And then, out of nowhere, the jungle thins.

The sun is reflecting off the water, and, I think I see the *Susannah*'s tall mast.

I break through the foliage to stumble onto the beach, and yes, there she is. Nico's boat.

My boat.

And there, standing in between me and salvation, are Eliza and Brittany.

They don't look surprised to see me, even as I lift the machete, the muscles in my arm screaming.

"Lux, stop!" Brittany yells, and then I see sunlight glinting on the gun Eliza points at me.

"Lux, Brittany is right," she says calmly. "There's no need for all of this."

"No need?" I choke out, almost laughing. "One of you fuckers killed Nico." My voice rises to a scream. "I know it was one of you!"

"And you killed Amma, but you don't see us making a big deal about it," Eliza answers, eyebrows raised.

I lower the machete, shaking my head. "I didn't. It was . . . she was holding me down, she was trying to drown me . . . it was self-defense. An accident."

The sun dances off the water, and it feels so close and so far away all at once.

Freedom. Escape.

"It doesn't matter anyway," Eliza says, her arms steady. "You're the one we want to talk to. To explain."

"Then don't point a gun at me."

"Fair enough."

She lowers it, and for a split second, I think about charging them. But there are two of them, one of me. Besides, I want to hear what she has to say. I need to make sense of this somehow.

Still, I keep my fingers curled around the handle of the machete.

"None of it was supposed to go down like this," Eliza says. "We were just looking to have a good time." She flashes that winning smile. "Have an adventure."

"Amma and I met her when we started traveling," Brittany adds. "Chloe. Well, Eliza. But when I met her, her name was Chloe."

"Brittany and I really hit it off," Eliza goes on, "and we had a similar . . . let's say, *philosophy* about life."

"Philosophy?" I echo, the word sounding thick in my mouth.

"The world takes a lot from us, doesn't it? Women like us. Women who don't get things handed to them. Women without a lot of options. So sometimes, you have to take *back*. You have to create your own options."

Her gaze sharpens on me. "I think you get that, don't you, Lux?"

I don't answer, the sound of my own heartbeat and the surf loud in my ears.

"So, one night in Rome, I lifted a wallet off these American assholes. They didn't notice, the cash let us have a little extra fun, no harm, no foul. It felt . . . satisfying, I guess. And then it became a little more. More wallets, a few watches, once a passport just to fuck with some guy. Then we went to Australia."

Her accent slips again, sounding like Jake. "That's where I met Jake again, and . . ." She raises the gun again, but she takes her eyes off me for a second, looking at the sky. "My mum spent ten years in prison because of that asshole's father," she says. "Ten years . . . because the guy she was in love with—the guy she also happened to *work for*—asked her to carry a fucking bag of drugs, and she did it, because she trusted him. Do you know where Jake's father spent those ten years?"

I shake my head, not that she expects an answer.

"Back in his mansion in Sydney," she says.

"Sterling Northcutt didn't even get ten years," Brittany says, her chin trembling. "The guy who killed my family. Amma's boyfriend. No prior record, good family, Florida's fucked-up sense of justice. He got five, and he'll be out in three. That's fucking *next year*, Lux. And where is *he* going to go? Back to his mansion in Connecticut. Back to Amma. Or he would have, if she wasn't . . ."

She trails off, and I see her throat move, but I can't tell if she's upset that Amma's dead, or just angry. I remember now: the fight on the boat last night, Brittany yelling at Amma about her boyfriend. Her boyfriend, who wasn't dead after all.

"She lied to me," Brittany goes on. "She got close to me for whatever sick reasons she had."

"Jesus Christ," I mutter, trying to make sense of it all, suddenly realizing that I never really understood any of these people, never knew the dark currents floating beneath their playful, shining surfaces.

Eliza looks at me then. "And do you know where Nico would've gone when he got tired of playing sailor boy? Back to the bosom of his family in his—you guessed it—mansion." She shakes her head. "And how the fuck is any of that fair?"

Brittany jumps in. "So, Chloe came up with a plan. She said she was going to sail to this deserted island with some rich asshole she knew from back home. And I should meet her here with Amma."

She gives me that sweet smile I'd found so warm and welcoming the night we met in Maui.

"So what, you brought her here to kill her?"

"Don't say it like that," Brittany insists. "Like it was *murder* we were planning. Like we just wanted to kill people for fun. Amma did something cruel. Something twisted. Jake's family ruined Eliza's life. When we killed them, it wasn't going to be murder."

"Accidents happen so easily out here," Eliza adds. "A million different ways to die in one day. Drink too much and you might drown. You eat the wrong thing, you get poisoned; you take the wrong path in the jungle—well, who knows what mess you might find yourself in. What a shame, what a terrible tragedy, losing the two of them out here, but hey, shit happens."

"And then you'd have the boat," I say, thinking it over. "Jake's boat. Jake's money. The two of you."

She nods, and I can see it, the way it all makes a kind of terrible, horrific sense. Except . . .

"Why bring me and Nico?"

"Brittany needed a way to get out here with Amma," Eliza says, shrugging. "Simple as that. And it wouldn't hurt to have a witness backing up our version of events. Brittany wanted to hire some crusty sea dog type, but—"

"But Amma wanted Nico," Brittany says. "And he wouldn't go without you."

I'm not prepared for how much that hurts.

I know Nico was not the guy for me. I know he was fickle and selfish and that he was always going to break my heart. But I had loved him, and he had loved me, enough to want me with him on this adventure.

"And then when I met you," Brittany goes on, "I knew. Knew that it was fate, and that you were coming with us for a reason. That all of us were coming to Meroe for justice."

Her gaze never wavers from me. "We deserved that. And so did you."

The world feels like it's tilting, and I blink, the sun bright, the sand hot underneath my feet and then my knees as I sink down.

"What do you mean?"

"Don't you get it?" she says softly. "You're like us. You've lost so much, and you kept going, kept trying to make something new, something beautiful. Nico was never going to give it to you. Eliza's right, he would've gotten tired of this scene eventually. I mean, look how fast he hooked up with Amma. Because they were from the same world. He was always going to pick someone like her over someone like you. I saw it that first night."

She steps forward, between me and Eliza now. "It's why I wanted you to come with us. Eliza and I lost our families. You lost yours. But we can make a new family. Together. Eliza free of Jake, me free of Amma, you free of Nico."

Her eyes go briefly to the machete, still loosely clutched in my hand, and when I look up at her, I see that something in Brittany has fractured and broken, maybe long before Meroe, but whatever it is that has her in its grip, it's not sane. Not even remotely.

"You," I say. "It *was* you I saw with Nico. It was you—"

"It was so easy to get him to go with me," she says, and somehow, her hazel eyes seem sad. "He didn't even resist when I kissed him. Not for Amma, certainly not for you. And you deserve better. I knew you were never going to be free, not really, until he was gone. For good."

Brittany. Sweet, funny Brittany with her big smiles and easy hugs, hefting a machete, smashing the back of Nico's skull.

"We'd laced the hash," she goes on, "so he was pretty out of it. He didn't suffer, I promise."

Was that true? I'd never know. Just like I'd never know if she'd killed Nico for me, or because it was another thing to take from Amma—just as Amma had, in Brittany's mind, taken from her.

"And the boat?" I ask, trying to fill the remaining gaps. "How did you—"

"Jake," Eliza supplies.

Jake. Where is he now? Is he out there, on the *Azure Sky*?

"Simple story, really. I told him Nico was asking about the drugs, how much we had, what we were doing with it. That he got freaked out, aggressive with Brittany, and she took care of things. Jake agreed with us that it was easier if you thought Nico had just fucked off rather than to tell you the truth, so he moved the *Susannah* for us."

It's almost too much to believe, how much these people lied to me, the secrets they'd been hiding this entire time. I had missed it all. I lean over, dry-heaving in the sand, my stomach cramping.

Stepping forward, still holding the gun, Eliza looks at me intently. "I know it feels hard now," she says, "but Brittany is right. You had to be free of him before he pulled you down."

I shake my head, thoughts spinning. "I don't want any part of this."

"But you do," she insists. "I see you, Lux. I see a woman who cleaned up other people's shit, literally, so that her rich boyfriend could cosplay as a sailor. A woman whose father abandoned her not once, but twice. I see a woman who deserves some kind of happiness, some kind of freedom in this world. The world took Brittany's family. It took yours. It took mine. So, I'll say it again: *we deserve to take it back.*"

There's a crashing sound and suddenly Jake emerges from the trees, and everything that comes next happens so fast.

Eliza swings her arm in his direction, Brittany is moving toward him, and there's a gunshot, so loud that I scream, my hands going up to my ears as I stare at Jake, waiting to see him crumple on the sand.

But instead, it's Brittany who falls.

# TWENTY-NINE

Brittany's blood spills into the sand, turning it from white to dark red, but overhead, the sky is still just as blue, the water just as clear.

It still looks like paradise, but I know now that it's hell.

Robbie, Amma, Nico, now Brittany . . . all dead, their blood seeping into Meroe's hungry sand. After the echoing gunshot, there's nothing but silence.

"Oh fuck," Eliza says to herself, her eyes wide, her hands at the side of her head. "Oh fuck, oh *fuck*—" She's whispering, moving toward Brittany's body.

"Eliza, what the *fuck*—" Jake starts, and then, before I have time to register it, she turns toward him.

The crack of the shot is loud, but it doesn't make me jump as much this time, even as Jake screams, clutching at his calf as he falls to the sand.

*His blood, too,* my muddled mind thinks. *Now Meroe has tasted all of us except Eliza.*

"This is your fault!" she shouts at him. "If you hadn't startled me, Brittany wouldn't be dead."

"She wouldn't be dead if you hadn't shot her, you bitch!" Jake seethes, clutching his bleeding leg. "You fucking *cunt*."

It's a clean shot, two neat holes piercing the meat of his calf, and his blood bubbles over his fingers as he desperately applies pressure to it.

"Isn't it crazy?" Eliza says to me, looking at Jake as he rocks there on the beach. "Men. They worship us, but the second we do something they don't like, we're bitches and cunts."

"To be fair, if you shoot me, I'm going to call you a cunt, too," I reply evenly, and that makes her smile a little, though her expression falters when she looks back at Brittany.

"It will be okay," she says, and I get the sense she's talking to herself again. "We can still do this. You and me," she says, searching my face. "That'll be okay, won't it?"

She kneels in the sand, leaning forward to gently close Brittany's eyes, a shudder running through her. "We can work with this. We worked with Robbie, we can figure this out, too."

"Robbie?" I ask, my voice dull. I'm still looking at Brittany, dead there in the sand.

She gestures at me with the gun, making me flinch. "Oh, yeah. You called that one right. Robbie hadn't left, had just parked around the other side of the island and was hiding in the jungle. Jake found him, though, didn't you?"

He doesn't answer, still panting and glaring at her.

"See, Robbie didn't just smash our radios, Lux. He actually stole some of Jake's drugs, too. Bet your ass that was the first thing he checked once we found the radios were destroyed. And if there's one thing Jake hates, it's people stealing from him. So he found Robbie and took care of it."

"But . . . the fish," I say. "Robbie ate bad fish and died from it."

Eliza looks at me with a mocking smile. "And who made sure you thought that, Luxy? Who led you directly to his body so that the two of you could *find* it, together, and you'd stop worrying about Robbie still being out there somewhere?"

Jake.

That afternoon, after the beach, after what we'd done, it had been his idea to take that path through the jungle.

He'd led me right to Robbie.

Eliza steps forward. The gun is right in front of my face, as she offers me the handle.

I take it.

The metal is warm from her hand, as heavy as I remember it being. "It's so simple now," she says, smiling.

Eliza who, for whatever reason, I still want to please.

That's her superpower. She presents you with a version of yourself that you could be, if you were just brave enough to try.

"You can shoot me," she says. "Kill me. Take Jake and sail back for Maui, tell the authorities the whole sordid story. Or . . ."

She steps back, spreading her hands wide. "You shoot Jake. He's the only person left, after all. We put all of them on the boat, we sink it. Drugs, too. All of it at the bottom of the fucking sea except for the money and the *Susannah*. We sail on. No one knows we were here, and if they ever find out, we have an easy enough story to tell." She widens her eyes, her lower lip trembling. "This guy showed up, and he was really creepy, and we decided to leave. Why, did something happen?"

Her guileless expression fades, replaced with something much more cunning. "What lucky girls we were, getting out before it all went so wrong. Too bad about the others." She clucks her tongue, shaking her head. "Good thing these two young ladies were so sensible."

I stand up, and she reaches out, her fingers brushing my hair back from my face. "It was supposed to be the three of us—you, me, and Brittany—but it can be just us, Lux. We can have it all."

She's right.

Months from now, we could be so far away, with all that money stashed on the *Azure Sky* in our pockets, and the *Susannah*—already mine on paper—underneath our feet.

Taking us anywhere.

Freedom. The one thing I always wanted. The thing Eliza was willing to kill for.

All I had to do was kill, too, and it was mine.

I lift the gun, and her smile is so bright. "There's a gi—"

She never finishes. I squeeze the trigger and the bullet hits her just under her jaw, her head snapping back as she falls to the sand.

Her heels drum once, twice, body twitching, and then it's over.

Next to me, Jake lowers his head to the sand, taking deep, shaking breaths. "Fuck," he breathes. "Fuck. Lux."

His eyes are as blue as the sky above, even though his skin has gone chalky white. "Thank you," he says, and gestures at Eliza's body. "Get her shirt, I need a tourniquet. The wound isn't bad, but I've lost a lot of blood."

Jake and I can leave together. Ditch the *Azure Sky*, take only the money, leave the drugs behind, the perfect motive for all this violence.

Jake and I can do that.

Jake, who killed Robbie.

Jake, who looked at Nico, bloody and dead in the jungle, and decided it was better for me to think my boyfriend had just abandoned me than to know the truth.

Jake, who might have been Eliza's prey, but who was, first and foremost, a predator in his own right.

Or, there's a third option.

I can take what Eliza created with both hands.

Money, freedom, choices—the entire world, opening up for me.

Jake is staring up at me, and the sun is hot on my face, and my hands are ice-cold, but they're also steady, steady like Jake taught me, and I see now that Robbie was right about one thing: this island doesn't twist people up. It just turns them into the purest version of themselves, hones them like a knife's blade.

I lift the gun even as Jake raises both hands, my name on his lips.

I aim. The trigger digs into my finger.

What am I when you strip everything else away?

I'm a motherfucking *survivor*.

INTERVIEW WITH JESSICA CARTWRIGHT, PASSENGER ABOARD VESSEL *EASY RIDER* RE: MEROE ISLAND. CONDUCTED BY DETECTIVE DANIEL KEKOA, MAUI COUNTY POLICE DEPARTMENT.

JESSICA CARTWRIGHT: I mean, I really don't know what I can tell you that the others haven't. I wasn't even the one who found them. That was Tucker. Have you guys talked to Tucker? (ED. NOTE— REFERRING TO TUCKER BRETT, OWNER OF *EASY RIDER* AT TIME OF INCIDENT.)

DET. D. KEKOA: We have, but we understand you were the first one on the island, so I just want to get a sense from you if you felt like anything was amiss, anything that felt off to you.

JC: I mean, the whole fucking—sorry. The whole freaking place felt off. Like, it was really, really pretty when we were sailing in, but as soon as Tuck dropped the anchor, I wanted to leave.

DK: Can you elaborate on that?

JC: It was just creepy, I guess. It felt haunted. I think part of it was that it was really quiet. There was stuff out on the beach. This tarp had been spread over some tree branches, and there were books, a cooler. It seriously looked like someone had just walked away for a second and would be back. We knew there were six people on the island based on that call, from the Australian guy who needed the radios. And I guess I thought they'd all be out there waiting on us or something? So it was just really weird that there was no one there.

DK: There were four of you on the boat, correct?

JC: Yeah, me, Tucker, and my best friend, Ashley, and Ashley's boyfriend, Bobby. Ashley's the one who found . . . you know. The first one.

DK: Can you be more specific?

JC: The first dead person. The first body. I don't know what you want me to say?

DK: The first male victim, Nicholas Johannsen.

JC: Right. He was . . . actually, can we take a break?

[INTERVIEW PAUSED FOR TWENTY-THREE MINUTES]

JC: Okay. Thank you. So yeah, Ashley had gone deeper into the jungle, I guess, she loves that kind of sh—stuff. We heard her scream, but I honestly thought it was just going to be a snake or something. I didn't think it was going to be a body.

DK: And what was the next course of action for your group after you found Mr. Johannsen?

JC: Bobby ran to get back to the boat to use the radio. Tucker wanted to keep searching around, which I thought was a dumb idea, but I was just kind of . . . numb? You know how they say on those shows, like *Dateline,* stuff like that, that people find a body and think it's, like, a mannequin? It wasn't like that. There was no doubt it was a body. I remember thinking that. Like, looking at him and being all, "That's a body. That was a person, and now he's dead." And when I saw the pictures later, it was so weird. Like, he was this really hot guy! I'm sorry. That's shallow, I guess, but that's what I thought. That he looked like someone I'd want to know, and now he was dead. Is that weird?

DK: Not at all. But if we can stay on track here—

JC: Right. Sorry. Anyway, we kept going until we got to this beach, and that's when Tucker found the others. I never really saw them because

Tucker pushed us back into the jungle, but I remember the smell, and . . . is it true? What it said on the internet about the crabs or the rats or whatever it was?

DK: The condition of the bodies was consistent with predation typical on that island.

JC: Jesus. Okay, that's one way to put it. [subject pauses] It's just so fucked up. It's so pretty there. Seriously, it was the most beautiful place I'd ever seen, like honest-to-god heaven or Eden or something, and then you find all that. [subject begins to cry] Why would anyone ever want to go there after this? Why haven't y'all like napalmed the shit out of that island? Because that's what I would do. Blast it off the fucking map.

DK: Ms. Cartwright, if you can—

JC: No, I'm serious. We went there to have a good time, and found six fucking dead bodies. And you know that other girl, the one they didn't find, is still there, too. Or in the ocean, or maybe those fucking crabs got her. I keep thinking about that. I keep seeing her in my head and—

DK: Let's take another break, okay?

[INTERVIEW PAUSED]

# IN THE AFTER

# EPILOGUE

Caroline wishes she'd never come to Thailand.

It's beautiful, sure, and loud and colorful, the sights and sounds are so different from her home back in Washington State. But she's sitting alone in this dingy bar, one ankle threaded through the strap of her backpack to ensure that on top of everything else, she doesn't get robbed, too, as she literally cries into her beer.

She's so fucking pathetic.

She never should have gotten involved with Tanner in the first place.

He's her roommate's ex, which is both a total cliché and a violation of Girl Code. It's what makes it even more disappointing that now, when she should be having the time of her life on the trip of her life, she is doing *this*—scrolling through pictures on Instagram of some girl she doesn't even know, some girl named Ainsley.

She keeps repeating the name in her head, a mantra. *Ainsley, Ainsley, Ainsley and Tanner, Tanner and Ainsley.*

Caroline can practically see the wedding invitations now.

Of course, it might not get that far. Maybe Ainsley, she of the shiny hair and colorful sundresses and golden skin, is just some distraction.

That's what Tanner had said last night at least, when he and Caroline were having their whispered argument in the hostel.

*I was drunk, it was just a little fun, we're on vacation!*

He's said that every time he's done some stupid shit on this trip. Bought dodgy weed from an even dodgier guy? *It's a vacation!* Forgot to double-check his booking at one of the hotels, so they ended up sleeping in a park? *I mean, it's an adventure, right? It's supposed to be a little unpredictable.*

Got caught with his hands up some other girl's dress in a bar bathroom last night?

Harmless fun! Vacation! No big deal.

Caroline hated when he said shit like that because it made her feel stupid and small and uptight, and she wondered why every time a guy fucked up, he did exactly this—made a girl think somehow it was *her* fault, that if only she were cooler and more fun, he might be satisfied.

Sniffling, she scrolls on.

Ainsley, with her perfectly flat stomach in a bikini in Italy. Ainsley, making some kind of symbol with her hand with her sorority sisters. Ainsley, brazenly holding a glass of red wine while sitting on a very white couch.

Caroline knows she needs to stop, but she can't. And she knows that Tanner and Ainsley are, even now, probably fucking in Ainsley's nice hotel room, because Caroline had seen the text while Tanner was in the shower this morning.

*3 still good?* Ainsley had written.

*U kno it.*

She'd waited all day for the moment when Tanner would suddenly have some errand to run, some friend from UMass to meet up with, some excuse for where he'd disappear to, some reason why Caroline could absolutely not join him.

It ended up being "friends of his parents."

Who didn't know he had a girlfriend. Too complicated to explain, he didn't want to make her feel awkward, he'd be back in a couple of hours, and then they could go drink beer on the beach. Wouldn't that be nice?

Caroline doesn't know what she hates more—how lame that story is, or how she hadn't called him on it, how she had just smiled through numb lips and watched him go.

Then she'd packed her stuff.

Except, she knows buying an earlier ticket home is going to eat up the rest of her money, and it's all just so fucking *unfair* and stupid.

Because when Tanner gets back, when she texts him and tells him she's leaving him, he isn't actually going to care that much. If anything, it might come as a kind of relief. After all, *he* has plenty of money. His trip will go on, and there will be other Ainsleys, and all Caroline will have from the last two weeks is a sunburn and a sad story.

She takes another sip of her beer, which has gone warm and flat.

Outside, it's started to rain, the sound echoing on the tin roof. Bikes whiz by, sending up sheets of water and filling the open-air bar with the smell of diesel and burnt rubber.

She doesn't want to leave.

There is so much more she wanted to do here, more to see and explore. She supposes she could always go back to the hostel, pretend she'd never seen the text, suck it up, and at least get *something* out of—

"Are you okay?"

Startled out of her misery, Caroline looks up to see a woman sitting on the stool next to her. She's pretty, with bright red hair framing an angular face and big green eyes. Her shoulders are bare and a little burned, and she has that kind of windblown, sun-streaked look that makes Caroline think she spends a lot of time outside.

"Yeah," she answers, sipping her beer even though she doesn't want to. "Just . . . a guy thing."

"Ah," the woman replies, nodding. "Boy trouble. The cause of at least eighty-five percent of all crying jags in bars."

That makes Caroline laugh. The woman seems nice. Friendly. There's an ease and confidence about her that Caroline wishes she could project, too—like she could fit in anywhere, talk to anyone.

"And," the woman goes on, leaning one elbow on the bar, "if you're *traveling* with a guy, that ups the percentage to a solid ninety-two."

It's her joke, and the inviting smile that accompanies it, that makes Caroline launch into her whole story. It's only when she's said it out loud that she realizes how silly it all sounds. How minor in the grand scheme of things.

But the woman isn't looking at her with pity or condescension. She *gets* it. Caroline can tell. It's something in her eyes, in the way she nods at certain details, like Ainsley's stupid fucking Instagram captions—*Fit to be Thai-ed!!!*—or the even stupider lie Tanner told.

"Anyway," Caroline concludes, "now I can either waste the rest of my money going home, or I can . . . I don't know. Go back to him, and get over it. I mean, I could try to get by on my own for the next three weeks, then meet up with him when it's time to fly back." The thought of having to deal with Tanner in any capacity is preemptively exhausting, but Caroline knows that's probably her best bet. Make her last few hundred bucks last as long as she can, and hope Tanner doesn't cancel her ticket.

But fuck, she hates that. Putting that power in his hands when what she really wants to do is ditch him entirely.

The woman nods again before glancing over her shoulder. "Or," she says with a shrug, "maybe there are other options?"

"Like what?"

The woman shrugs again, then smiles. "There are always options. Particularly when you let go of the version of yourself that got here in the first place. You can cling to the before, or you can try to live in the after, you know?"

*In the after.*

Caroline isn't sure what it means, but she likes the sound of that.

She likes this girl, too.

By the third beer, she's not a stranger anymore, though. She has a name, an unusual one that Caroline has never heard before.

She also has a boat.

And that night, when Caroline steals back to Tanner's room at the hostel, she knows that she *does* have options. Her new friend has just shown them to her. She'll take Caroline on her boat, sail her anywhere she'd like to go. Caroline just needs to do one thing first.

She finds the money clip in a drawer, underneath his underwear.

She picks it up, sliding it into her bag, then slips back out into the night, toward the bar and her friend, and her freedom, and it surprises her how easy it is. How there was a before, when she was sad and miserable and trapped—and now, just a few hours later, there's this glorious after.

Caroline steps into it.

# ACKNOWLEDGMENTS

This is the book I've been wanting to write since I was twelve years old and first came across a copy of *And the Sea Will Tell* in my local library. I can still see the turquoise cover, the leering skull. To finally get to write my own "boat murder" book is a (slightly macabre) dream come true, and I am so thankful to everyone who helped make it happen!

Holly Root has been my agent for more than a decade, and I hope she will still be talking me off ledges and helping to steer my ideas into port for decades more to come. This book particularly benefitted from her excellent notes early in the planning stages, and I am so grateful for her expertise.

Sarah Cantin understood this book from the first pitch, and then pushed it to be so much better and more ambitious than I'd ever hoped for. This might be the most complicated novel I've ever written, and were it not for Sarah's editorial genius, I think it—and I—would have fallen to pieces many times over. Thank you so much, Sarah, for all your work and for never stopping me from using roughly 354 nautical puns whenever I emailed you about the manuscript.

Thank you also to Sallie Lotz, whose notes are always so smart and whose eye is so sharp.

The entire team at St. Martin's Press is a dream to work with, and I am beyond fortunate to have them at the helm. My books and my career are in such good hands with all of you.

Thank you, as always, to my friends, especially, in this case, Ash Parsons, Kerri Muñoz, and Vicky Alvear Schecter, all of whom heard about this book in its earliest stages and cheered me on. Hopefully by the time this one is out, we're all back at the convent again, walking mazes and scandalizing nuns.

And of course, for my family. I love y'all.

## A GIRL LOOKING FOR LOVE...

When Jane, a broke dog-walker newly arrived in town, meets Eddie Rochester, she can't believe her luck. Eddie handsome, rich and lives alone in a beautiful mansion sinc the tragic death of his beloved wife a year ago.

## A MAN WHO SEEMS PERFECT...

Eddie can give Jane everything she's always wanted: stability, acceptance, and a picture-perfect life.

## A WIFE WHO JUST WON'T STAY BURIED...

But what Jane doesn't know is that Eddie is keeping a secret – a big secret. And when the truth comes out, the consequences are far more deadly than anyone could ever have imagined...